4

ANA
ON THE
EDGE

BY A. J. SASS

LITTLE, BROWN AND COMPANY
New York   Boston

Little, Brown and Company
Hachette Book Group
1290 Avenue of the Americas, New York, NY 10104
Visit us at LBYR.com

First Edition: October 2020

Little, Brown and Company is a division of Hachette Book Group, Inc. The Little, Brown name and logo are trademarks of Hachette Book Group, Inc.

The publisher is not responsible for websites (or their content) that are not owned by the publisher.

Interior curly swishes © NazArt/Shutterstock.com
Emoji icons © Cosmic_Design/Shutterstock.com

Library of Congress Cataloging-in-Publication Data
Names: Sass, A. J., author.
Title: Ana on the edge / by A. J. Sass.
Description: First edition. | New York: Little, Brown and Company, 2020. | Audience: Ages 8–12. | Summary: Twelve-year-old figure skater Ana strives to win competitions while learning about gender identity—Ana's own and that of a new friend—and how to navigate the best path forward.
Identifiers: LCCN 2019056117 | ISBN 9780316458610 (hardcover) | ISBN 9780316458634 (ebook) | ISBN 9780316458641 (ebook other)
Subjects: CYAC: Ice skating—Fiction. | Gender identity—Fiction. | Friendship—Fiction.
Classification: LCC PZ7.1.S26476 An 2020 | DDC [Fic]—dc23
LC record available at https://lccn.loc.gov/2019056117

ISBNs: 978-0-316-45861-0 (hardcover), 978-0-316-45863-4 (ebook)

Printed in the United States of America

LSC-C

10 9 8 7 6 5 4 3 2 1

*To anyone who's ever answered "no"
when asked, "Are you a boy or a
girl?"—or even just thought it silently
to yourself.*

I see you.

JANUARY

Breathe In

I stand alone at center ice. Around me, the audience is quiet. Seven judges sit in front of me, fourteen eyes ready to follow my every move.

Breathe in, breathe out. Shoulders down.

Black, glossy fabric encases my white skates, part of my one-piece costume. I look down at the National Championships logo underneath layers of ice. Knots unfurl in my stomach and flutter upward, even though I just chewed a ginger tab to settle my nerves.

The opening notes of my music drum rhythmic and low. I aim a smile at the judges before gliding forward, extending one leg behind me in a quick arabesque. I push thoughts of the large crowd in the stands, of my mom sitting among them, of how this is my first-ever Nationals, out of my head. It's time to focus.

My step sequence begins. I carve deep edges and quick, controlled turns in a winding, S-shaped pattern.

I catch sight of my coach, Alex, by the boards. His

eyes bore into me as I turn into my first jump, a simple double flip. It's not the highest-scoring element I'm capable of, but it's a great way to get my feet under me at the start of my program.

It also comes right before the tricky triple toe loop.

I take a steadying breath, then tap my toe pick into the ice for my double flip. One, two rotations, and I land strong, back arched.

I lift my arms as the music builds. There's no time to get excited yet.

Everything comes down to this next jump: the triple toe loop.

Turn, bend, tap. I recite the toe loop's takeoff technique in my head, then turn backward, preparing to spring off the ice. Once I'm airborne, muscle memory will have to get me through the rest.

My left leg reaches behind me, blade tapping. I launch into the air and snap my ankles together, arms crossed tight over my chest.

The audience cheers. Relief floods through me, and a smile tugs at the corners of my mouth. It vanishes a second later as I twist into my next combination spin.

To the untrained eye, I'm just an effortless blur of

glossy black fabric, gold-and-red chiffon fluttering from my costume. But I know each crisp position comes from years of repetition in private lessons with Alex, lessons that Mom worked long hours to pay for.

Shoulders relaxing, I exit my spin to more clapping. My smile is less rehearsed, more genuine. The ice feels more like home now, instead of slippery and foreign.

I lean on a deep edge and tap my toe pick into the ice for my three-jump combo. Launch and land, launch and land. Repeat again. It's over in a matter of seconds, my movements smooth and fast.

Out here, all my problems vanish. The judges seem to disappear, and I can no longer hear the crowd roar. The world falls away once I get into character. My steps perfectly match the music.

I land two more jumps, right on the beat of my music, then finish with a crowd-pleasing spin. My short hair whips against my cheeks as I grab my skate blade, lifting my foot high behind me in a vertical split. I end with a flourish as the audience rises in a standing ovation.

I bow to the judges, then exit the ice. Warmth forms in my stomach and spreads outward as Alex uncrosses his arms and reaches out for a quick hug. He looked stiff during my performance, shoulders tense under the gray business suit he wore especially for this event. Not anymore.

We head to the Kiss and Cry seating area, where skaters receive their scores. The cameras catch all the drama here, every tiny reaction recorded. I'm still breathing hard by the time we sit down, but I wave at a nearby camera livestreaming the event.

In just a few seconds, I'll know how I placed.

Alex nudges me and offers a water bottle. I take a sip as a volunteer hands me flowers and stuffed animals that members of the audience threw onto the ice. I've seen this happen for famous skaters, but it's the first time anyone besides Mom has thrown things for me.

"Now the score for Miss Ana-Marie Jin's free-skate program." I sit up straighter, trying to ignore a prickle of discomfort. "Ana-Marie has earned a total of sixty-eight point five eight."

The steady thrum in my chest skips a beat. I was the last skater who performed today, and that's higher than any of the scores I overheard while I warmed up. I turn to Alex, who squeezes my arm. His gaze stays on the results screen. It'll refresh soon. Until then, nothing's official.

I look up to the stands and spot Mom. Unlike others around her, she isn't clapping. Her eyes are fixed on the huge digital scoreboard looming over the ice. I hold my breath and keep watching her. I want this win for her as much as I want it for myself.

A roar of approval fills the rink and Mom's eyes widen. She stands with the rest of the crowd, hands flying to her mouth. My gaze flickers to the final results.

ANA-MARIE JIN: 68.58—1ST

I jump out of my seat as Alex rises and pulls me into another hug. I hug him back, bouncing in his arms. All those months of intense training, of sore muscles and hard falls, were worth it to get to this moment. My heart's racing again, but this time it has wings. I'm soaring.

I look back to the stands and find Mom. I blink fast, and she smiles at me like she knows I'm trying to hold back tears, her eyes crinkling at the corners.

The announcer speaks again, and Alex catches me

by the elbow. "Medal ceremony." He nods toward the ice where a group of workers is setting up a podium.

We make it to the ice by the time the bronze medalist is announced. Silver comes next, her program music playing softly in the background as she takes the ice and curtsies to the crowd.

"Soak this all up. Enjoy every second." Alex pats my shoulder. "Tomorrow we'll fly home and get you back on your regular training schedule. Think you can top this next season?"

My program music plays, low at first, then strong and brassy. The other medalists already stand on the podium in sparkling dresses. The top spot is empty, waiting for me.

The announcer calls my name. I step onto the ice, then turn back to Alex. I give him a quick thumbs-up before gliding off to accept my gold medal.

"Definitely."

JUNE

Chapter One

Sunlight glimmers across the ice through the San Francisco rink's floor-to-ceiling windows. I squint, trying to find my best friend, Tamar. She's on the far side of the rink, working on spiral positions, just like I'm supposed to be doing. I scan the ice, making sure Alex is nowhere in sight, then wave her over. She skids to a scratchy stop in front of me, brown curls bouncing in her loose ponytail.

Her skin is usually pale, but right now it's flushed pink from the cold rink air. She twirls her index finger, brows raised. "You first."

"I'm always first," I shoot back, but Tamar doesn't budge.

We're supposed to be practicing Moves in the Field— exercises that focus on power, body alignment, and edge control—but there's no one around to call us out for goofing off. Also, I never back down from a challenge. Swizzling a few feet away from Tamar to make sure my sharp blades don't nick her, I raise both arms. I plant one toe in the ice, reach down, and perform a perfect cartwheel. Tamar applauds, and I bow like I've just skated my winning program at Nationals.

"Ana!" Alex calls.

I freeze mid-bow. Tamar's eyes dart past me, up to Alex in the viewing stands. He's right next to my mom.

Alex beckons to me. I look at Tamar for help, but she's zipped away, back to her corner of the rink.

I grab my stuff and slide on my blade guards at the edge of the ice, then open my phone to the calendar app Mom and I share. There's nothing about her visiting the rink over lunch today. She should definitely still be at work.

I climb the metal steps up to the stands. Mom pats the seat next to her and I sit down, waiting for her or Alex to lecture me about my cartwheel. I fiddle with my hair, trying to tuck it behind my ear. The strands are a little too short to stay put.

Shoulders tense, I glance toward the ice, but Tamar's focused on twizzles. They're supposed to look like mini–traveling spins, and most of hers do—until the last set. She hits her toe picks and loses her balance.

Alex clears his throat to get my attention. "Your mom and I wanted to discuss some things now that

the new season is fast approaching. You've been showing progress all spring during the off-season, learning harder jumps and getting more consistent. And
of course, we're both proud of how you performed at
Nationals a few months ago."

Relaxing a little, I look between them. It doesn't
seem like I'm going to get in trouble for my cartwheel
after all.

"You'll definitely be moving up a level next season,"
Alex continues. "You've got the skills to be competitive
as an Intermediate lady."

Competition announcers always call Juvenile skaters boys and girls, then it switches to ladies and men
starting at Intermediate. I already knew this, but it still
sounds weird.

"Even so, this will be a big leap for you. You only
needed a free-skate program in Juvenile, but Intermediate also requires a short program, with very specific
jump and spin requirements."

I nod to show I'm still following along.

"The plan is to convert your Juvenile free skate to
an Intermediate short program. It's a real showstopper
the way you perform it."

My chest swells at the thought of performing my program in front of a huge crowd again, and I share a look with Mom. The corners of her eyes crinkle, just like at Nationals.

"You're also going to work with a choreographer to create an Intermediate free-skate program so it has a different feel and layout. The judges will want to see your range as a performer."

My eyes widen. Alex has always been the one to choose my programs and map out where the steps, jumps, and spins will go. But all the best skaters have choreographers.

"Lastly, we've decided to move your home base to Oakland. Their management team has been asking me to coach there on a more full-time basis for quite some time, as you know."

Mom nods.

"Plus, our offer was just accepted on a house in Temescal."

"That's a great neighborhood," Mom says. "I know you and Myles have been searching for a new house for a while. Congratulations."

"Congratulations," I echo.

"Thanks." Alex turns to me. "I'll still be your main coach. There are changes going into effect next season that we'll need to keep on top of. For example, in the past, medaling first at Regionals and then at Sectionals would qualify you to compete at Nationals—but starting this season, Nationals has been cut for all but the highest levels. Instead, top Intermediate skaters will attend a training camp to build skills and determine eligibility for international competitions down the road."

No more Nationals? I listen carefully, trying to memorize as much of this new information as possible.

"Both your mom and I want to make sure you have room to grow. Oakland has two rinks. No more competing for ice with the hockey teams, which should give you plenty of practice time to get your skills even more consistent for Intermediate. Your mom has also signed you up for some great off-ice stretching and dance classes."

"For real?" I look at Mom. She nods again, and I can hardly believe it.

"For real," Alex confirms. "You'll start your new training schedule next week. How's that sound?"

"It sounds great. Like a dream come true, actually."

Beaming, I glance back toward the ice, first to the floor-to-ceiling windows, then to where Tamar's practicing twizzles across a patch of sunlit ice. My hands tingle as I imagine telling her everything.

"I'm glad you're excited." Alex stands and looks down at me, one eyebrow arched as his expression gets serious. "Now, back to work on your Moves in the Field. No more cartwheels. Last time I checked, you were a figure skater, not a gymnast."

Chapter Two

Tamar and I sit side by side on my bunk bed as the closing credits from *The Mighty Ducks 2* play from her iPad. On the opposite end of our studio apartment, Mom sits at the kitchen table with her work laptop.

Tamar rests her head on my shoulder and sighs. "The rink is going to be so boring without you and Alex."

"He'll still be around for your synchro practices."

I feel her nod. "For now, I guess. I'm having a tryout lesson with a coach he recommended tomorrow, too. Still, it's going to be weird without you."

"At least there's less chance you'll get in trouble for on-ice cartwheels?"

"Like I can even do them that well." She laughs and leans past me to grab her iPad off its perch on my pillow. "I'm not multitalented like my BFF, the last national Juvenile champion in the history of ever."

I roll my eyes. "There'll still be national champions at Junior and Senior. I'll just be trying to qualify for the national training camp at Intermediate instead."

Tamar gestures to the wall, pointing at my gold medal. It hangs right beside a Michelle Kwan poster so old it's curling at its yellowed corners. Michelle was the first Chinese American I ever saw skate, so she'll always be my favorite.

"Last. Ever. Juvenile. Champion."

Shaking my head, I can't help smiling.

"But the camp does sound cool," Tamar says as she scrolls through iPad notifications.

"Yeah. If I skate well there, I could get picked to compete internationally as a Novice-level skater the season after."

At this, Tamar looks up. "Okay, that would be awesome."

"Definitely awesome."

All I've wanted since I started skating is to represent the United States in competitions around the world.

Tamar checks her texts. "Mom's downstairs." She scooches toward the ladder at the edge of my bed as I twist around to glance at my Nationals medal. It never gets old to look at. That's when I notice the photo missing from its spot behind my poster.

"Hey," I call to Tamar. "Do you see a picture down there?"

"I'll check!"

Mom's mattress squeaks below me as I scramble down the ladder.

"Found it!" She studies the photo before handing it back to me. "You look a lot like your dad."

"Really?" I glance at the two teenagers in the picture. Mom's hair was longer back then, but just as straight. Beside her, Dad's graduation cap tilts above a mess of wavy, dark blond hair.

Tamar nods. "Same smile. And nose."

"I guess." It's a super-old photo, from Mom and Dad's high school graduation. They had me a couple of years later, but it's just been me and Mom for as long as I can remember. Dad moved away when I was a baby.

A chair leg scrapes against the floor. I look past Tamar, over to Mom.

"How was the movie?" she asks. "It was that hockey one again, right? You two must be close to a record number of views by now."

Tamar and I glance at each other. "Yeah, probably," we say, totally in sync.

Tamar grabs her backpack from the foot of the bed. "I should head downstairs. Mom's waiting." She turns to me. "Walk me out?"

She waves to my mom, then grabs her shoes from a rack near the door.

Outside, we give each other our usual goodbye hug. "Let me know how it goes with the trial coach?"

She takes a few steps away, walking backward. "Only if you let me know all about your first day in Oakland."

My stomach twists at the reminder that we won't be skating together anymore, but I push away the feeling. "Deal!"

Mom's in the kitchen when I return. "I thought we'd have a special treat before your big first day." She waves me over. "Help me mix the batter?"

Soon, the griddle's hissing. I stand next to Mom, collecting plates and silverware for dinner.

"I've set the alarm for six tomorrow." She nudges her spatula under the first pancake, then flips it. "Alex arranged a car pool with a family who just started taking lessons with him. Mrs. Park drives to Oakland every day with her daughters, Faith and Hope. They'll pick you up at seven thirty in front of my office."

"I know Faith. She competed against me a few times last year."

"That's wonderful." Mom covers her mouth to yawn, but it's not because she's bored with our conversation. She works all day, plus teaches Mandarin to private school students on weekends and evenings. Nowadays, she's almost always tired.

Flipping the final pancake, she turns to me. "Start setting the table, Ana-Marie, please?"

I look down so Mom can't see my frown. I wish she'd just call me Ana like Alex and Tamar do, but I'm not sure how to tell her. We spend a lot of time apart now. Talking to her doesn't feel as easy as it did last year.

"Are you excited about tomorrow?" Mom asks.

My eyes dart over to her, then back to the plates in my hands. My stomach was a little fluttery with Tamar in the hall, but now it feels like it's performing somersaults.

"Yes." I head for the table.

"Nervous?"

I chew on the inside of my lip and lay out two place settings. "A little."

Okay, a lot. It's weird how you can want something so much but still be all jittery when you finally get it.

We sit down across the table from each other, under our apartment's only window. A light breeze makes me shiver. Hot days are rare in San Francisco, even in June. For me, summer is less about warmer weather, more about being done with my online homeschool classes until the fall, plus skating lots with Tamar. It's also when Alex puts together my new program before Regionals in October.

Except now I'll be at a different rink and have a choreographer.

My stomach flips again and I fidget, rubbing the charm on the necklace I always wear. My phone chimes in my pocket. Mom looks at me.

"Sorry." I silence it.

"Would you like to say the blessing tonight?" she asks.

"Sure."

We never used to recite a blessing before meals, but I started practicing prayers in Hebrew school a few months ago to prepare for my bat mitzvah. Mom thought it'd be a good idea to recite some at home, too.

As soon as I'm done, Mom picks up where she left off. "Alex will arrive in Oakland by midmorning, after your off-ice classes."

I take a bite of my pancake.

"I'm sure Faith and Hope will help you get settled in beforehand."

Swallowing hard, I try to imagine tomorrow. New skaters. Different rink. A choreographer I've never met. I overheard Alex tell Mom on the phone that she's flying in from Florida. Mom turned off the speakerphone when he mentioned her choreography fee, but not before I heard we'll be splitting her travel costs with the other skaters who hired her.

I glance past Mom, beyond the kitchen, and to our bunk beds on the opposite side of the apartment. Our entire studio could fit into Tamar's living room.

"How are we going to pay for everything?"

I can't help asking, even though she'll probably just tell me that it's her job to pay for things and mine to focus on training. But I know a low-income families sports voucher made it possible for me to learn to skate, and that she split Alex's coaching fee with Tamar's parents for a year after we passed all the levels in our skate-school.

Mom looks at me like she's trying to decide something. "Do you remember that big case I helped out with last April?"

"When I stayed at Tamar's house for, like, a week?"

"Yes, exactly. Work just won a large settlement. My boss gave me a bonus to thank me for my help."

"Seriously?" I lean forward. "That's awesome!"

Mom doesn't smile. "This doesn't make us rich, Ana-Marie. Far from it. I'm only sharing this with you because you're old enough to understand the costs of your training, and I don't want you to worry. Focus on your skating, and train hard this summer."

"Okay." I sit up a little taller. "I'll train hard. Hard squared."

"I know you will." Mom keeps her eyes on me, pausing long enough to make me wonder what's going on. "Now I have a question for you: If you had the chance to help pay for your skating, would you be willing?"

"Yes." I don't even have to think about it.

"Good." Mom nods, as if she's made a decision. "I've already paid for your practice ice tomorrow. Alex will explain more later."

"Explain what?" How am I possibly going to get any sleep between my current nerves and this new mystery?

Mom smiles a little, and I know she's amused by my impatience.

"Eat, Ana-Marie" is all she says. "It's almost time for bed, and you'll need your rest. You've got a big day ahead of you."

Chapter Three

I wake up an hour before my alarm is set to go off. Closing my eyes, I steady my breaths and roll from my back to my side, but sleep feels out of reach. My head swirls with thoughts.

Nationals. The Oakland rink. Cars honking on the street. The high-pitched whine of bus brakes. Money. New choreography.

For a while, I stare at my Michelle Kwan poster. Eventually my eyes drop lower, to my parents' photo. Mom and Dad both smile back.

The alarm finally goes off. "Time to get up, Ana-Marie." Mom's drowsy voice floats up from the lower bunk.

Mom takes the bathroom first and emerges in her freshly ironed work clothes. Then it's my turn to get into a T-shirt and my comfiest stretchy leggings. Alex once told me the Iowa rink he trained at as a kid would make girls wear skirts or dresses to practice. I'm glad there are no rules like that at the rinks here.

We eat a quick breakfast and head out.

The Number 5 bus will take us to Mom's office, but we only ride it on special occasions. Walking is free. Homeless people sleep or sit huddled under aged brick buildings, reminding me how lucky we are. I slip my hand into Mom's. Even if our studio is small, it's safe and comfortable.

As the Financial District looms closer, cars honk more often. The sidewalks get busier, too. We're weaving our way around people dressed in business suits when a fluttering movement catches my eye. Rainbow flags line the sidewalk, but someone's tied a second flag to this lamppost. White, blue, and pink stripes whip back and forth in the wind.

"Look." I point it out to Mom.

"How pretty. I always love Pride month. It feels so festive." Mom smiles. "Do you remember Alex and Myles's wedding?"

"Kind of." I was seven and it felt like the whole city

was celebrating, because two women or two men could officially get married for the first time. "That's when Alex and Myles started calling me Bean."

"I almost forgot about that." Mom laughs. "You would've danced all night if I'd let you."

I grin.

Mom's office is in a tall building downtown, complete with Samuel, the security guard. He always wears freshly pressed suits and keeps his hair trimmed so close to his brown skin that he looks like he's ready to attend a wedding himself.

He waves to us. "Good morning, Ms. Jin." I brace myself as Samuel turns to me. "Hi, Miss Ana-Marie."

I wince at the *Miss*.

Looking up at Samuel, I remind myself he's just being polite. "Morning, Samuel."

"Big day today, right?"

I nod. My phone vibrates. There's a 99 percent chance it's Tamar, already checking in.

"But you're not wearing a dress? On an important day like this?"

I tense. "Not to practice. Almost no one does."

Before Samuel can respond, Mom steps toward the

street, arm up. An SUV with tinted windows pulls to a stop at the curb in front of us.

Mrs. Park gets out of the driver's side and shakes hands with Mom.

"Bag in the trunk," says Mrs. Park. Her words are curt, like how my grandma Goldie talks. She grew up speaking Mandarin with her parents and didn't learn English until she moved to Hawaii as a teenager.

The trunk already contains two designer skating bags. Skaters can sit on the hard frame while lacing up, plus the wheels sparkle when you roll them. My duffel bag looks drab next to them. I press my shoulders back and tell myself it doesn't matter. It holds my skates just as well as any expensive bag.

"See you later." Mom ruffles my hair. "Listen to Alex. Work hard and take lots of notes."

"Okay," I call, making my way around the SUV. I hop into the back seat and come face-to-face with a wide-eyed girl. Her dark hair is pulled back behind her ears in two pigtails. It's been a couple of months since the last time I saw Faith Park, but this definitely isn't her.

"Hi!"

"Hey," I say back. As Mom's building disappears

behind us, I recognize the girl in the front seat. A ballerina bun holds her hair above her slender neck. Headphone cords snake down from her ears into the iPad that rests on her lap.

I can see only part of her face, but it's enough to recognize Faith.

When we stop at a light, Mrs. Park glances back at us. "Introduce yourselves to Ana-Marie."

"You can just call me Ana," I say.

"Hi, Ana. I'm Hope." The girl beside me waves. "I'm nine and a Pre-Juvenile, but I want to test up to Juvenile this summer so I can compete at real Regionals!"

Hope is practically bouncing. Behind her, rainbow flags zip by through the window, a blur of vivid colors. Hope looks from me to Faith, who still hasn't said anything. She leans forward and pokes her on the shoulder.

Pulling one headphone speaker off her ear, Faith raises an eyebrow at Hope.

"Introductions. Your turn!"

"We already know each other." Faith glances my way. Her headphones go back on after I confirm with a small nod.

Hope flops back against the leather seat and sighs. "Faith is competing Intermediate this season. She had to move up a level because she turned thirteen in April, even though she didn't make it to Juvenile Nationals. You're doing Intermediate, too, right?"

"Yes."

Hope looks like she expects more of an explanation, but I'm not sure what to say. When I imagined how this morning would go, I assumed I'd be talking to Faith, not her little sister.

"And you take lessons from Alex?"

I nod.

"We just started with him last week." Hope doesn't give me a chance to respond before she chatters on. "I loved our old coach, but she retired and doesn't teach anymore."

We ascend a ramp onto the Bay Bridge, which connects San Francisco to the cities of the East Bay. If you hold your left hand up, palm toward your face, San Francisco would be at the tip of your thumb, Oakland at the crease where your index finger connects to the rest of your hand. The bay we're driving across is the empty space between.

"What triples can you do?"

"Hope! Don't pester." Mrs. Park shoots her a look in the rearview mirror.

"Sorry," Hope says, but she's still smiling.

"It's okay. I can do triple toes and salchows. My loop's usually okay, but I cheat the landing sometimes. I'm still working on flip and lutz."

"That's so cool." Hope sounds genuinely impressed. "Alex says I need to land a clean double axel before I can try triples. How long did it take you?"

"A few months."

Not even that long. I don't want to brag, though, especially in front of people I don't know very well.

"It took Faith almost a year!" Hope crows. A smile tugs at the corners of my mouth. Faith doesn't respond as we enter a dark tunnel, her eyes focused on the glow of her iPad.

Oakland spreads out in front of us as we exit back into the light. To the right, rows of metal cranes loom over the Port of Oakland. On the left, hills stretch across the horizon, dotted with houses.

We get off the freeway and arrive at the rink within

minutes. I thank Mrs. Park for the ride, then grab my bag out of the trunk after Hope and Faith.

Faith is taller than I remember. She's always had super-skinny legs, but they used to look like they'd get tangled during jumps and spins. Now she looks like a runway model.

"Ready at three thirty," Mrs. Park calls. "Church youth group at five tonight."

Hope and I trail behind Faith as she takes off toward the rink, the wheels of her roller bag shimmering blue and red. Beyond the front door, kids sit on benches and roller bags, lacing up their skates. I can just make out a sign with directions to Oakland's two sheets of ice, one on the left, the other to the right.

Faith disappears inside. My stomach feels like it's home to a hundred wriggling bugs. It's almost like I'm about to compete.

Breathe in, breathe out. Shoulders down.

I hold the door open for Hope, then follow her through it.

Chapter Four

Rinks are like cities, each one unique. This isn't my first time at the Oakland rink, but now that I'm officially training here, I study everything like I'm seeing it for the first time: the lobby, with its picnic benches and concession stand; two rinks side by side, one for freestyle skaters, one for hockey; a studio on the second floor, complete with mirrored walls above a ballet barre.

I follow Faith and Hope to the studio for thirty minutes of stretching class, then forty-five minutes of off-ice dance. I still feel like dancing after we're dismissed. It's hard to tell if I'm more excited about training in Oakland or being done with school for the summer.

Last year in San Francisco, I skated an hour each morning, then Alex dropped me off at Mom's office. Mom's boss let me use an empty cubicle to watch videos from my online homeschool classes while Mom worked. Tamar and her mom would pick me up in the afternoon, I'd skate a couple more hours, and then Mom would come get me.

Summer's different. I can stay at the rink all day and train. No video lectures for three whole months. No homework, either, except taking notes after lessons with Alex.

I sit on a bench across from Hope, who's perched on the edge of her roller bag. She slips a gel sock over her ankle. It's just like the ones I wear to prevent blisters. I reach into my bag and pull out my own pair, along with my phone.

Tamar texted this morning, like I'd guessed. She also sent another message during off-ice classes.

7:29 a.m.: Good luck today!!! Plz also tell my parents it's too early to be fighting

9:40 a.m.: Hi for real this time b/c I went back to sleep lol. Summer is awesome

"Don't forget to check in with the ice monitor." I look up from my phone and over at Hope. "If your mom paid already, they can just mark you off on their list."

I'm glad Hope is explaining this, because Faith isn't. She finishes lacing her skates between two chattering girls, then pulls out her headphones and iPad in the minutes before the Zamboni finishes.

I put my phone away and lace my skates.

Nearby, a door clicks open. I look up at a familiar face.

"Alex!"

"Hi, kiddo. How's it going?"

I steal a quick glance at Faith, then shrug.

"Give it a few days." It's like Alex can read my mind sometimes. He pats my shoulder, then calls Hope and Faith over.

"You probably already got to know each other a little on the drive over." He waits until we all nod. Hope's head bobs the hardest. "What you may not know is, you're my only Oakland students who commute from San Francisco."

Hope beams. I glance at Faith, who tilts her head a little.

"This summer has some big changes in store for all of you. Ana's obviously getting used to a new training environment here, but Faith and Hope just started taking lessons from me, as well. The more you support one another, the better your chances at success this season."

"Like a team?" Hope asks.

"Exactly." Alex nods. "Help each other out and cheer one another on. Not only will you develop a strong mindset for competition, it should make practices more fun."

"Okay!" Hope dances in place, then looks at Faith and me. "We should come up with a name."

"That's a great idea." Alex smiles at her. "But first, go get on the ice and start your warm-up."

Hope and Faith head toward the rink entrance as Alex turns to me. "You and Faith are at the same level, so it'd be great if you used that to your advantage and learned to train together."

I watch Faith as she skates away from us. I have no clue why Alex thinks she'd want to train together when she's hardly said anything to me all morning.

"Do you remember some of the jump exercises I taught you last year, like the split jump into a single toe loop?"

"Yep." How could I forget when Tamar videoed my millions of attempts? For weeks, I had a stream of flailing arms and hilarious wipeouts on my phone, until I finally figured out the timing.

"Wonderful. Now, there's someone I want to introduce you to before I start Hope's lesson. Meet me at the music box after you get yourself situated."

I check in with the monitor, peeking at her list while she puts a check mark beside my name. The cost of the practice ice is listed at the top. Fifteen dollars per hour. That adds up fast when I skate four sessions a day.

I tuck my necklace under my warm-up jacket's collar, then pull off my blade guards and make my way to the boards. I set my tissue box and water bottle on the top ledge. My eyes scan the ice as I glide toward Alex.

This rink is a very different type of city. Even the skaters behave differently here. No one stops to chat or sneak in a cartwheel behind their coach's back.

Alex stands in front of a white woman in a puffy pink jacket that looks like it's half swallowing her. She rests her elbows on the ledge that separates the ice from a long bench behind the boards.

"Ah, Alex," she says as I skid to a stop. "This must be your little prodigy, yes?"

Her heavy accent makes me think of fur-lined coats and castles capped in snow.

"Indeed." Alex turns to me. "Ana, this is world-renowned choreographer Lydia Marinova. Lydia is visiting for the next—"

"Miss." Lydia interrupts Alex, but her eyes stay on me like a hawk.

"Of course." Alex recovers fast. "*Miss* Lydia will be choreographing several skaters' programs and offering costume consults while she's here over the next week. You'll have your first lesson together tomorrow."

When I was little, Mom wanted me to say "Mister" before Alex's name. But Tamar never called him Mr. Alex, so after a while I stopped, too.

Miss Lydia's title seems a whole lot less optional.

"Yes," Miss Lydia says. "Tomorrow you will work hard."

"Great," Alex says. He smiles and I copy him, even though I can't tell if her comment is a promise or a threat. "I hate to cut this short, but I've got to start my first lesson."

As Alex skates off, Miss Lydia turns back to me. The playful bounce of her tightly wound, dyed-blond curls doesn't match her frown.

"Your skirt."

"My skirt?" I look down at my leggings, confused.

"Yes." The word cuts through the air like a skate blade, a deep edge into soft ice. "Wear it tomorrow."

"Um. Okay."

I don't have a skirt, not in my duffel bag or at home. It's been years since I even wore one at a competition.

Miss Lydia dismisses me. A lump forms in my throat as I glide away. Where am I going to get a skirt on such short notice? Besides, it's not like I'll ever wear it after Miss Lydia's gone.

I spot Faith nearby, working on quick-twisting rocker turns. I skate past, not quite sure I'm ready to talk to her yet. Darting around slower skaters, I pick up speed. Arms out and shoulders down, I focus on strong edges and posture.

After one full circuit around the ice, I hop backward. The air feels colder than I'm used to, the ice harder. It crunches under my blades each time I shift my weight between the inside and outside edges of my feet. One more circuit of alternating backward edges, then I move on to basic turns and twizzles. The moves loosen my joints and warm my muscles.

I notice Hope watching me. Alex says something that snaps her to attention, but her gaze shifts back to me after a second. I raise my eyebrows, like Alex does when he catches me daydreaming. Hope grins, then refocuses on her lesson.

"Hope's been talking about meeting you for, like, two whole weeks."

I whirl around, surprised to see Faith behind me. She looks down, sliding the cuffs of her warm-up coat sleeves over her hands.

"Really?"

"Ever since she found out we were all going to be Alex's students."

"Team Alex." She looks up at my comment, and I shake my head. "Never mind."

"You don't think he'd like us calling it that?"

We're skating together now, gliding slowly side by side.

"I think he'd probably tell me I can be more creative. Or that it should be about us, not him, or something."

"That make sense, I guess."

We both go quiet, keeping our eyes on other skaters. Some wear official Team USA jackets. Most have on the same stretchy leggings as Faith and me, but my gaze keeps drifting to an older girl. She stands in front of Miss Lydia for a lesson, wearing tights, a leotard, and a flowery wraparound skirt.

My stomach twists. I force myself to look up at Faith instead.

Alex mentioned jump exercises, but I don't want Faith thinking I'm a know-it-all, demonstrating things before Alex teaches them to her. I have another idea, one that seems safer. "Do you want to run through jumps together? Like, singles, then doubles, and combos and stuff?"

"Okay." She nods. "Start with a waltz jump, then I'll do mine."

We fly across the ice, performing simple single-rotation jumps with legs extended behind us to practice strong landings. We move on to doubles next, which require better focus and timing.

My doubles spring off the ice, explosive with tight, fast rotation. Faith's are precise but slower, gracefully arcing through the air. The longer I skate with Faith, the easier it is to learn my new rink's unspoken rules. When to avoid crossing another skater's path. Who's in a lesson. Which skater is practicing their program to music.

By the time Alex calls Faith over for her lesson, we've gotten through most of our jump combos. She waves to me, then skates off as an instrumental version of a pop song plays over the speakers. With nothing else to do, I perform a series of bunny hop jumps in time with the song, then a one-foot turn into an edgy power pull to pick up speed.

If Tamar were here, she'd probably join in, making up choreography with me. Today, I'm alone, letting the music guide my movements. Deep edges. Quick turns. A rapid blur of twizzles. I step forward and leap into a big single axel. The rink air nips at my cheeks. I breathe it in, then out in a fine mist, waiting for the next song.

My mind erases Miss Lydia's scowling face. The skirt request feels like a distant memory.

This is what I love about skating.

I slip into character as the music changes to a selection from *Carmen*, adding sharp arm movements to my landings. Right hand on my hip. Left arm arched over my head. I step forward, preparing to spin, but stop when I spot Alex.

"Looks like you've managed to settle in some." He glides closer to me. "Session's done. Grab your stuff. I want to run something by you."

We pass the benches, then walk through the door I saw Alex exit into before the session started. I immediately recognize it as a coaches' lounge.

"Have a seat," Alex says, gesturing to a chair, "and let's get down to—"

Bzzzrr!

"Just a sec." Alex pulls out his vibrating phone. "It's Myles."

While Alex and his husband discuss weekend plans, I slide my duffel bag off my shoulder, drop into the chair, and unlace my skates partway. Now that I'm off the ice, the whole morning comes back to me, from my pre-alarm jitters to Miss Lydia's skirt request.

I take a deep breath and let it out fast.

As Alex talks, I fish through my bag for my phone. Tamar's sent even more texts.

11:38 a.m.: The suspense is killing me . . . How's everything going?? (Answer when u can, no pressure)

11:39 a.m.: OK some pressure. I'm bored and you've only been gone like 3 hours

Where do I start? There's so much to tell her.

"Ana?" Alex points to his phone. "Want to say hi?"

"Oh, sure!"

Alex rotates the screen, and Myles's smiling face greets me. His head is completely shaved, brown skin contrasting with the collar on his light pink shirt.

"Hi, Bean. How's it going?" His southern accent makes each vowel sound long and special.

"Good." I flex my ankles in my skates.

"You must be real excited about—"

"Hold that thought." Alex cuts in. "I haven't had a chance to tell her yet."

"Ah, my mistake!" Myles shoots me a wink. "My lips are sealed, too, then."

After a quick goodbye, Alex ends the call. "All right, let's talk skating." I drop my phone into my lap, leaning forward in my seat.

"I'll work on revamping your old Juvenile program later this week to make sure it's competitive for Intermediate. Your mom said you'd be fine keeping last year's costume." I nod but keep quiet. I want him to

· 45 ·

explain what Mom and Myles both know that I don't. "Now, remember when I said things would be changing in the qualifying competition pipeline this season?"

"You said there's a training camp instead of Nationals."

"I did, indeed. But there's more." Alex leans back in his chair, crossing one leg over the other. "Starting this year, skaters have a chance to skip Regionals and go straight to Sectionals based on their scores at select summer competitions."

I sit up straighter.

"Regionals will remain the same, with the top four skaters qualifying for Sectionals," Alex explains. "But I wanted to make you aware that they'll be tracking scores at your first competition this summer in Los Angeles."

I stare at him, eyes wide. "You mean if I skate well there, I could automatically qualify for Sectionals?"

Alex nods. "I want to be clear, though, Ana. Your mom and I aren't having you compete in Los Angeles with that as a goal, not so soon after moving up a level and giving you a new program. If you qualify for

Sectionals, great, but the main objective is to develop endurance and consistency in your new programs this summer. Understood?"

"Yes."

"Good. That's settled. And one more thing..."

I barely hear him. I know Alex said we won't be focusing on trying to skip Regionals in October, but I can't help thinking that Mom wouldn't have to take as much time off from work if I did. She also wouldn't have to buy another set of plane tickets if I advanced straight to Sectionals this November.

"Your mom and I had a talk a few weeks back, while we were discussing the move to Oakland. As much as she wants you to focus solely on skating, we know you're aware of the high cost of your training. The rink manager has offered to help offset some of these expenses by covering your ice-time."

"Free ice?" My thoughts about skipping Regionals grind to a halt.

"Yeah." Alex gives me a small smile. "Here's the deal: Rink management will offer you ice-time in exchange for your help with their Tuesday night skate-school classes.

You'd be my assistant, working with kids who need individual attention and demonstrating skills."

He pauses just long enough to confirm that, yes, I'm listening. I really am—as if he couldn't already tell from my mouth hanging open.

"The summer semester starts tomorrow. One of the skate-school instructors who lives in San Francisco will drive you home in the evening since the Parks will be gone by then. Her name's Jen. You'll get to meet her tomorrow. Any questions?"

I do some quick math. At fifteen dollars an hour and four hours on the ice every weekday, that'd save Mom three hundred dollars a week—over a thousand each month!

"I just have to help out one night a week? For all the freestyle ice I want?"

Alex nods. "They may have other requests, but management knows they have to work around your training schedule." He looks at me straight on. "Can I assume that poorly concealed grin means you'll accept their offer?"

I am *this* close to rolling my eyes at him.

"Yes!"

He mouths the word *excellent*, rubbing his hands together like a cartoon villain.

I roll my eyes for real this time, pull my lunchbox out of my duffel bag, and look inside. This day keeps getting better! Mom packed bao. A steamed bun filled with bean paste, the bao is technically my dessert. But since I'm old enough to help pay for my training now, I should also get to decide what order I eat things in. The bao comes first.

"Do you still have those boot covers you got at Regionals last year?" Alex asks. I nod, mouth already full. "Bring them with you tomorrow, along with a warmer pair of pants. It gets cold fast when you're teaching. The rink will provide an instructor coat."

"O-tay," I say, mouth full of bean paste filling.

Alex checks the clock on his phone. "I've got to head back to the ice. Watch the time, but feel free to stay here and finish your lunch. You're officially a rink staff member. Between working with Lydia and assisting skate-school students, you're going to have your hands full this summer. Think you can manage?"

"Definitely." I polish off the last of my bao. "Oh,

and, Alex," I call in my sweetest, most innocent tone. He pauses, hand on the doorknob. "It's *Miss* Lydia."

He shakes his head but doesn't hide his grin. Then he's gone, leaving me to my dessert-first lunch.

For the first time today, my smile is 100 percent genuine.

Chapter Five

Later in the afternoon, the Parks drop me off in San Francisco. I wave to Samuel on my way into Mom's office building. The elevator doors slide open, and I tap the button for the fourteenth floor. My stomach drops as the elevator zips up, like I'm riding a roller coaster in reverse.

The doors ping open, and I greet the receptionist as I head into Mom's law office. Her desk sits in a maze of paralegal cubicles in the center of the room—two rights, one left. I poke my head around the corner of Mom's desk.

"You made it back!" She looks up from her computer. "I can't wait to hear all about your day. We can leave in about forty-five minutes. Do you have something to do while you wait?"

Normally, the Parks will drop me off at home so I can eat dinner and do chores while Mom's still at work. But Mom asked Mrs. Park to drive me to her office today instead so we can walk home together and talk about my first day at the Oakland rink.

I nod, and Mom's gaze moves back to her screen. "I'll come get you as soon as I'm done."

I'm off again, this time to a cubicle at the edge of the maze. It's empty, except for a coffee mug that says *I'd rather be skating* in curly blue letters. It's filled with pencils and pens Mom bought me when I started taking online homeschool classes last year.

I grab a pen, then pull out my notebook and phone from my skate bag.

I send a quick text to Tamar.

4:22 p.m.: Boo to your twizzles! Call you when I get home?

I turn to my notebook and flip to a clean page. I was really planning to do this earlier, but my thoughts kept spinning back to what Alex said during my lunch break.

Fifteen dollars per ice session, times four sessions a day, five days a week. That's twelve hundred dollars saved a month. It could buy tons of groceries. Help with costs for flights and hotels at competitions. Maybe we could even save up enough to fly to Hawaii and surprise Grandma Goldie. Then I could skate well in Los Angeles and save us more by getting to skip Regionals....

Focus!

I scribble a tip I learned in off-ice stretching class about breathing before deepening my splits. Faith sat in front of me today, legs long and straight, toes pointed. I jot down those details, too.

Looking up, I try to remember anything I could've forgotten. The office where Mom's boss usually works is empty, lights off. Sun pours in through windows overlooking the Bay Bridge.

I twirl the pen in my hand, wishing I'd gotten to talk to Faith more today. But after the morning freestyle, then lunch in the coaches' lounge with Alex, we both had lessons. Then, she put her headphones on the moment we climbed into Mrs. Park's car, while Hope talked my ear off about team name ideas.

My phone screen blinks with a thumbs-up emoji from Tamar. I get back to my notes. By the time Mom's ready to go, tips and diagrams fill my paper.

At street level, people crowd the sidewalks. Most make their way toward the BART subway station that will take them out of the city. Mom and I walk in the opposite direction.

Once we're past the noisy crowd, I look up at her. "Are you tutoring the Millers tonight?"

"Just the oldest boy. The younger is away at a sports camp."

That reminds me of the national training camp I'll be trying to qualify for later this season. I wonder how much a Team USA jacket costs, or if you get one for free at the camp. Do they pay to send you to international events, or is that something else Mom'll have to figure out?

We stop at a street corner, and I look up at Mom. At least this year, I know how to help. I slip my hand into hers. "Alex told me about how I can get free ice-time."

"Oh, good," Mom says as the light turns. "What did you think about his idea?"

"I think it's awesome. I can skate as many freestyle sessions as I need. Plus, it'll be fun to help teach other people to skate."

"I bet you'll be a wonderful assistant." Mom smiles. "How was the rest of your day?"

"Good. I liked my off-ice classes and got used to the ice pretty quickly on freestyle."

"That's wonderful." Mom squeezes my hand.

The walk sign flickers on. I take a step forward, but Mom pulls me back as a car whips past.

"Careful!" She doesn't loosen her grip, even after other people move into the crosswalk. "These drivers, sometimes."

She shakes her head, lips pursing into a thin line. It reminds me of Miss Lydia this morning.

Should I tell Mom about needing a skirt?

As we reach the gate at our building's entrance, I still don't have an answer.

"I met my new choreographer."

"What was she like?" Mom asks as we enter a small lobby.

"Intense," I admit. "Alex said our first lesson is tomorrow."

We take the stairs up to the fourth floor. By the time we enter and slip our shoes off, I've made my decision. Mom doesn't have time to buy me a skirt tonight. Plus, she said to focus on training hard. I don't need a skirt to do that.

"That reminds me," Mom says. "I need to take your measurements for Mrs. Park. She's handling everything with the seamstress your choreographer recommended. I don't think you've grown much since Nationals, but I'll double-check this weekend."

She drops her purse on the kitchen table, rushing around as she talks. I set my duffel bag by the door, then perch at the edge of her bed.

"I'm going to get changed before I head out for tutoring. Now, where did I put that red...ah!" Her eyes light up, and she takes the shirt I hold out. "Thank you. We make a good team, you and I."

As Mom disappears into the bathroom, I think about training with Faith today. I wonder if we'll ever become a real team like Alex wants.

"There are leftovers in the refrigerator." Mom's voice pulls me out of my thoughts. She heads my way, then kisses my forehead. "If you need anything, Mrs. Lee is around tonight, just down the hall. I'll be home in a couple of hours."

After Mom leaves, I head for the kitchen. Magnets from skating events cover the refrigerator, plus photos from each new city Mom and I visit. I open the door with one hand, video-calling Tamar with the other.

Tamar appears, hair still pulled back in a ponytail from skating.

"Anaaaaa."

I pull a sealed bowl off the top shelf. "Tamarrrrr."

"So, I was right. Practice was hecka boring without you and Alex."

"Oh no." I make sure she can see my big pout. "Weren't you supposed to have a tryout with a new coach, though?"

"I did." Tamar's head bobs up and down. "Her name is Kell. I think it's short for Kelly. She seems nice. Knows her stuff. Made me practice tons of brackets and twizzles."

I set the phone on the counter, peel back the bowl's plastic wrap, and pop it into the microwave. "But that's good, right? Haven't they been giving you trouble?"

"*Always.* But whatever." Tamar rolls her eyes. "What about you? How was your first day in Oakland? Did you meet any Olympians?"

"Not sure about Olympians, but there were lots of good skaters there. I even saw a couple of Team USA jackets. And a lot of older kids can do triples, so maybe they have jackets, too, and just weren't wearing them."

"So cool! Have you—"

The microwave dings, drowning out the rest of what Tamar says. I grab the bowl and a pair of chopsticks, then head to the table.

"Sorry, say that again?"

"I asked if you've met your choreographer yet."

"Oh. Yes. Kind of."

"That doesn't sound good. Is she mean?"

"She seems a little strict, but I don't really know yet." I take a bite of tofu. "I met her for, like, less than five minutes."

"Gotcha." Tamar flops on her bed and the video bounces with her.

I suddenly realize how tired I am. My legs feel like jelly. It's the good type of exhausted from training hard, but I can hardly keep my eyes open.

"I think I'm going to pass out soon. Can I tell you more when we hang out on Wednesday?"

Tamar grins. "You better."

I finish the rest of my dinner, take a quick shower, and crawl into bed, determined to wait up for Mom. I twist toward my wall, eyes on Michelle first, then my parents' graduation photo—on Dad's smiling face. I glance at the Juvenile championship medal hanging on its own special pin, then back to Dad.

I wonder if he knows I'm a national champion. What would he think about me training with a famous choreographer? Mom used to talk to him on the phone every Sunday night when I was little. Then it dropped to once a month, and now I can't remember the last time he called her.

My eyelashes flutter. The photo blurs out of focus.

The next thing I know, the door clicks open. I blink, eyes bleary. Mom dims the lights and makes her way to my bed.

"Did you eat?" Her voice is a comforting murmur. I nod, and she smooths the hair on my forehead. "Go back to sleep. I need to make our lunches for tomorrow."

Mom opens the window on her way to the kitchen, then sets a pot of water on the stove. I listen to the bubbling water until my eyelids shut, and everything fades away for the second time today.

Chapter Six

It's not until after Tuesday's off-ice classes that I start questioning my decision not to bring a skirt for my lesson with Miss Lydia.

I spot Faith at a nearby bench, skirt already tied around her waist. Hope perches on her roller bag. A glittering skirt lies on the bench beside her.

What if Miss Lydia refuses to choreograph my program without one?

I scan the other skaters, but Faith's too tall, and I don't know anyone else well enough to ask if I can borrow from them. Only one option left.

"Hey, Hope? I forgot to bring a skirt. Do you maybe have an extra?"

"Oh, sure!" She leans forward to unzip her roller bag. "I've got lots. What's your favorite color?"

Before I can answer, she pulls out a handful of gauzy wraparounds. She sifts through her stash, then holds up a purple skirt bedazzled with crystals.

"This one is my favorite." She glances down at the pink skirt on the bench. "Okay, second favorite, technically."

I thank Hope, then quickly wrap her skirt around the band of my stretchy pants. It's lightweight. Pretty, even. But I can't make myself look down as I glide over to Miss Lydia.

"Your old footwork sequence," Miss Lydia calls from the boards when I'm still half a rink away. "Show me."

No greeting. No small talk.

I get going, wondering how Miss Lydia plans to demonstrate my choreography if she doesn't step onto the ice.

"Go!" she shouts.

I pretend Miss Lydia is a competition judge and start my footwork. I imagine the low, subtle beats at the start of my Nationals program. Soon, it's like I'm skating at an event, performing for an invisible crowd. I forget about the skirt and Miss Lydia's harsh words, instead focusing on steady edges and controlled turns.

I complete the sequence with a showy stop, spraying snow a few inches in front of me.

Miss Lydia's expression doesn't change. "Again."

I stare at her. I skated it just fine the first time.

She pinches the bridge of her nose. "*Now.* Go, go."

The skirt flaps at my hips as I repeat my step sequence. It feels like a flag on a windy day, fluttery and distracting.

Miss Lydia doesn't give me a chance to skate back before barking another command. She has me perform Moves in the Field patterns next, ordering me to skate the Intermediate-level spiral sequence. For almost our entire lesson, I extend my leg behind me, performing every possible variation, on inside edges and outside, skating both forward and backward.

With five minutes left, she waves me over and tells me to lift my arms in front of me, one after the other.

"Now down," she says.

I drop my arms to my sides.

"Up."

I comply.

She orders me to do this what feels like a frajillion times. Up fast, down slow. In reverse. Both arms forward. One behind my back, the other rising at an angle, finger pointed toward the clock on the rink wall.

"Don't move."

I do as I'm told, convinced people are staring. Just

what I need: a choreographer who isn't choreographing and every skater out here watching me point at nothing.

"Your lesson is done." Miss Lydia dismisses me with a flick of her wrist.

I hesitate, but her focus has already shifted to Faith. I hop off the ice but stay by the boards, peering out through the plexiglass.

Miss Lydia walks on top of a long bench to avoid the line of skate bags stored behind the boards. In her thick bubble gum–pink coat, she totters along like an overstuffed doll.

She makes it to the music box, and soon the *tluck-tlick* of a string instrument plays through the overhead speakers. She calls something out. Faith turns backward and picks up speed before reaching for one skate blade with the hand on the opposite side of her body. The ties from her silver skirt flap like butterfly wings. Lifting her leg into a vertical split, Faith flies down the ice, head tilted back. No sign that the skirt is bothering her.

Faith stops in front of Miss Lydia, one arm behind her, the other lifted. It's just like the position Miss Lydia told me to hold, except Faith is less rigid. She radiates grace, from the arch of her back to the tip of her out-stretched finger.

I turn away, my face suddenly hot. Faith doesn't seem to be struggling with Miss Lydia's directions like I just was. Making my way toward a bench, I tug at the tie on Hope's skirt until it unknots. Free, for now.

Sitting, I pull out my phone and text Tamar.

11:01 a.m.: I had my first choreography lesson. Tell you more when we hang out tomorrow.

I look back toward the ice in time to see Faith copy Miss Lydia's arm movements with perfect precision. She receives a small nod, something I didn't manage after a full hour. Faith's been in her lesson for less than five minutes.

I untie my skates, reminding myself it was just the first day of choreography. I'm never perfect the first time Alex teaches me something new, either.

A surge of determination travels out from my chest as I grab my bag and head to the coaches' lounge for lunch. I'll work hard and get Miss Lydia to nod at me, too. Hard squared. By my next lesson, she'll be just as impressed with me as she is with Faith.

Chapter Seven

After our final freestyle session, Faith and Hope head out, but I don't leave with them. I make my way to the rink bathroom to change into thicker pants and a fleece-lined jacket.

Only a few people still sit at the tables between the two rinks when I get back—including Faith and Hope.

Hope spots me first and waves. As I get closer, I notice the pencil and paper in front of her. Faith sits across from her, an electronic pen hovering above her iPad.

"Mom's running late," Faith explains.

"Did you want to sit with us?" Hope asks. "We're taking notes on stuff Alex taught us."

It definitely wouldn't hurt to see how much of Miss Lydia's lesson I remember. Maybe writing it down will help me figure out how to make her happy.

"Sure." I take a seat across from Hope, next to Faith. I pull out my notebook and flip to a blank page, then create a list of everything Miss Lydia asked me to do today, from each spiral down to the tiniest arm movement.

Beside me, Faith leans forward, pen swirling across her iPad screen, and I can't help stealing a peek. She isn't taking notes, at least not like Hope and I. Lots of horizontal lines and dots fill her screen.

"Is that music?"

Faith nods slowly. "It's the intro for my free program. I'm trying to memorize what steps go with the rises and falls of the melody."

"Whoa." I don't even have my program music yet. Am I even more behind than I thought? "Does Miss Lydia want everyone to do that?"

"I'm just doing it for fun. Hope definitely doesn't do this kind of off-ice work, right?" Faith looks at her sister.

"Nope!" Hope shows me her sheet of paper. It has a line with Alex's name on it, but it's mostly filled with doodles. They don't look related to skating at all. She shrugs. "Mom says I get distracted very easily."

"That's the truth," Faith says, and Hope sticks out her tongue. Her phone chimes. "Mom's here." She looks at me. "You're not coming with us, right?"

I shake my head. "I'm helping at skate-school tonight.

It's just on Tuesday, so everything'll be back to normal tomorrow."

"Cool." Hope jumps up. "Bye, Ana!"

Faith glances back at me, too. "See you."

I say goodbye, then pull out my phone and realize Mom's sent me a text, asking how my first choreography lesson went.

I know I should tell her the truth, but I don't want her to think she made a mistake letting me switch rinks.

5:22 p.m.: Good!! Lots of work on spirals and edges for my new program!

That should do it. I check it over again, so I don't arrive home to a lecture on proper English spelling and grammar, then tap send.

I head into the coaches' lounge, and Alex looks up from his salad. "Hey, you."

I sit beside him, then pull out my own dinner. Mom packed a big container of noodles today. No bao this time around, but I'll survive. Probably.

"How'd your first lesson with Lydia go?"

I catch Alex's flub but don't point out Miss Lydia's proper title. Correcting him felt like a game yesterday. Today, I don't feel like playing.

"Practicing in a skirt felt weird. Plus, she made me do Moves in the Field for almost the whole lesson." I make a face at my noodles. "She didn't choreograph anything."

"It sounds like you're going through a normal adjustment period. My hunch is that Lydia wants to get a sense of how the skirt looks while you skate so she can tweak your steps as needed. Watching your Moves will also help her learn your strengths as a skater. That's pretty standard for new choreography students."

I guess that makes sense. It also explains why Faith got to skate to music today. I bet she worked with Miss Lydia last season.

Maybe the lesson wasn't 100 percent awful.

Except for the skirt. If Miss Lydia wants to see how I move in it, she might be making mental notes for the seamstress she works with. That could mean a *dress* in my future. Not something I want. The skirt is bad enough. I grab my chopsticks and peel the lid off my food, wondering how to mention this to Alex.

The door opens, and a white woman with shoulder-length blond hair steps into the lounge.

Her face lights up when she sees me. "You must be Ana-Marie."

"Yep, that's me." I glance at Alex. He's smiling, too.

"I'm Corinne, the skate-school director. We're so excited you'll be helping out this semester."

If Corinne is the director, that means she's a big reason I get free ice-time. I balance my lunch container on my lap and reach out to shake her hand.

"Follow me, sweetheart. I've got some stuff to go over with you before classes start."

Corinne waves me over to a tall table with cubbies above it. I stow my container under my seat, then move to join her. The table reaches my chest, even on tiptoes.

"Our classes each have one instructor and sometimes an assistant like you," Corinne explains. "For the most part, you'll be assisting Alex. Everyone in tonight's classes should be around your age since we hold group lessons for younger kids on a different day."

I nod to let her know I'm listening.

"We're lucky that someone so accomplished is giving back to our community. I also hope you might consider performing in our end-of-session recital this August."

She studies a row of coats hanging on a nearby wall. "This might be a little large for you, but it's the smallest we have." She pulls a jacket off a wall peg and passes it to me. The rink's logo is sewn on the back. "No need to decide about the recital now, of course, but we would be honored if you'd give it some thought."

I glance from Corinne to the jacket. They're giving me free ice-time in exchange for a few hours of my help. I'll be saving Mom twelve hundred dollars a month, and all they want is for me to skate in a recital?

"I don't need to think about it," I tell her. "I'll totally do the recital. And anything else you need help with."

Corinne beams. "Wonderful, sweetie. Now, some more things you should know." She reaches into a plastic jack-o'-lantern bowl at the center of the table and pulls out a glossy rectangle. "It'll be your responsibility to help students who're struggling to keep up with the rest of their class. Wear this in a visible place, so everyone can learn your name."

She hands me the tag. It has my name etched out in big, bold letters.

I slip my arms into the oversize coat, then pin on my tag as the door opens again. Corinne announces the name of each instructor as they file in.

There's Taj and Kaitlyn, Etsuko and Victor-who-goes-by-Vic. Nicole arrives on her own a minute later.

Corinne sits and starts lacing up. I return to my chair and take a big slurp of noodles before grabbing my skates.

The door flies open, and a woman rushes in. Her hair is short and brown, skin a little darker than mine. "Oh man, bridge traffic was intense." She grabs an instructor jacket from the wall and plops into the seat next to me. Her eyes scan my name tag. "Hey, Ana-Marie! I'm Jen. It's super nice to meet you." She unzips her bag as she talks. "We're all stoked you'll be helping out."

Around the room, a couple of instructors nod as Jen's eyes fall on them.

"Hi," I reply back. I glance at Alex, then back to Jen. She looks familiar, even though we just met. "Alex said you're driving me home tonight?"

"That's right. I even had a nice chat with your mom last week." Jen grins. "She officially knows I'm not a child abductor."

Alex rolls his eyes, and I laugh.

Jen pulls two gel socks and one scuffed-up skate out of her bag. "You know, Alex and I used to perform together, before he settled down and coached you to a national title."

I sit up a little straighter. "Did you ever do a show in France? In a white lacy dress?"

Jen studies me, a bit perplexed. "Yes, we did—"

"Although only one of us wore a dress." Alex shoots me a wry smile. "How did you know about this?"

"Tamar and I found a video of you online. She said you looked like you were in love with your partner... with Jen." My cheeks heat up as I look between them.

"Better not show that to Myles, then!" Jen winks at Alex before sliding on her gel socks.

"I was acting." Alex shrugs, but he's still smiling. "Not that Jen made it easy. She'd eat spicy food right before the show, then huff her horrific breath on me for the entire number."

I look back at Jen. "You seriously did that?"

"Hey now, don't judge. You have no idea how dull being on tour could get. I was just spicing things up! *Spicing*—get it?"

Before I can answer, Corinne steps into view. "Sorry to interrupt. Mind if we trade seats, Ana-Marie?"

I grab my stuff and hobble to a chair across the room, one skate half-laced and still loose. Jen stops rummaging through her bag as Corinne holds out a clipboard and pen.

"There's a student in your first class whose mother called this afternoon." Corinne leans toward Jen and lowers her voice. "She asked us to update the name on our roster and make a note to use male pronouns."

My ears prick up. I know we've gone over pronouns in English class, but it's summer now. My mind's sluggish, reluctant to remember school subjects.

"The front desk printed tonight's class lists this morning, but I promised her I would give you a heads-up. Everything will be corrected by next week."

Jen grabs the clipboard and looks it over.

"This one." Pointing, Corinne passes her pen to Jen. "Last name: *L-U-B-E-C-K*. Change the first name to Hayden."

"So, I call this kid 'he' instead of 'she'?"

"Yes." Corinne nods. "Exactly."

"Got it." Jen scratches out a line and scribbles a note to herself.

I look down fast before anyone catches me staring. My cheeks burn, like earlier today when I saw Faith effortlessly execute a pose for Miss Lydia that I wasn't even close to mastering. Except, this feels different.

Can people really ask others to call them whatever they want? I can't imagine asking Mom to even call me Ana instead of Ana-Marie.

"The Zamboni's about done." Victor-who-goes-by-Vic peers out the door. "Heads up—it's chaos."

"Ready, Ana?" Alex calls.

"Yep!" I slide on my black boot covers for added warmth and head out the door with him.

Outside the lounge, kids hop over benches, chasing one another in the seating area, while their parents check out skates at the rental counter.

"Level three, this way," Vic says in a booming voice. He hops onto the ice and glides past a crowd of people, waving his clipboard over his head.

"Level one!" Jen calls. "Meet by the vending machines."

I stop in my tracks, looking toward the snack area.

I sort of remember my own first day of skate-school, back when I was five. It's when I met Alex. Before we were allowed to get on the ice, Alex taught my class the safe way to fall and get back up. This must be what Jen will teach first, except these kids are older than I was. No one looks under ten.

The students in Jen's class face away from me as she rounds them up. I rock to the tips of my toe picks to get a better view, but I'm too far away to see much. Even if I knew what Hayden looked like, he'd be impossible to spot.

I'm not sure why I'm so interested in someone I don't know. It could be because I've never met someone with a different name from the one their parents gave them. This feels bigger, though. Maybe it doesn't have much to do with Hayden at all.

"Hurry, Ana!"

Alex is already at the rink door. I dart forward, dodging around people to catch up. He wastes no time getting me up to speed.

"We've got a combined class of levels five and six first." Alex and I glide past orange cones that divide the rink into a few sections. "This group should be comfortable with all types of forward skating and able to skate backward, almost ready to learn two-foot spins and single jumps. We need to evaluate everyone today to make sure they're in the right class. If anyone's struggling, let me know after."

Kids swizzle over. Each student wears a sticker with their name in blocky black letters. Elsie, Simone, and Priya stand in front. The rest of the class clusters behind them. All girls. They look about my age, although I'm one of the shortest out here.

Alex introduces himself, then me.

The class warms up on our private strip of ice. They glide back and forth and back again, practicing lunges, dips, and slaloms. On our fourth pass, I spot Jen. She's by the rink entrance, helping her students onto the ice. I slow my glide. Jen extends a hand to one girl after another while a boy waits nearby, already on the ice. With his back to me, all I see is blond hair and a dark red sweatshirt.

That must be Hayden.

A throat clears. I whirl around, noting Alex's arched eyebrow. The class has moved on to forward crossovers without me. "Push with the side of your blade, Priya, not the toe pick," I call.

Focus, focus, focus.

When class finally ends, Alex's students skate away, only to be replaced by another set. I look across the rink again, but Jen's students are already off the ice.

My mind circles back to Hayden for the rest of the night. I can't stop thinking about how his mom called the rink and how Jen had no problem calling Hayden "he" instead of "she." By the time Jen drops me off at home and I get into bed, I'm no closer to figuring out what Hayden's name and pronouns have to do with me.

Chapter Eight

Mom and I take the bus to a neighborhood nestled in San Francisco's northern hills after skating the next day. Walking is free, but even Mom won't risk getting sweaty before tutoring.

We hop off the bus and walk a block together, before heading in opposite directions. "I'll be back in a little over an hour," Mom calls. "Have fun with Tamar."

"I will!" I half sprint, half skip down the street. It's only been a few days since I saw Tamar, but we've got a ton to catch up on.

Tamar lives in a house instead of an apartment. It looks like a castle, with a circular turret on one side, its roof sloping to a conical point. I ring the bell and the click-clack of canine toenails draws close, followed by barking. I've visited enough to know that the higher yips come from Pixel, while the throatier yaps are all Poncho.

"Pix! Ponch!" Tamar's voice is muffled, but her

annoyance travels through solid wood. "Away from the door. Get gone!"

The door opens a sliver. Tamar pokes her head out.

"Hey! You hungry?"

"Yeah, a little." I almost never turn down food at Tamar's house. Her kitchen's always full of leftovers from parties her mom throws.

Tamar pushes the door open a bit more, still blocking the bottom half with her legs as a flurry of white and gingery orange whizzes back and forth behind her.

I slip in before either dog can escape, pausing to look at my feet out of habit. Mom and I store our shoes on a rack by our front door, but no one in the Naftali family seems to care about taking their shoes off. I leave mine on, following Tamar into the kitchen.

"The walker canceled, but Mom and Dad argued about something dumb this morning instead of calling the backup. These fluffy goofballs have been antsy all day." She glares at both dogs. "Then *someone* didn't walk them when Mom asked."

Tamar's older brother, Eli, is perched at the breakfast bar wearing sweats, plus a tank top that emphasizes his narrow shoulders. His hair is shorter than

Tamar's but just as frizzy. Eli doesn't look up at first, just pauses a video on his iPad.

"She could've meant you." His curls bob above thick brows. For a split second, his gaze turns to me as Pixel and Poncho weave around my feet. "Hey."

"Hi," I return, but Eli's attention is already back on his tablet.

Tamar makes a clucking sound with her tongue, then heads for the refrigerator. "Doubt it. I had skating practice all day."

When Eli doesn't respond, Tamar sighs, then pulls open both refrigerator doors.

"Take whatever you want," she tells me. "The caterer left a ton of samples."

I peer in. Pastries line the middle shelf, in rows of frosted blues and pinks. I reach for a cupcake swirled with a blend of both colors. "What're they for?"

"A gender reveal party. Mom's organizing it for someone on one of her nonprofit boards."

I pause with my arm still halfway in the fridge. "Wait, people have events to reveal their gender? How? I mean, *why*?"

Tamar looks at me with one brow raised. "It's for a baby, Ana."

"Ohhh. I thought you meant someone was trying to—I don't know—announce that they're a boy or a girl. Or something."

My expression must be comical because Tamar laughs. "That'd be super weird. Everyone already knows what they are when they're born."

"Right." I think of Hayden and something twists inside me. It's a relief when Tamar grabs a brownie decorated with an intricate pink flower, then heads upstairs. Conversation over, I take a bite out of my too-sweet cupcake and follow her.

Tamar's bedroom is on the second floor at the front of the house, in the castle turret. It has custom furniture designed to fit its rounded walls, which are painted a pale lilac. Posters from some of our favorite sports movies line the walls: *The Mighty Ducks 1* and *2*, *Bend It Like Beckham*, and *Ice Castles*, even though we both joke about how fake the skating scenes look.

"I can't believe we haven't seen each other in three whole days. Tell me everything."

As Tamar drops onto her bed, I slide into a dark plum armchair in front of her wardrobe closet.

"Everything? We just talked yesterday."

"Texted," she corrects. "And yeah, *everything*. How's Oakland? What's your training schedule like? Do the girls gossip a ton? How cute are the boys?"

"Um." I study what's left of my cupcake. I could say, *Okay, fine, really busy, and I haven't noticed anyone super good-looking*, but Tamar probably wants more. "It's good. The rink management is going to let me have free ice-time."

"Aaaaand you had a lesson with your choreographer. Lydia Marinova, right?" I nod as Tamar rolls onto her stomach, propping her chin on open palms. "She's *such* a huge deal. You're so lucky you get to work with her. I heard she used to choreograph for all of Russia's top skaters before she moved to Florida."

I lean back and cross my arms, not sure how to respond.

"Did you get your new program?"

"We've mostly worked on some arm stuff, plus footwork. She hasn't let me listen to my music yet, but..." I frown, remembering my first lesson.

"What?"

I take the last bite of my cupcake, chewing slowly. "She told me I have to wear a skirt during our lessons."

"How *dare*." Tamar shoots me a grin before her expression turns serious. "What's it been, like, three years since you wore one?"

"Yeah." My eyes travel to her bulletin board. It's covered in skating photos. Most are group pictures with Tamar and her synchronized skating teammates. Action shots of the team gliding in crisp formations. Full makeup and frilly, flowery dresses. Tamar's curly hair pulled up in a tight bun, her pale cheeks flushed. It reminds me of how Faith wears her hair to practice, so poised, both on and off the ice.

That gets me thinking. Tamar's got an opinion on everything. Maybe she'll have some thoughts about my new choreography.

"Hey." I hop up. "How does this look?"

I rise onto my toes, arms out and rounded in front of me. I imagine Faith's graceful posture.

My ankles wobble. I shoot an arm out to the edge of Tamar's desk to avoid toppling over.

"That needs some work." Tamar giggles from her

bed. "But I bet it'll look great when you get the hang of it."

"Faith made this look so easy yesterday," I mutter. If I can't do this on the ground, how will I ever manage on less than an inch of steel blade?

"Who?" Tamar tilts her head.

It takes me a second to remember what I said. "Oh, Faith Park. She's another skater who just started taking lessons with Alex. We ride to the rink together."

My calves ache as I hold the position again.

Tamar sits up, watching me carefully.

I drop onto my heels. "What?"

"You just never mentioned her before." She looks down at her lap for a second. "Never mind. Maybe you're trying too hard. Do it again, but make sure to breathe."

I rise one more time. My breaths get faster as I start to tip over.

"Ana, nooo!" Tamar starts laughing. "You look like you're hyperventilating." She heads over and puts a hand on my shoulder. "Again."

I take my time, lifting my arms, then rising to my toes.

Tamar steps back. I hold the position for one, two, three more seconds, eyes drifting back to her bulletin board. All those synchro skaters and their glittery costumes. My eyelids flutter closed as I try to imagine myself performing in a dress like that.

I lose my balance again.

"Not bad." Tamar drops onto her bed. "Although I'd suggest keeping your eyes open next time."

I trudge back to Tamar's armchair and let myself sink into the plush cushion. I tuck my knees to my chest and hug them, thoughts still on flowing skirts and bedazzled dresses.

"So, what's the catch?" Tamar finally asks.

"Hmm?"

"With the free ice."

I didn't realize we were done talking about my opening pose, but I'm happy to move on if it takes my mind off skating costumes. "I'm helping with the rink's skate-school classes."

She wrinkles her nose.

"It's actually kind of fun. I get to help people and demonstrate moves, and I'm pretty sure half the girls already have a crush on Alex."

"Oh my gosh." Tamar sits up. "I wish I could see their faces when Myles stops by the rink to pick him up."

I try to smile, but my thoughts shift to Hayden. I want to tell her there's a skate-school student who used to have a girl's name and now uses boy pronouns, but that feels private. I also wouldn't know how to explain why it even matters to me.

"Are you still bummed about that skirt rule? I bet you looked fine. More than." I don't say anything, but Tamar doesn't seem to notice. "Maybe Lydia wants to get you to try something new. Show the judges a different side of you?"

Alex did say something about the judges wanting to see a skater's artistic range between the short program and the free skate. "I mean, it's fine. I'd just rather wear leggings."

"I never would've guessed. I totally didn't see your costume at Nationals."

I narrow my eyes but know Tamar's teasing.

"How much longer are you working with her?"

"My final lesson's next Tuesday. Then Mom said Miss Lydia will email Alex a document with all my steps and arm positions in case I forget something after she leaves."

"Okay," Tamar says. "You've got, like, four more

lessons. Then you'll have an awesome program choreographed by someone who's basically famous, *and* you won't have to practice in a skirt anymore."

When she puts it that way, I guess that doesn't sound so terrible.

"You've got this, no problem." Tamar throws me a thumbs-up. "It's a piece of cake, just like landing a triple toe. For you, not me, obviously. Hey, want to see a video of my synchro team's new intersection?"

She waves me over. I flop down beside her, eyes fixed on her phone as two lines of girls in identical warm-up jackets glide toward one another, connected at the shoulders. Dropping their arms at the last possible second, they twirl and pass through the spaces that open up between them.

"That's cool," I say, but my mind's still on lessons with Miss Lydia.

Like Tamar said, it's only four lessons. I can do this. Piece of cake.

No, *bite of bao*.

I smile to myself. That's more my style.

Chapter Nine

When I enter the rink today, I can't find Miss Lydia—she's not behind the boards in her usual spot.

"Ana-Marie! Come."

Ugh. Now I see her. She's by the music box.

"Listen," Miss Lydia says when I arrive.

All I hear is rink noise at first. Skaters greet each other by the boards. Coaches call out technique critiques. The *crunch-chrip* from a deep-edged step sequence filters in, followed by the *shicka-shicka-shicka* of a tightly centered spin.

Then, a clue: an airy lilt of a flute. There's something familiar about the soft thrum of string instruments that soon joins in. I imagine songbirds, can almost see cotton-candy clouds floating past a dazzling castle. A minute later, I'm still waiting for a tempo change or swell in the song's volume.

When the music stays soft, I wring my mittened fingers.

That's when the singing starts. A sleepy chorus. The track ends as drowsily as it began. No flair whatsoever.

Miss Lydia looks at me, arms crossed. "Now you see the graceful edges, the dainty arm movements, how they come together."

I try to visualize my opening pose to this music, arms rounded beautifully. An image of Faith appears instead. Faith balanced on her blades, gazing over one shoulder. Faith performing a lovely, deep-edged spiral while Miss Lydia looks on and nods.

Miss Lydia steps onto the ice, marshmallow coat, snow boots, and all. As she shuffles her way to center ice, I finally remember where I've heard this music before. I glide behind her, calves already tense.

"Was that from the *Sleeping Beauty* movie?"

"Yes. A classic composition based on the Russian ballet. Tchaikovsky." Miss Lydia seems to expect me to say something, but all I can do is swallow hard. She clucks her tongue, then continues her slow shuffle.

"First, arms," Miss Lydia says when we reach the center circle. She plays the music again, this time from her phone.

Arms out, I look over one shoulder and rise onto my toe picks, just like I've practiced at home all week.

"Arrogance," Miss Lydia calls over the music. "You are a princess, the world at your fingertips."

I hop sideways to keep myself upright, feeling ridiculous. The song fades out, then loops back to the opening notes.

"Again," orders Miss Lydia. "Again, again."

The more I attempt my starting pose, the harder it is to stay balanced. Skate boots are stiff. They don't make it easy to point your feet.

We move on. Miss Lydia's lips are a thin line, her words clipped as she maps out the next forty-five seconds of my music. This takes almost an hour, through the end of my lesson.

Then I'm dismissed. Miss Lydia moves on to her next victim.

I head for the boards, grabbing my water bottle before rushing into the hockey penalty box. Normally it's a big no-no to leave the ice in the middle of a freestyle session, but I need a minute.

That music was *bad*. Alex said Miss Lydia would evaluate my strengths based on how I skated last week.

She must think I'm slow and boring if this is the song she chose for me.

"Hey, Bean." Alex glides up to me. "How's your new program coming along?"

"It's okay," I say automatically. As Alex attaches his phone to an aux cord snaking out of the music box nearby, I scoot closer. "What do you think about the music?"

"It was a little quiet."

I nod eagerly, waiting for him to continue, but his eyes are fixed on Hope at center ice, standing in her opening pose. "We might have to adjust the volume on the digital file, but that shouldn't be too much trouble."

My heart sinks. Hope's program begins and Alex skates off.

Sighing, I slouch on the bench and take a sip of water, letting my eyes travel across the ice. I pick at the bow on Hope's purple skirt.

Two more days of this. Then Miss Lydia goes home.

But I'll still be stuck with this program.

Skaters whip by, blurs of black stretch pants and jackets. Someone runs their program to a selection of *Carmen* music. I remember creating choreography for that song only a few days ago. It's not my favorite, but I'd take it over my no-energy music.

I rock on the bench, trying to figure out what to do next. I thought working with a famous choreographer would take my skating to the next level. Maybe the judges will love Miss Lydia's music and my new flowery arm movements, but I don't.

Nearby, blades click together. I refocus in time to see Faith push herself back to standing. She brushes snow off her leggings, then circles the ice to set up another jump.

I stop rocking. I've seen Faith skate lots of times, even before I started training in Oakland. Her competition programs were always artistic, but she'd score lower on the technical portion. This is the first time I've seen her try a triple jump. She turns backward, bends, and taps.

She falls again, half a revolution short on her triple toe loop.

She gets up and attempts the jump a third time. Same result.

I watch, transfixed. It's weird to see someone as

graceful as Faith struggling on a part of skating I've always found easy.

She keeps trying—and falling, falling, falling. I wouldn't be happy taking that many spills, either, but Faith looks totally over it, like she doesn't want to be here.

I look around, but Alex is across the rink working with Hope. Faith's on her own.

I get up before I can second-guess myself and glide over.

"Hey." I offer her my hand. "Are you okay?"

She lets me help her up. "Yeah. My timing just feels off."

"And your head," I say, then clamp my mouth shut. She didn't ask for help.

She wipes a clump of snow off her thigh. "What about my head?"

"It's just, you're turning it in the wrong direction when you take off."

She puts her hands on her hips. I brace myself for an argument, but all she does is sigh and drop her arms to her sides. "Like how?"

"Like"—I reach my leg back like I would right before a takeoff, then turn my head over my left shoulder—"this."

"*Oh*. I never even noticed I was doing that."

"I used to do the same thing when I was learning the double. Alex would ask what was so interesting on the other side of the rink every time I turned my head the wrong way."

To my surprise, Faith grins.

I'm about to make another suggestion when Alex glides past. Next to him, Hope slides to a stop and crosses her arms, pretending to look stern. "Less talk, more practice!" she calls in a low, deep voice, probably meant to mimic Alex.

Faith and I exchange a look. She turns to Alex. "Ana was helping me with my triple toe."

"I totally was." I nod. "I was about to show her your toe loop takeoff exercise, too, if she wants."

Alex nods back. "Ten minutes, you two. Then back to work on your programs. You've only got a couple of days left to learn all the steps." He glances toward the boards, where Miss Lydia stands watching another skater's footwork.

We glide toward an open part of the ice.

"This looks simple, but it might take a second to get," I tell Faith. "It's three back outside edges into your toe loop takeoff, but instead of pulling in your ankles right away, you do a split jump and then snap your legs together to finish rotating."

She practices the edges in front of me, hesitating when she's supposed to tap in her toe pick. "Then I do a split jump here?"

"Yep. You know how the toe loop's technique is *turn, bend, tap*?" Faith nods. "This exercise makes it *tap, split, snap*."

"*Tap, split snap*," Faith repeats. "I like that." But she doesn't move to try it. "Can you show me first?"

"Sure!" I glide backward, extending my free leg behind me. Shifting my weight, I switch feet and repeat the movement. Edge, extend. Edge, extend. One more time, then I tap into the ice. I twist forward to perform a midair split, then snap my ankles together and land backward.

I skate back to her. "Your turn."

Faith looks like a ballerina when she springs into the air, but she doesn't snap her ankles back together in time on the way down.

Surprise floods her face when she lands forward instead of backward. "This is hard!"

"Yep! Alex says it's all about timing—but once you figure it out, it'll make your toe loop so much bigger."

By the time our ten minutes are up, Faith's got the basics down well enough to practice it on her own.

Then it's back to my new choreography for the rest of the session. I start with my opening pose, one hand on the boards to keep my balance.

My arms are still too stiff. My ankles still wobble.

I skate off, working through the new steps Miss Lydia laid out earlier. Background music fills the silence in the last minutes of the session, but I barely notice. I definitely don't make up choreography for it.

The session ends. I unlace my skates, rolling my ankles in circles to work out the kinks. I feel like I've been riding a roller coaster, flying high when I helped Faith on her toe loop, only to plummet while practicing my program. Faith glances at me as she passes, then takes her usual seat at one of the tables.

Hope sits down next to me.

"Miss Lydia told me to give you this." She passes

me a thin envelope. "Your program is going to be really pretty."

"Thanks," I mumble.

I set the envelope down and swipe a towel across my skate blade extra fast. Icy slush takes flight, landing a few feet away with a soggy *splat*.

"Her choreography is really hard. But it'll earn you lots of points with the judges."

I turn away from Hope slightly. This isn't something I want to discuss when I don't know how to feel about it myself. Is it the music I hate, or the princess everyone will see when I perform to it?

I slide a soft guard onto my blade, then reach for the envelope. It isn't sealed. I untuck the flap and slide out a single sheet of paper. It's a bill from Miss Lydia to Mom.

Wide-eyed, I read it again, but nothing changes.

Miss Lydia charged Mom four thousand dollars for a handful of lessons, my music cut, and a phone consultation with a seamstress?

The air around me feels thin. My breath comes fast, like I just skated a double program run-through. This is way more than Alex's fees. We haven't even seen my new costume yet, since the seamstress Miss Lydia prefers lives in a different state.

I set the bill in my lap, trying to control my breath.

"Hey, hurry up. It's time for lunch," Faith calls to Hope. Her eyes land on me. "Do you want to come?"

"Where?" I'm surprised I can speak at all right now.

"The diner across the street," Hope jumps in. "We eat there sometimes with other skaters. You should come!"

"Oh, um." I look down, catching sight of the bill again. Mom gave me twenty dollars last week, but it's supposed to be for emergencies. I reach for my bag and pull out the lunch she packed this morning. "I have food already."

"You could eat it there with us." Faith's expression is friendly and open. Hope nods, pigtails bouncing.

On any other day, I'd tuck my lunch back into my bag and join them. But after seeing the bill, I'm not in the mood to be social.

"Thanks." My gaze drops back to the bill in my lap. "But I think I'm going to stay at the rink today."

The girls depart in a collective sparkle of roller bags. Skaters who can afford designer bags probably wouldn't blink at a bill like this. I peek at it one more time, hoping I misread a decimal point.

Nope.

I stow it away in my duffel and head for the coaches' lounge.

Four thousand dollars. That's more than the cost of my ice-time for the entire summer. The money I'm saving as a skate-school assistant definitely won't cover this.

Mom got a bonus at work, I remind myself. *She told me to focus on training. She said not to worry.*

I swallow over the thickness in my throat and enter the lounge. My heart still thrums faster than normal.

Even if Mom has this all figured out, there's still a problem: I don't know if my slow music and boring choreography are even worth all this money.

Chapter Ten

After my final choreography lesson with Miss Lydia, I try to focus on jumps, but my thoughts drift away from takeoff technique to money and music. Mom seemed fine after I gave her Miss Lydia's bill, but my stomach churns just thinking about her spending money on something I don't even like.

I'm too distracted to lose myself on the ice today. I land a solid triple salchow, then snag my toe pick the moment I step forward. That gets me a small amused grin from Faith. I smile back.

Then I remember my new program.

I should practice it now that I know all the steps. I glide toward the music box, but stop, letting another skater go ahead of me. I hover nearby. When another skater approaches, I pretend to work on spirals by the boards.

The session ends, and Faith offers me a small wave before leaving the rink with Hope for the day.

Only half the lights are on when I enter the coaches'

lounge. Alex sits in a dark corner, skates off. I plop down next to him with a frown. Something seemed wrong with Alex all day. He didn't joke as much or smile.

"Bad practice?" he asks.

"It was okay. I landed most of my jumps. It's just..." I fidget and reach for my necklace. "I'm not sure....I mean, I don't know how I feel about my program."

Alex offers me a small smile. "It's certainly a change from your last one, isn't it?"

"Yes." That's exactly it. I think? It doesn't feel right. I open my mouth to explain, but Alex winces. "Are you okay?"

"I can't seem to shake this headache." He rubs his temples. "I'm going to head home before this turns into a migraine. I texted Corinne, and she confirmed one of the older assistants can take over my classes. She'll have you help Jen, just for this week. Is that okay?"

What else can I do except nod?

As I trudge toward the bathroom to change into warmer clothes, I remember that Hayden's in Jen's first class. Maybe I'll get to meet him.

I change, then find a seat at one of the front lobby

tables and pull out my notebook. Miss Lydia's bill is a good reminder that I have to write everything down. I can't afford to waste time repeating something I've already learned when my training costs Mom so much.

I write *triple flip* in big letters, underlining it twice.

I stare at the header, wishing my practice notes would write themselves. When they don't, I grab my phone out of my duffel. I don't really feel like talking to anyone, but maybe a text or two will make me feel better.

Tamar responds almost immediately.

5:08 p.m.: Heyyy what's up

Lots of stuff, that's what. But first things first.

5:10 p.m.: I'm bored and don't want to finish my practice notes.

I can imagine her laugh when she sends back her next message in all caps.

5:11 p.m.: LOL

5:11 p.m.: Miss u

I miss her, too. Tomorrow is the day we usually hang out, but Mom's Mandarin student canceled so we'll probably stay home.

Before I can respond, Tamar texts again.

5:12 p.m.: Hey want to hang out Saturday after I get back from ship?

5:12 p.m.: ship

5:13 p.m.: SHUL!

5:13 p.m.: Autocorrect faaaaail

I grin. She could've just typed *temple*. Usually I'd be at our synagogue on Saturday morning, too, but Mom and I have both been so tired from work and skating that Saturday's become our sleep-in day lately.

An ellipsis appears. Tamar texts faster than I spin.

5:13 p.m.: Brb, dinner

5:13 p.m.: Talk more later???

The rink's front doors open and a pair of hockey players file in, rolling huge bags behind them. They head toward the other side of the building.

Maybe I need a change of scenery.

I follow the stream of hockey players into the second rink, where a dozen kids warm up on the ice. I take a seat halfway up in the stands and pull out the sandwich Mom packed for me.

Helmets and thick padding make it hard to tell

whether these players are girls or boys. A pang of jealousy shoots through me. People will think I'm a girl the second my free-skate program begins.

I freeze, sandwich halfway to my mouth.

Why would that bother me? I *am* a girl.

What else could I be?

Pap, pap!

Two hockey sticks clash. I try to relax as I take a bite of my sandwich. My eyes stay glued to the players tearing circuits around the rink, but my mind is a million miles away.

If I'm not a girl, then...what?

I hunch forward, elbows digging into my thighs. I take a bite of my sandwich, then another and another. By the time it's gone, I still don't have an answer.

Hrrnnng!

I check the large digital clock above the goal net. It flickers from 00:00 back to the actual time: 5:56.

Skate-school starts in less than five minutes!

I tear downstairs to the coaches' lounge in record time.

"There you are." Corinne looks up as I burst through the door. "I was wondering if you'd gone home, too."

"I'm here," I pant. "Sorry!"

I swipe my coat from the rack and lace up my first skate, fingers flying.

"Did Alex explain that you'll be assisting Jen tonight?"

I look up long enough to nod.

"Wonderful. See you on the ice, then." Corinne and the other instructors file out. I shove my foot into my second skate. After fastening my boot covers in place, I dash toward the door, only to come to a stuttering stop.

Name tag. Duh!

I sprint to the pumpkin bowl. Peer in and scan the labels. Different instructors teach classes on other nights, so there are several still inside.

WHITNEY. SANDRA. KYOKO. FINN.

KATHLEEN. E-something I can't read the rest of. CHRIS.

Finally, I spot one that starts with an *A*. I'm out the door lightning fast, hopping on the ice where students have already started their warm-up. I pin the name tag to my coat and skid to a stop behind Jen and her students.

Jen glides backward, calling out instructions while her students practice scooter pushes in a row. She doesn't introduce me, probably because I was late, but we catch each other's gaze for a second and she winks.

I move to one side of the line, prepared to offer tips, but my stomach jumps when I spot the boy I saw last week. He's skating on the far side of the line. The row of girls partially blocks my view, but I'll find out for sure if this boy is Hayden soon.

First, one-foot glides.

The students march forward, then lift one foot for as long as they can. I follow behind, eyes on their feet. "Too high," I tell one girl with strawberry-blond hair. "Try lifting your skate just to your ankle." She lowers her free foot like I suggested and holds her glide for twice as long.

I move on. The other students seem to be doing all right on this skill.

Except one. The boy struggles to balance. His ankles sink inward, knees knocking.

I skate over to him.

"I think your skates are loose. They might also be a size too big."

"Huh. I thought I was just bad at this." The boy lowers his free leg and attempts a two-foot glide. Still wobbly.

He turns toward me, and I glance at the skate-school sticker on his University of Minnesota sweatshirt:

HELLO, MY NAME IS
HAYDEN

I knew it!

Hayden is white, and he seems about my age, maybe a bit older. Taller than me, too, by several inches. Mom would call him lanky. My hair sticks out if I don't keep it super short or long enough for gravity to take over. Hayden's blond hair lies naturally around his ears, falling just above his eyes.

It's hard to believe he used to have a girl's name. Or used to be a girl? I'm not totally sure how that works, but Hayden looks like any other boy I've ever seen, so that's how I'll treat him.

He turns toward the rental counter. "You think I should ask for smaller skates?"

I have just enough time to count six small freckles on the bridge of his nose before his gaze shifts. Now we're looking right at each other.

"Let's try tightening them to see if that helps." Caught staring, I drop my voice to a mumble, but Hayden seems to have heard. He follows as I zip over to the boards. When I turn back, he's still march-glide-marching his way over to me.

"Wow, you're fast." His eyebrows rise, disappearing under his hair. "How long have you been skating?"

His voice is deeper than mine, but not by a ton. I clear my throat. "A...while."

I answered automatically when Hope asked what jumps I can do. With Hayden, it's hard to finish a full sentence for some reason.

He takes a seat in the hockey penalty box so I can re-lace his rental skates. The leather doesn't offer much support, but I don't think that's the issue.

"My family just moved here." Hayden shifts so I have better access to his second skate. "Most guys played hockey back in Minnesota. I wanted to do that, too, but Oakland's league coach said I needed to learn basic skating skills first. Do you live near the rink?"

I look up at him. Boys don't usually go out of their way to include me in conversations. The ones I train

· 108 ·

with are high school age or older. They're all focused on their own skating.

"I live in San Francisco, but it doesn't take that long to get here." I tighten the bow on his second skate. "See how you feel now, but I think they're probably still too big."

Hayden seems better balanced when he rejoins Jen's group. They've moved on from one-foot glides to backward skating in our absence. Hayden and I don't talk for the rest of class, but he grins at me whenever our eyes happen to meet.

Corinne blows a whistle to end classes. I follow Jen to the exit, making sure everyone gets off safely. An older girl with hair dyed a tropical blue green waits by the door.

Hayden heads to her, then waves me over.

"No broken bones? Injuries requiring stitches?" Hayden shakes his head, and the girl pats his shoulder. "Awesome. Congrats for not dying. Mom'll be thrilled. Dad, too."

Hayden rolls his eyes, then turns to me. "This is my sister, Cynthia."

"Cyn," she corrects, extending a hand. I shake it.

"I was teetering all over the place until Alex helped me with my skates." Hayden nods toward me.

...Alex?

I look over my shoulder. Scan the rink to be sure. Alex left hours ago.

And how does Hayden even know Alex's...wait.

I look down at my jacket. The letters are upside down, but the error is obvious. There are four letters on my badge.

I open my mouth. No words come out.

"I still don't think Mom and Dad want you losing all your teeth playing hockey." Hayden dodges as Cyn tries to tousle his hair. Neither of them seems to notice my silence.

"Yeah, well, Alex skates, and I don't see him missing any teeth." Hayden looks at me expectantly.

Boy pronouns. My short hair. Black boot covers over my white skates.

He thinks I'm a boy named Alex. They both do.

This is an easy fix. All I have to do is explain how I grabbed the wrong name tag. Except I'm not even sure if I want to say anything.

The shock is wearing off, but it still takes a second to offer the toothy smile Hayden seems to want.

"See? All there."

I laugh as Hayden thrusts his index finger at me and Cyn shakes her head. After a week of Miss Lydia's "princess-this" and "damsel-that," being seen as a boy settles my discomfort better than a ginger tab.

"Anyway, nice to meet you, Alex." Hayden waves again as he and Cyn head toward a bench.

"You too!"

I head back to Jen's section of ice, still smiling. As I glide up to the boards, she grabs her clipboard from the ledge. "Nice job helping that kid with his skate problem." She flips to the next attendance sheet, then glances at me, eyes dropping to my name tag. "Alex?"

My whole face heats up as I follow her gaze. "I guess I grabbed the wrong badge."

"No big." Jen waves over her next batch of students. "Might want to take it off for the rest of the night so you don't confuse anyone, though, myself included."

"Because I look *so* much like Alex."

As Jen takes attendance for her next class, I slip the

name tag into my pocket. I'll set the record straight with Hayden next week.

Until then, I plan to enjoy the fact that not everyone I meet takes one look at me and automatically assumes I'm a girl.

Chapter Eleven

It's a rare warm Saturday in Golden Gate Park. Beach towels below us, blue skies above. Tamar and I eat lunch while Mom and Mrs. Naftali chat behind us under the shade of a redwood tree.

"What do you think?" Tamar hands her phone to me, just as a gust of wind blows her hair into her eyes. She collects her tangled strands and twists them tight.

I study the green sleeveless dress on the screen. It cinches at the waist, then widens all the way to its knee-length hem. "It looks a little old?"

"You mean *vintage*." Tamar takes a bite of her sandwich. "Kell's really into fashion from the forties and fifties, so I thought I'd see if I could find anything online that would make a good bat mitzvah dress. It's cute, right?"

It takes me a second to remember that Kell is Tamar's new coach.

"It's nice. The color would look good with your hair."

"I was thinking the exact same thing." Tamar's expression turns thoughtful. She lays her arm across my shoulders. "Any idea what you'll wear to your ceremony?"

I ball up a napkin in my hands, eyeing a pair of teenagers playing Frisbee nearby.

"Not yet."

"But not a dress."

"Not a dress," I echo.

"Figured." Tamar laughs, rocking me side to side. "You are such a tomboy sometimes."

My shoulders tense. Suddenly, I remember what she said the last time I was at her house: *Everyone already knows what they are when they're born.* I wonder what she'd think about Hayden changing his name and pronouns.

I look away, toward two trucks that have parked on the clearing's edge. Their drivers unload large stereo speakers with the help of nearby picnickers. My fingers twitch. I rip my napkin into strips.

"The ceremony's not for months. I'll decide later." My words are sharp, reminding me of Miss Lydia.

Our final lesson together was on Tuesday. No more borrowed skirts or on-ice lectures. I should feel like celebrating. But her parting advice continues to stump me:

Feel the music. Become *the princess.*

What does she want me to do, sprout a crown? Order people around?

Tamar drops her arm off my shoulders. "Is everything okay?"

"Yeah, sorry. I'm just annoyed with my new program."

"I still don't get what the big deal is. *Sleeping Beauty* might be a little old-school, but the music's not that horrible. Plus, the choreography sounds amazing."

Tamar's missing the point. Boring music isn't my only problem. I tuck my knees up under me. "I'm still not sure it's right for me."

"Then tell your mom. Or Alex."

I don't know how that would fix anything. My first competition is in four weeks. There's hardly time to get comfortable with my current program. Asking Alex to choreograph a new one is out of the question, especially if I want to score well enough to skip Regionals. "We'll see."

Tamar would probably side with Alex and Mom about wanting me to focus on my performances, not the scores. But I'm thinking bigger. Free ice is just the beginning. I want to save Mom as much money as I can.

Plus, Sectionals isn't until November. If I get to skip Regionals, I'll have plenty of time to figure out how to tell Mom I don't like my program, then ask Alex to choreograph a new one.

Tamar sets her phone in her lap. "I seriously wish not liking my program was all *I* had to deal with. My parents have been fighting a ton this summer. Like, nonstop."

"Oh no. About what?"

"Nothing. Everything. Who even knows?" She shrugs. "Mom gets mad when Dad doesn't come home from work on time because they arrive late to her events. Then Dad tells her his job is more important than her dumb parties, which just makes things worse. I don't even know what they were arguing about last week, but Pix and Ponch's walker canceled and they didn't remember to call a backup for three days, even after I reminded them, like, ten times."

"I remember that." I let my shoulder bump hers. If my dad ever fought with Mom, I was too young to have any memory of it. "That must be really awkward for you."

"So awkward." Tamar sighs. "I'm trying to ignore them and just focus on skating, but Kell signed me up to test my Intermediate Moves next month, so I've also got that to stress about."

"Do you need to pass it to be on your synchro team next season?"

"I do if the coaches decide to move us up a level." Tamar fiddles with the corner of the beach blanket. "I just want to get it over with. The judges totally freak me out at tests. They're so . . . judgy, you know?"

I lean back onto my elbows, remembering the trouble she had on her twizzles last week. "Could I maybe help?"

"Yes, please!" Tamar's expression brightens instantly. "When can we skate together?"

I pull up the calendar app on my phone. "Mom wants me in bed pretty early during the week. Plus I've got skate-school on Tuesdays. I'm actually not sure if I can make any of your rink's freestyle sessions."

Tamar's face crumbles.

"But! You could video your Moves. Then we could watch the clips and figure it out together."

"That's perfect! And then a movie? Kell said you're

not really living until you see *A League of Their Own*. I think it's about girls playing baseball in the 1940s."

"That sounds awesome."

"See, this? Totally why we're friends." Tamar points at herself, then me. "That, and people are impressed that my BFF is the national Juvenile champion."

I snort.

"Soon to be national *Intermediate*, um...team training camp attendee?" Tamar tilts her head. "Is *attendee* even a word?"

I roll my eyes at her. "Not unless I learn how to skate my program a whole lot better. The steps are totally perfect for someone graceful like Faith Park. Me? Not so much."

Tamar goes still beside me. "Are you and Faith friends now?"

"Um, I don't know. Maybe?" I squint at Tamar through the sun. "She invited me to lunch last week, but I didn't go."

"Oh." Tamar looks down at her phone.

Did I say something wrong? I try to catch Tamar's gaze but she avoids my eyes.

"Skate-school's keeping me busy, too," I offer, hoping a change of topics will help. "I assisted Alex with his classes on the first day and worked with a different coach this week."

"Mm." Tamar's eyes stay down. She opens a music app on her phone and plays a song.

I could switch subjects again, ask about synchro practices or where she'll be going on vacation this year. I look around the clearing instead. To my left, the stereo speakers are almost set up. On the other end, a group of teenage boys lies on their backs, shirts off and hands behind their necks.

I wonder if Hayden is allowed to do that. I don't need to wear a bra yet, but there's no way I could take my shirt off in public without someone saying something.

"I met a boy at skate-school, too...." I trail off. My thoughts about Hayden are so jumbled.

He's a boy—but at one point, people saw him differently. That means sometime in the past Hayden was still figuring things out.

"Earth to Ana." Tamar pokes me in the side.

"Sorry." I drag my gaze back to her. "What'd you just say?"

"It was what *you* said."

I stare at Tamar.

"Something about a boy."

"Oh! Yeah. I met him in the skate-school class I helped out with this week."

"And?"

Tamar's my best friend. But I'm still not sure how to explain what I've been feeling.

"I was in a hurry and grabbed Alex's name tag instead of mine. But I didn't notice until this boy introduced me to his sister after class. I'm pretty sure he thought I was also a boy."

"Wow, awkward! He must've been hecka embarrassed."

"Yeah." I look back across the clearing, avoiding her gaze.

Tamar twists onto her side, phone forgotten. "Was he cute?"

"Huh?"

"OMG, Ana, keep up. The skate-school boy: cute or no?"

"Oh, um. I don't know." I press my lips together, thinking. "I guess?"

"So oblivious." Tamar shakes her head. "Okay, let's start with the easy stuff. What does he look like?"

"Messy blond hair. Tall-ish, kind of?"

"That's a start. Eye color?"

For real?

"I don't know! I was just trying to help him with one-foot glides."

"All right," Tamar says. "I know it's summer, but I'm giving you homework: Pay more attention next week and report back with your findings. Take a pic if you can sneak one in."

She has to be joking on that last one, but it's hard to tell sometimes.

A song blasts out of the speakers across the clearing, louder than the music on Tamar's phone. She pauses her app, then hops up and turns toward our moms.

"Ana and I are gonna go dance."

I shield my eyes with one hand, looking up at Tamar. "We are?"

"Yes, ma'am."

Ma'am? I make a face. "What if I don't want to?"

"Then you'd be disappointing your very best friend. Pleeeease?"

People already surround the speakers, swaying in time with the music. Some wave brightly colored flags. At least we won't be the only ones dancing.

"Okay, fine."

Along the way, someone offers Tamar a small rainbow flag. She asks for another and passes it to me. We stop near the edge of the crowd, and a kaleidoscope of colors fills my vision as a light wind tugs at flags of all colors, shapes, and sizes.

Tamar twirls in front of me. I pause at first, remembering all of Miss Lydia's critiques. Tilting my chin toward the sky, I let the wind tickle my face.

Then I copy Tamar, lifting my flag as I twirl faster and faster.

Next week will be better. I'll talk to Hayden at skate-school and tell him I'm Ana, and we'll laugh about his mistake. Maybe I'll even get used to my free program.

Right now, I twist and turn, letting the music take over my movements. Tamar bumps into me, and we giggle, swaying together with arms wrapped around each other. For now, nothing exists outside this clearing.

JULY

Chapter Twelve

Before I can set the record straight with Hayden tonight, I have to get through a full day of training.

Alex signals me over to the music box at the start of our afternoon ice session. "Your first event is in Los Angeles at the end of the month. Let's spend this lesson focusing on your program."

I ran my short program yesterday, so I know he's talking about my free skate. I fiddle with the zipper on my warm-up jacket as I skate to the middle of the rink.

Alex gives me a thumbs-up. I rise to my toe picks, arms extended, hoping this position looks less awkward than it feels.

It could be worse—I could be wearing a skirt.

Focus!

My short program is familiar after skating it last season. My free skate is different—I still have to think about each step. Instead of bold statements, my movements feel like nervous questions.

I hear the fourth note first, and teeter on my toe picks as Alex turns up the volume. Pushing hard to catch up with the music, I feel less regal by the second as I prepare for my triple salchow.

Turn, bend... I kick my free leg through too soon, taking off tilted. There's nothing I can do except flip forward to keep from falling.

"Shake it off," Alex calls. "Don't stop."

I suck in a shuddery breath and launch into my first spin. My shoulders are tight, and I don't realize I've been holding my breath until the corners of my eyes sparkle with stars.

I dash off to start my footwork but skid to a stop. I'm on the wrong side of the rink!

It's only when I whirl around to get back on track that I realize I haven't performed a single arm movement.

Too late now.

My program turns into a to-do list of spins and jumps that I check off in the last ninety seconds. Jump combo, jump, another jump, final jump sequence, combo spin—DONE.

I strike a sharp end pose, arm up like I'm saluting

someone. So much for portraying a princess. I feel like a soldier returning from war.

Hands on my hips, I look down as I catch my breath.

"That was an unusual interpretation of your music." Alex smiles at me, a look I don't return. He skates over and lays a hand on my shoulder.

"Hey, I know that wasn't your best, but this program is still new. You'll get better with practice."

I'm not so sure. A princess is someone who oozes grace, from fingertips to feet. Someone who wears frilly dresses and powders blush on her cheeks. That's not me. I'm a strong skater who lands jumps on perfectly timed crescendos. That's why my short program works. It's all about speed and power instead of portraying a delicate character.

I want to tell Alex this. So badly.

Except, he might just explain that sometimes we have to play roles that don't fit perfectly, like the romantic duet he performed with Jen in France. Acting is a part of skating.

"Let's focus on your salchow for a moment," Alex says, pulling me out of my thoughts. "The takeoff was a bit rushed. Are you getting thrown off by the steps leading up to it?"

"They're fine," I huff. It's the princess part of the program that's messing me up.

"Okay." Alex raises his eyebrows like he's not sure he believes me. "Then go try it again. Start right after your opening pose so you can build up some speed."

I glide off, grateful I don't have to balance on my toe picks again. I perform a quick twizzle, then a crisp rocker turn from forward to backward. One crossover, then I turn into my takeoff position. My right leg extends back, kicks through, and *snaps*.

Alex claps.

I perform my next couple of steps, stopping right before my first spin.

"You were right," Alex calls as he glides over to me. "The steps flow well into that jump. Now you just need to land it to music." I know he's just teasing me a little, but I'm not in the mood.

"That's it for your lesson." Alex pats my shoulder. "Good job today."

It didn't feel good. A performance like that won't cut it if I want to skip Regionals.

Faith looks at me with a tentative smile as I grab my bag from behind the boards. It only makes me feel worse. I cut past her without a word, ignoring the other skaters on my way to the coaches' lounge. I don't feel like talking to anyone.

I eat my dinner alone in the coaches' lounge. When Alex arrives after his final lesson, I grab my bag and get up.

"Gotta change for skate-school." I slip out before he can say anything. It's not a lie, but it also isn't the full truth. I need time to plan exactly how to tell Hayden I'm Ana tonight.

I've got everything figured out. If I stick to three easy steps, I'll be fine.

One: Grab the correct name tag. For real this time.

Two: Catch Hayden before classes start and tell him the truth.

Three: Don't freak out about Step Two.

Alex is already wearing his name tag by the time I get back to the lounge. I find my badge and pin it to my own coat.

Step One: Done. That was easy.

Step Two requires patience. I lace up my skates, pretending to listen as Jen jokes with the other coaches.

Leaning forward, I arch my back and exhale. I wish I had some ginger. The thought of telling Hayden I'm a girl fills me with the same nerves I get at big competitions, but I'm determined. Step Three will not get the best of me.

I follow the instructors out of the lounge, eyes darting from bench to bench, then back to the badge on my jacket. It feels like there's a spotlight on me, tracking my path.

I trail behind Alex, scanning the seating area.

No sign of Hayden.

I help students get onto the ice. When there's no one left for me to assist, I reluctantly glide off to join Alex's class.

I've imagined this moment for days, but Hayden isn't here. This is something I didn't plan for.

I follow behind Alex's students as he leads them through a warm-up.

"Chin up, Priya," I call as I skate past, then slow to demonstrate the proper arm position to Elsie. My eyes drift back to the entrance as Alex brings the class to a stop in the middle of the ice.

"Has anyone done a two-foot spin before?" A few

students raise their hands. "Great. Does anyone want to demonstrate?" Their hands go down fast. Alex shoots me an amused look. "Then it's a good thing we have our very own talented assistant. Ana?"

This is just the distraction I need. Stretching my arms out, I bend my knees, wind up, and pull my arms and feet toward my body.

"Pretty cool, right? Can you imagine doing that soon, Simone?" Alex winks at her. "How about you, Elsie?" Both girls blush as Alex continues to give technique tips. They must not have seen him and Myles together yet. Or maybe they have and it doesn't matter. I make a mental note to tell Tamar. Either way, she'll think it's funny.

"Now, Ana," Alex continues. "Just for fun, do a fast scratch spin."

I'm off again. Soon I'm nothing but a dark blur of short hair, baggy instructor jacket, and black boot-cover fabric. The students fade away. For a moment, it's just me, my blades, and the ice. I've missed this during the last couple of weeks of practice.

People clap as I finish—and not just the students from Alex's class. Across the rink, Jen has paused her lesson. Her whole class watches in awe.

Even Hayden.

Our eyes lock and I lean back on my heels, almost losing my balance. He waves, then turns back to Jen.

Alex moves on, too. We have twenty minutes left, but they pass fast now that I know Hayden's here.

"Back in a sec!" I call to Alex the minute he dismisses his class.

Step Two: time for a redo.

I swizzle past the cones separating Vic's section from Jen's, then stop. Hayden's back is to me but he's still on the ice. My stomach flips again as I study my name tag with a tucked chin.

One word. Eight letters. People see it and think they know my whole story. Ana-Marie equals girl.

Hayden thought the opposite, which isn't right, either. But it definitely beats being seen as a princess.

My hand reaches up to my jacket like it's got a mind of its own. I unpin my name tag before I can stop myself and slip it into my pocket. I already feel lighter as I glide over, like an invisible weight's been lifted off my shoulders.

Jen spots me first. "Well, hey. Fancy running into you in this corner of the rink."

I say hi to her as Hayden turns. I should be memorizing details of his appearance for Tamar, but my mind goes blank the second I see him.

"That was a cool spin."

"Thanks." I study him as we glide toward the rink door. No evidence of wobbly legs today. "Your skates seem like they fit better."

"Yeah." He looks down at his feet. "I asked for a smaller size. You were right that my last ones were too big."

We wait at the back of the line as students file off the ice. Now is the perfect time to tell him. Step Two awaits.

"Skate fit is super important. I had to try a few pairs before I found the right ones."

I glance down at my skates, but there's nothing to look at since they're under my boot covers. I need to just tell Hayden about the mix-up, but the words stay stuck in my throat.

"Well, maybe if I make it into the hockey league someday, I can convince my parents to buy me my own skates."

"That'd be cool...."

"I probably have to get a lot better first, though."

"It's hard when you're only here once a week," I offer. "My best friend and I practiced on public sessions outside of skate-school classes when we were younger. That's how we improved a ton."

"Good idea," Hayden says. "Of course, I'd need to make a friend for that to work."

"Oh, um." I'm not exactly an expert when it comes to making friends.

"I have an idea." Hayden looks at me. "Maybe we could hang out sometime?"

"Hang…what?" I stare at him. "Like, skate together?"

"Sure. Or hang out somewhere else. I haven't met anyone since my family moved here. Except you. Maybe I'll get to know more people when school starts, but that's still a ways off."

Hayden's talking so fast, I can hardly keep track of what's being said. When I finally catch up, I can't think of anything to say other than a quiet, "Oh. That stinks."

"Yeah." Hayden nods. "Want to swap phone numbers?"

I pat my pockets. My name tag digs into my hip like it's sending me a pointy message. "I totally left my phone in the coaches' lounge."

"It's cool." Placing his hands on either side of his mouth, Hayden hops off the ice and yells, "Cyn! My phone!"

My fingers curl around the edge of the plexiglass. Alex's next class is about to start. I can't follow Hayden off the ice.

"I'm not your servant." Cyn appears in a flurry of blue-green hair. She shoots Hayden an irked look, then spots me. "Hey, Alex. That spin was awesome. I would've hurled."

I wave, then drop my gaze. That's not my name.

"My phone?" Hayden holds his hand out.

"Chill." She digs through a large bag. "I'm looking."

"Cyn takes her time with everything," Hayden informs me. "That's why I missed half of class today."

"California drivers are terrifying. Drive yourself next time. Oh, right. You can't, so maybe stop complaining."

Despite her comment, Cyn doesn't seem angry. She and Hayden remind me of Tamar and Eli. She finally pulls out Hayden's phone and hands it to him.

"Okay, what's your number?" Hayden asks, ignoring Cyn.

I tell him and he types in my name—Alex's, actually.

Do something!

"Just *A*."

Hayden pauses as he looks at me. "Just the letter *A*?"

I could say, *My real name's Ana, but I prefer A.* It'd be better than him thinking my name's Alex. But then what about pronouns?

I nod, throat dry. *What am I doing?!*

Hayden backspaces. "Last name?"

I spell it for him.

"Okay, cool. I'll text you."

"Ana!"

I whirl around. Alex gestures at me from the far end of the ice. Chest tight, I glance back at Hayden. His eyes are still down on his phone. I push away from the boards, my arms tingling with relief.

"I should get back to class." I smile at him, but it feels like I'm grimacing.

Hayden waves as I skate back toward Alex, head down, eyes on the ice.

Three easy steps?

Yeah, I totally blew that.

Chapter Thirteen

It's spring rolls for dinner tonight. Sit-down dinners are rare in the middle of the week, but Mom's Mandarin lesson canceled again. It feels like I've seen Mom more this summer than I did all last year.

"How was practice today?"

"Good."

Mom looks like she expects me to say more. It used to be easy to tell her everything on my mind. Now I feel rusty.

We worked on my free program, but that's not something I feel like talking about. "I landed some triple flips during my afternoon lesson with Alex."

Mom lifts the cutting board at an angle, using her knife to nudge chopped cucumber sticks into an empty bowl. Unlike her favorite chive pancakes and some of her noodle dishes, this isn't a recipe Mom learned from Grandma Goldie. It's something she found online, but I can't remember the last time we made it together. Nowadays, I usually eat before Mom gets home from work and tutoring, and she makes our lunches after I've gone to bed.

"On or off the harness?"

"On. One of the other coaches has a pole harness that he let Alex borrow."

A harness helps skaters learn new jumps. A rope is attached to the belt I wear around my waist, which usually extends up to a wire track on the rink's ceiling. Alex pulls on the rope so I can learn how the rotations feel on a new jump. The belt comes off when I'm ready to try without help. The pole harness is almost the same, except it's not attached to the ceiling. We can practice jumps anywhere on the ice.

"Sounds like fun."

"It was." I arrange our food at the center of the table. "I'm super close to landing it on my own."

"And you're taking notes, so you can refer to them when you're not working with Alex?"

"Tons of notes." Since Miss Lydia left, I've been less distracted. Tips from Alex fill my notebook. Diagrams line the margins with proper jump takeoff and landing edges. "If I keep working hard, Alex said we can maybe add it to my program in the fall."

He actually said by Regionals in October, but I leave that part out. If everything goes according to plan, I can debut my triple flip in November at Sectionals instead.

Mom nods. She places the cutting board in the sink, twisting the faucet knob to wash her hands.

Blrrriing!

My phone blinks brightly from the nook by my bed.

"How's Tamar?" Mom asks as I head across the room.

"Good, I think." I stand on my tiptoes and grab my phone. "We've both been busy, but we're going to meet up this weekend."

We haven't hung out since our picnic in the park last weekend. Saturday can't come soon enough.

I unlock my phone and scan the message.

6:02 p.m.: Hey A! 👋 It's Hayden, how are u?

The corners of my lips twitch up. Part of me thought Hayden had forgotten to text when I didn't hear from him right after skate-school.

I send back a quick reply.

6:03 p.m.: Hi, I'm good! How are you?

I spell all my words out. Mom's nearby, and so are her expectations about proper English.

Hayden's answer comes back fast.

"Dinner, Ana-Marie."

I hunch my shoulders, eyes fixed on Hayden's ellipsis. I set my phone down on Mom's bedside table as slowly as possible, waiting for his response.

No luck.

"Do you want to say the blessing?" Mom asks when I return to the kitchen.

I shake my head. "You can do it this time." It's been hard to avoid thinking about my bat mitzvah ceremony ever since Tamar showed me that vintage dress. Mom lets me wear nice pants whenever we go to Shabbat services, but I'll be in front of the entire temple for my bat mitzvah ceremony. I can't help wondering if she'll ask me to wear a dress for that.

My phone chimes again. I cringe.

Mom raises her eyebrows.

She recites the blessing same as always, but something feels off. Maybe it's because we haven't been to temple in a while. I dip the thin rice-paper wrap into a bowl filled with warm water. It softens on contact. After adding ingredients, I fold the wrap around them like a blanket.

Blrrriing!

"Sorry!" I hop up. "I'll put it on silent."

It chimes again before I reach it, then twice more in my hands.

I'd planned to silence it fast, but since I'm here, and since it's Hayden, I stop to skim the texts.

6:15 p.m.: Sorry I didn't msg sooner

6:15 p.m.: Lost track of time working on my cosplay

I don't know what a cosplay is, and there's no time to ask.

6:15 p.m.: But question for u

6:16 p.m.: Want to hang out this weekend?

Yes! One hundred percent.

"Ana-*Marie*."

I flinch, then whirl around, phone still in hand. Mom taps the table.

"Sorry," I say again. One swipe, two clicks. I silence my phone for real this time.

"What's so important that Tamar can't wait until after dinner?"

I plop back down, then dip my spring roll into peanut sauce.

"It wasn't Tamar. I met a kid at skate-school who asked if I wanted to hang out this weekend."

"Ah." Mom's jaw relaxes. "I'm glad you're making new friends."

"Yeah." If I made friends with anyone in Oakland, I would've guessed it'd be Faith. I'm glad Mom hasn't asked about her. I'd have to explain how Faith's been nice and even invited me to lunch, but I didn't go.

"Hayden just moved here with his family. He's in the level one class."

I take a big, crunchy bite of my spring roll.

Mom looks at me. "Your new friend is a boy?"

I swallow hard. "Yes. That's okay, right?"

"Hmm." Mom folds her arms. "He's your age, Hayden?"

I actually don't know. He didn't look *too* much older than me, though.

"Pretty close." I try to act cool while assembling another spring roll but can't bring myself to look across the table. "I think."

I chew slowly. Mom stays silent. Finally, I look up.

"All right."

My legs bounce. This is going to be awesome.

"But I have a condition."

I go still.

"I want to speak to his mom or dad first."

"Mmmrilly?"

"You know how I feel about talking with food in your mouth, Ana-Marie."

I take a big swig of water and chew furiously fast.

Mom can't call Hayden's house. If she does, he'll know I was lying the second one of his parents gets off the phone and says my real name.

"Why do you have to talk to them?"

"Because not only do I want to ensure there'll be a parent around to supervise, but I'm not about to leave my only child in the hands of strangers without learning more about them."

I stare at Mom, silently begging her to reconsider.

She looks back with a slight shake of her head.

"Fine." I give up. "I'll ask him for their number."

Mom gives me a quick nod, then reaches for a second rice-paper wrap. I stare at my plate as she chooses her vegetables.

I'm glad one of us is still hungry.

Chapter Fourteen

I should be skating a few clean run-throughs by now, but I'm not even close. It's one thing to fall on a triple jump when I'm competing. As long as I rotate three times in the air before landing, I get credit for the jump, minus a deduction for falling.

But at practice this morning I *popped* more than half my jumps—meaning my timing was so off that I didn't rotate enough. There's no deduction, but in a competition, I'd earn next to nothing.

Alex keeps telling me to relax, that this is a new program with harder transitions between jumps and spins. Still, the real problem is my free-skate music. I'm not sure I hate it, just how it makes me feel when I skate to it.

I exit the ice and stop in front of a bench, wondering how Alex felt while pretending he was in love with Jen during their duet in France. Maybe the video will give me a clue. I sit down and pull out my phone, skipping texts from Tamar. I'll text her back after I watch the duet.

Alex's and Jen's smiles fill the screen once it loads. I move to the part where Alex puts his hand on Jen's cheek, then kisses her during a lull in the music.

I watch it again.

I know it's just acting, not how Alex really felt. Maybe skating as a princess in my free program doesn't say anything about me, either.

I really wish I could believe that, but Alex got to be himself again after his performance. Between skating and Hayden, I feel like I'm stuck between two things that both feel wrong.

As skaters leave the ice, I set my phone down and look away. Besides my program, I have something else to worry about today. Mom's going to call Hayden's parents during her lunch break.

"Ana!" Hope sails off the ice, skidding to a stop in front of my bench. "Mom called. She's meeting us at the restaurant across the street!"

I look up at her. It's not even noon. Mrs. Park isn't supposed to pick us up for hours.

Hope kicks off one of her skates, then hops closer to me. "Come on. *Hurry.*"

I untie the top rungs on my skate, then glance at

Hope. She's already got her second boot off. "What's going on? Why is your mom here so early?"

"It's the first week of July." Hope says this like it means something. I shake my head as she swipes a towel across the slush on her blades. "Our costumes arrived. Mom's handing them out at lunch!"

"Ohhh."

Mom told me the seamstress shipped them out to Mrs. Park a few days ago. Then Hayden invited me to hang out and I forgot I had even more stuff to worry about.

I pick up my pace for Hope's sake. Faith walks ahead of us with a pair of girls around our age. We cross the road and enter a diner. Vintage knickknacks line the walls.

Mrs. Park sits at a booth near the back. She drapes a large garment bag across the table, then pulls garbage bags out of her purse. "For later, to keep the dresses clean on the ride home." She opens one of the garbage bags. There's a hole in the center of the bottom seam where a hanger can be slipped through.

Mrs. Park unzips the garment bag, and thousands of crystals reflect light from the overhead lamp in a shimmering spectrum of silver, black, and red.

"Faith first. For her free skate."

Mrs. Park lifts up the deep red dress, trimmed with black crystals and a hint of lace around the neck. Faith reaches out and lays the dress flat on the table so the rest of us can admire it. This would be a good time to tell her how perfectly this new dress matches her music. Maybe that would make up for turning down her lunch invitation, plus all the times I've avoided her lately.

A second dress emerges before I can form the words. Mrs. Park holds it up before passing the dress to its new owner. I swallow. My throat feels thick, like someone's wrapped a hand around it.

My phone vibrates. As Mrs. Park pulls out another outfit, I skim over a text from Mom.

11:34 a.m.: I spoke to Mr. and Mrs. Lubeck. You may spend Saturday with Hayden. We'll discuss more later.

I reread her message, studying it for hints about what Hayden's parents might have said.

Hope nudges me. I look up, and a powder-blue dress fills my vision. Everyone waits for me to react.

Shimmery white Lycra lines the chest and shoulders. The skirt sways as Mrs. Park holds it out to me. I hesitate before reaching to accept it.

"It's sooooo pretty," Hope says. She's right. A champion would wear a dress just like this on the top step of the podium.

I blink fast. Bite my lip. I could get used to it. Maybe.

"What's wrong?" Faith asks.

Hope's eyes flicker from the dress to me. "Don't you like it?"

"I"—swallowing again, I look at the dress in my hands—"thought it would be pink."

"It's okay." Hope pats me on the shoulder, like she's trying to reassure a little kid. "Princesses don't always wear purple or pink. You'll still look really pretty."

Hope twists to look when Mrs. Park pulls out another costume, but I barely notice. My eyes are still on my dress, plus a small envelope attached to its hanger. I pick at the tape until it opens. It's a bill from the seamstress.

For sixteen hundred dollars.

My heart nose-dives into my stomach. It's not just the cost that's making me feel sick. This is the first time I can imagine how I'll look at the skate-school recital. Lots of people will be there watching me, like Cyn and the rest of the Lubeck family. What will Hayden think if he sees me perform in this?

"Ana?"

A hand waves in front of my face. I blink the table back into focus and look over at Faith.

"We're going to order lunch." Faith watches me carefully. "What do you want?"

Hope passes me a menu before I can answer. Most of the entrees are over ten dollars. The appetizers aren't any cheaper. I still have the twenty Mom gave me, but this definitely isn't an emergency.

Our waitress taps a pencil against her notepad. The plastic bag crinkles as I slip my dress in and move it to my lap, on top of my phone with Mom's text about the Lubecks. I still don't know if Hayden knows my secret. What I *do* know is that this bill will make things harder for Mom, even if I save us money by qualifying to skip Regionals.

"Thanks, but I'm good." I reach under my chair for my lunch bag. Forcing a smile, I place it in front of me. With a heavy sigh, the waitress moves on to another table.

Chapter Fifteen

Tourists crowd the BART subway station as Mom and I stop near the outbound platform. She paid a fare to come through the gates with me, even though I told her I'd be fine.

"It takes seven minutes to get through the tunnel before your stop at West Oakland. Please text the moment you meet the Lubecks so I know you made it there safely."

"I will."

A gust of air shoots across the platform, blowing people's hair into their faces. The brakes of an approaching train squeal before it comes to a stop.

"Have fun. Don't forget to text." Mom watches as I board the train. I keep catching her staring at me like something's off. I first noticed it at dinner last night, and it happened again after I got dressed this morning. I wear these black shorts and my Nationals T-shirt all the time. It must be more than my clothes.

The train car is almost empty. Normally, I'd find a

seat, but I'm not sure I can sit still, even for seven minutes. I stay by the doors, still thinking about Mom even after they close. I was so sure we'd have a talk after her call with the Lubecks. But all she said last night was that Hayden's parents seem like "very nice people."

The train zips out of the station and into the Transbay tunnel. I tuck a strand of hair behind my ear, and it stays put. Any longer and it'll distract me while I skate, so it's probably time for another haircut. I scroll through texts on my phone, gripping the rail with my free hand to keep my balance.

The most recent message is from Hayden, sent last night. Hanging out: achievement unlocked!

I scan my other messages, eyes snagging on Tamar's name. She's third from the top, below Hayden and Mom, but the text is still bold and unread. I tap on it, and messages from yesterday fill my screen.

11:34 a.m.: I've been practicing moves in the field for a flippin hour

11:34 a.m.: Send help, why are inside twizzles so hard??

11:35 a.m.: Anyway, can't wait to see u tomorrow and watch a new movie!!

My body goes stiff, hand tightening on the rail in

a white-knuckled grip. How did I miss these? Yesterday was hectic, but I've never forgotten a hang-out date with Tamar. Never squared. I text her back fast.

9:52 a.m.: I can't meet today. I'm sorry! Can we do tomorrow?

"Approaching West Oakland." The intercom crackles to life with the conductor's tinny voice. "Next stop: West Oakland station."

I pocket my phone as we exit the tunnel, rising above the edges of the city. I hop off the train into the glow of midmorning sun. The San Francisco skyline peeks out across the bay through a cloud of perpetual fog. Following the trickle of passengers down an escalator from the elevated platform, I swipe my fare card at an electronic reader.

"Hey!" Hayden waves to me. "We're parked over here."

Seeing him makes me feel like skipping. I pick up my pace as he slides open the back door of a minivan and hops in. I take a seat next to him in the middle row.

"Good morning!" A woman twists around in the driver's seat. Her blond hair is a shade darker than Hayden's, but their smiles match.

I say hello back, then buckle up before remembering

I still have to text Mom. As the van turns out of the parking lot, I let her know I found the Lubecks. No reply from Tamar yet.

"Hayden mentioned you go by A?"

"Yes, ma'am."

"Such a gentleman," Hayden says. I can tell he's teasing me, but last week's delight at being seen as a boy now twists into guilt. Sticking out my tongue, I try to ignore it.

"A it is, then." Mrs. Lubeck looks back through the rearview mirror. "Boys, introduce yourselves."

I glance behind me at two boys in the back seat. The older boy wears glasses and is focused on a phone, the younger a tablet. Their blond hair and fair complexions make them look like younger versions of Hayden.

"*Boys.*"

"Mat—"

"—liot."

They speak over each other. The older boy looks up first.

"I'm Elliot." He slides his glasses higher onto the bridge of his nose, then points to the smaller boy. "That's Mattie."

Elliot looks like he's eight or nine, Mattie about five. Elliot nudges Mattie, who finally drags his eyes away from his device. He meets my gaze, eyes narrowing. "What kind of name is A?"

"Mattie!" Mrs. Lubeck calls. "Remember your manners."

I actually don't mind. It's better than other questions Mattie could be asking.

"I don't know. A short one?" I shrug.

Mattie shoots me a gap-toothed grin, then looks down at his tablet again.

"So." Hayden clears his throat. "We were going to take you to this cool outdoor arcade, but I got outvoted because *someone* decided they wanted to see a puppet show. Two someones." He glances toward the back seat. Mattie and Elliot ignore him.

"That's okay. Where are we going instead?"

"It's this place near Lake Merritt, called Fairyland. Have you ever been?"

"*Fairy*land?" I shake my head.

"Don't worry. It's not super girly—or else Mattie and Elliot wouldn't want to go, either."

I stay quiet. Girly isn't usually my thing, but that doesn't automatically mean it's bad.

"It's supposed to be like Disneyland," adds Elliot.

"That sounds cool." I've never been there, either. All our money goes toward skating expenses.

A lake comes into view. People are out picnicking, just like on a nice day in Golden Gate Park. It takes Mrs. Lubeck a few minutes to find a parking spot.

"Electronics, please, boys." Mrs. Lubeck holds out her hand.

Mattie and Elliot pass over their devices without protesting, eyes fixed on a sign with oversize letters. FAIRYLAND. It's spelled out in a wacky font and a rainbow of colors.

We head toward an arch in the center of a tall row of plants. I look closer and realize the leafy greens are shaped like a dragon. As Mrs. Lubeck rummages through her purse in front of the ticket booth, I slide a red paper envelope out of my pocket.

Each winter, Grandma Goldie sends me a crisp ten-dollar bill, plus a red-and-gold hongbao for Chinese New Year. I haven't decided what to spend that money on yet. Plus, I still have the emergency twenty and another fifteen dollars Mom gave me specially for today.

I pull out the twenty and catch Mrs. Lubeck's eye.

She waves it away. "This is my treat. I'm glad Hayden's made a friend so soon after our move."

"Mom," Hayden groans, cheeks turning pink.

Mrs. Lubeck just smiles and passes us both an admission ticket.

We enter under an arch carved into the plant-dragon's side. Mattie, Elliot, and Mrs. Lubeck turn down a path. Hayden and I trail a few feet behind.

"Momma!" Mattie waves his arms. Mrs. Lubeck leans down and he whispers something to her.

She straightens. "Quick detour before the puppet theater."

As she leads us down another road, I look at Hayden, who shrugs. "He probably needs the bathroom. Mattie has to go, like, every five minutes for some reason."

The rest area comes into view. Mattie makes a dash toward the boys' bathroom on one side of the building, while Hayden follows Elliot. He hesitates at the entrance.

"It's okay, Hayden," Mrs. Lubeck calls. "You can go in. I'll meet you boys outside when we're finished."

I hesitate, too, as I stare at signs I've seen thousands of times before. Signs I never thought twice about—until now.

In front of me, there's a bathroom for boys, another for girls. I stand in the middle, eyes darting from one to the other, with no clue which one to use.

Chapter Sixteen

"Are you coming?" Hayden glances back at me.

I need to decide fast.

Looking down, I kick at some loose gravel in a sudden surge of anger. Why does everything have to be a choice between one thing or another?

It would confuse everyone if I entered the girls' bathroom. Plus, the boys' room will probably have a stall, but I don't know for sure—I've never used it before. I'm frozen in place, unable to move in either direction.

"I'm fine," I lie. "I'll wait for you out here."

Once everyone's finished, we return to the main path, and my anger turns into frustration. Hayden's already made the choice to use a boy name and pronouns. For me, it doesn't feel that simple.

Mattie and Elliot take off at a run, following signs toward the puppet theater. Brightly colored structures line the road on either side of us. I spot an old woman peeking out of a huge shoe-shaped house, then a small carousel called the Wonder-Go-Round.

"Mattie! Ell! Slow down." Mrs. Lubeck sighs, then turns back to us. "I have a hunch you're not going to want to sit through the puppet show, correct?"

We both nod.

"I figured. You two can feel free to do your own thing, as long as you promise to stay inside the park. Meet us back by the theater in about half an hour."

She takes off down the path, in pursuit of Mattie and Elliot.

"Let's find a map," Hayden suggests. "I think I saw one near the entrance."

It's quieter without the rest of his family around. Now would be a perfect time to tell Hayden my real name.

Before I can say a word, he points toward a big wooden board. "Found it!"

We stand in front of the map for a few silent seconds. A million ways to say what needs to be said run through my head. Too bad my mouth's gone completely dry.

"Want to check out the"—rising to his toes, Hayden

reads off the small print in the upper corner of the map—"Jolly Trolly?"

"Sure." The word comes out high and squeaky, but he doesn't seem to notice.

"Looks like it's on the other side of the park, so maybe we can find another ride before we get there."

We follow the signs and before long, we come across a statue of the White Rabbit from *Alice in Wonderland* standing in front of a tunnel.

Hayden and I glance at each other. We enter together.

Light floods the tunnel from both ends, highlighting artwork on the walls. I recognize scenes from Alice's adventures, like the door she tried to chase the rabbit through once she arrived in Wonderland. Beside it, there's a tiny bottle that says *Drink Me*. Hayden points out a painted biscuit marked *Eat Me*.

We head farther in, past a wall of flowers beside a window cutout. It's fenced off, but we can still peek through to the outside world.

"Sorry if this is boring." Hayden's eyes drift to the playing cards painted on the tunnel's ceiling. "Mattie and Elliot like the same things, which means I almost always get outvoted."

"What about Cyn?"

Hayden shrugs. "She used to have my back when we were younger. Now that she's almost done with high school, she spends more time on her own doing whatever, you know?"

I don't. Tamar and Eli don't really do much together, either.

We press up against the wall to let a group of kids pass.

Why is it so hard to switch subjects and get this over with?

Hayden glances back at me. Heart hammering, I catch up to him. Now or never.

"So, I need to tell you—"

"Do you have any—"

We both stop mid-sentence, waiting for the other to finish. I open my mouth at the same time that Hayden repeats the first two words of his question.

His laughter bounces off the tunnel walls. "You first."

I shake my head with a sheepish grin.

"You sure?" I give him a stiff nod. "Okay. I was just wondering if you have any brothers or sisters."

Relief replaces my jitters. "It's just me and Mom. My best friend, Tamar, is almost like a sister, though. We both skate and hang out a ton, plus our families go to temple together."

Hayden nods, encouraging me to continue.

"I have some friends through my homeschool program, too, but it's all online. Most of them don't live in San Francisco."

My phone buzzes in my pocket. It's almost like Tamar knew I was talking about her. She's not free until tomorrow afternoon, according to her text.

I type up a response.

10:28 a.m.: Movie night then?? (I need to get a haircut too btw)

Tamar's response buzzes in fast.

10:28 a.m.: OK YES

10:29 a.m.: I can be your stylist!

10:29 a.m.: Alsoooo I videoed my intermediate moves for your review

"That's cool." Hayden watches me text with interest. He looks like he's waiting for me to say something.

"What about your friends?"

Hayden looks away. "I haven't made any yet here,

except for you." He takes a few steps forward, following the tunnel's curve.

"I mean where you used to live. Back in Minnesota."

"Oh." Hayden doesn't say anything at first. His gaze moves from the phone in my hand to the tunnel walls, where the playing cards have sprouted legs and arms. "It's—I don't know—hard to keep in touch when we're so far apart."

This seems like a weird answer. Even if he doesn't want to write letters, he could text.

The tunnel ends before I can say anything. We step out into the sunlight. Life-size playing cards tower over us, creating a barrier from the rest of the park.

"It looks like a maze," Hayden says. "I wonder if it's actually hard to find your way out."

We explore it, guessing which way to take when we have a choice, backtracking when we find a dead end. Eventually, we stop in front of a wall of playing cards that have fun-house mirrors across their stomachs.

Hayden leans close to one and his head doubles in size. I jump, arms up. My reflection stretches tall and thin. We're both grinning by the time we find the exit.

From there, it's only a short walk to the café and the

train. As Hayden orders a hot dog, I rub my hongbao between two fingers, then step forward before he can pay, and order popcorn. "I've got this."

A high-pitched whistle pierces the air. Hayden and I board a compartment near the back of the train, taking a seat across from each other.

Hayden unwraps the silver foil from his hot dog. "So, I was curious about something after your mom called my parents."

"Yeah?"

He tears off a piece of hot dog bun and leans closer. It only takes him a couple of seconds to chew and swallow, but in that time my heart leaps from my chest to my stomach and back again.

"Yeah. I was curious how good of a skater you are."

"Um." What does this have to do with the phone call with Mom?

I shake my popcorn bag, letting the un-popped kernels settle at the bottom. "Are you asking, like, on a scale of one to ten? Or ... ?"

"Anything. Like, are you trying to make it to"—his eyes drop to my shirt—"US Nationals?"

"Kind of. Except there are no more Nationals, at least, not at my level." I purposefully don't tell him that I won last January. I don't want him looking up the list of champions. No one named Alex won in any division last season. "Now I'll go to a special training camp if I qualify. If I do well at the camp, they might ask me to represent the US in another country one day."

"Whoa." Hayden's eyes widen. "I so want to see you skate someday."

An image of myself performing in my new dress flashes through my mind. I chew on my lip.

"I bet you don't have cones to separate skaters when you're practicing."

"Nope. Everyone does their own thing on freestyle ice." The train whistles again as it chugs back to the station. "My last session is about an hour before skate-school starts, if you ever want to watch. There are lots of really good skaters who train on it."

"That'd be awesome. I'll see if I can get to the rink early sometime."

The train slows to a stop and Hayden hops down fast, crumpling up his hot dog wrapper as he heads away from me. He lifts his hand like he's dribbling a basketball, jumps up, and slam-dunks his hot dog wrapper into a trash can. He turns back to me, brows raised.

I know a challenge when I see one.

Balling up my popcorn bag, I lift my arms and lunge forward into a cartwheel, spinning on my heel once my feet hit the ground. I drop my trash into the can with a flourish that'd definitely get a nod from Miss Lydia.

"Okay, you win." Hayden grins. "I would land on my head if I tried that. Race you back to the theater!" He takes off running, and I tear after him, dodging people the same way I zip around skaters at the rink.

Without warning, Hayden slows. I skid to a stop, calves burning.

"I'm glad we met," he says once he catches his breath. His eyes are fixed on the ground, voice quiet. "Maybe this sounds dumb, but I didn't want to move here this summer. Then my great-aunt Becca died and gave us her house, so..." He kicks a stone. "It's not like Minnesota was all that great, either. It's just hard to make friends in a new place, you know?"

My pulse slows. It's almost back to normal, but a

heaviness stays, just under my rib cage. In the distance, Mattie and Elliot appear under the puppet theater's sign. They spot us and take off in our direction.

Hayden turns to me. "I know you've got your skating and Tamar and other stuff, but maybe we could hang out again sometime? If you want."

In the seconds before his family reaches us, I nod. "That'd be cool. Plus, there's still a lot of the park we haven't seen today yet."

His expression brightens, and my insides twinge a little. Maybe I'm not a boy like he thinks, but it doesn't feel right to call myself a girl, either. I need to find a word that describes this in-between feeling.

Until then, I'll have to keep pretending.

Chapter Seventeen

"Okay, it's official," I tell Tamar. "Baseball is brutal. And I think I have a new favorite movie line. It was... something about how sports are hard because if they weren't, everyone would do them?"

"It's your favorite, but you can't even remember the exact words?" Tamar laughs and I shush her, glancing toward the kitchen table where Mom's working from her laptop.

"But you liked the movie, right?"

"It was good." I nod.

"My favorite quote is the 'no crying' one because you can use it for skating, too," she says. "Everyone thinks skating's this prissy sport. Especially hockey players. But we compete with blisters and have to do these complicated jumps. Plus, the spins twist our bodies into pretzels, and then we have to pretend we're not exhausted after our programs? There's no crying in skating!"

"Except in the Kiss and Cry area," I point out.

"Okay, fair." Tamar pulls up Google on her iPad. A screen of photos loads, all from high-level skating competitions. The skaters were caught on camera right after seeing their scores. Tamar enlarges an image. "I was looking for actual tears, but these are better."

Their expressions range from angry to embarrassed. Somewhere between the ice dancer glaring at her guilty-looking partner and a glitzy Senior-level lady rolling her eyes directly at the camera, we dissolve into giggles.

"You two seem to be enjoying yourselves." Mom watches us from the table with a tired smile.

"Are we being too loud, Mom?"

"Sorry, Ms. Jin," Tamar chimes in.

"I'm just glad you're spending time together. It's been a busy summer for all of us." Mom moves toward my bunk bed. "That said, Ana-Marie, you should head out if you still want your hair cut today. I checked you in at the salon a moment ago." She pulls out her wallet as Tamar and I climb down the ladder. "How much did you spend yesterday?"

"Um." My eyes dart to Tamar, cheeks flushing. "I think I have about eighteen dollars left. And my ten from Grandma."

Mom hands me a new twenty and a five. "Keep what's left after your haircut for emergencies. The ten doesn't count. It belongs to you."

"Thanks." I pocket the money, then head for the door. I can feel Tamar's eyes on me but can't bring myself to look at her.

Halfway down the stairs to the ground floor, I sneak a peek at her. "Oh, dang. I forgot to look at your Intermediate Moves clips before we left."

Tamar shrugs. "You can watch them when we get back."

We exit the building and walk in silence. Tamar finally turns to me when we stop at a crosswalk. "What were you doing yesterday?"

I shuffle my feet. Tamar and Hayden feel like they're part of two separate worlds. It was easier to tell Hayden about Tamar yesterday, because she has nothing to do with my secret. But if Tamar knows I hung out with Hayden, I'd probably have to explain how I never corrected him about my real name. The light turns green and we step into the crosswalk.

"I was in Oakland." Tamar's eyes stay on me. "...With a friend."

"Oh." Hurt flashes across her face.

"It's my fault. I've been so busy lately I totally forgot we had plans. I'm really sorry."

"It's fine." We stop in front of the hair salon, and Tamar nudges the strap of her messenger bag higher onto her shoulder. Bells jangle above the door as a customer exits. Tamar catches it with one hand. "Come on. Let's find you the perfect look for your competition."

I slip inside and make my way to the front counter. The hairstylist waves me back to her workstation. Tamar pulls her iPad out of her bag as I climb into a cushy chair in front of a big mirror.

"This is your first event at Intermediate, so you'll want to look awesome." Tamar pulls up an image on her iPad. "Good thing I found tons of cute options."

She holds her iPad out while the stylist snaps a big black cape around my neck. The material billows in front of me, settling over my legs. I watch the stylist in the mirror's reflection as she glances at Tamar beside me.

"Oh, that's precious." She looks down at me. "Are you a dancer, sweetie?"

My fingers ball up at my sides, tense shoulders making the cape rise a bit. "Figure skater."

"I love ice-skating. I watch the Olympics every four years, like clockwork," she gushes.

I aim a fake smile at her, look down at the iPad, then up at Tamar. "I'm not sure about bangs. They might get in my eyes when I'm spinning."

"What about this?" She flicks to the next image. The model's hair is curled into tight ringlets. She has more makeup on than I've ever worn. "It'd be perfect for your program. You could even clip in a tiara."

My fingers squeeze tighter. "Wouldn't it be easier to just shave it all off?"

Tamar's expression clouds. "That'd be—I mean, don't you think that's a little extreme?"

"I'm joking." Her expression relaxes, but now that it's out there, I start to wonder what I'd look like with that short of a haircut.

"Hey, can I look at your iPad?"

As Tamar chats with my stylist about all things ice-skating, I pull up a new browser tab and search for boy haircuts. I had no idea there were so many, from short-cropped to complicated-looking longer styles. Gelled and formal to messy-on-purpose.

I scroll and scroll, studying each photo. I stop on one, and my heart performs a blur of twizzles.

"This one."

Behind me, Tamar and the stylist stop talking and lean forward.

"That's an interesting choice." The stylist seems to be choosing her words carefully.

Tamar shakes her head fast. "That's for boys."

My cheeks felt hot after we left the apartment, but now my whole upper body heats up. "It doesn't have to be. There's no law that says girls can't get boy haircuts."

Tamar flinches like I slapped her.

"That's right." The stylist keeps her voice smooth as she reaches for an electric razor. "Hair is hair. You can cut it however you like."

"Are you sure?" Tamar scrunches her brows. "I saved other pictures if you want to look at more. You don't have to get bangs or curls."

The stylist flips on the razor. It buzzes above my head as she waits for my decision.

I look at the mirror, at my short hair that's about to get shorter. My pulse dances with excitement.

"Totally sure."

Six minutes later, the cape comes off. I walk up to the cash register, holding a tiny tin of hair gel. Tamar follows behind me without a word.

As I'm rung up, I catch my reflection in the mirror behind a shelf of styling products. My hair is shaved short at the nape of my neck. The stylist used gel on the top, which I kept a couple of inches longer. It spikes up in tufts.

I'm handed back my change, and we head toward the exit. I raise my eyebrows as I pass another mirror, smiling at myself.

Hair is hair, like the stylist said.

But still. I absolutely love how I look.

We walk back, still not talking. Finally, I look over at Tamar, who nearly trips on the curb when our eyes meet.

"What?"

"Nothing," Tamar says quickly. "I'm just getting used to it. You look good."

"Yeah?"

She nods, then pulls her phone out as we round the corner to my building. She sighs as we enter the lobby.

"What's up?"

"It's Eli." The corners of her mouth turn down as we start climbing the stairs. "Mom and Dad are arguing again, I guess."

"Did he say about what?"

I reach up to feel the back of my neck, letting Tamar get a few steps ahead. My hair's so short there it prickles my palm. What if Mom hates my new look? I remember how hard it was to get her to let me cut my hair short the first time, when I was nine. She thought I might get upset after they cut it, maybe cry. I wasn't and I didn't.

But if Tamar didn't want me to get a boy haircut, maybe Mom won't, either. We're all the way to the third floor before I realize Tamar's done talking and I didn't hear a word.

"Sorry." I shake my head, still enjoying how light it feels. "What'd you say?"

"Never mind." Tamar doesn't look back at me. "It's no big deal."

Her gaze drops when I catch up to her. It stays down while I fish out my key and unlock the door.

Mom's in front of the oven, cooking dinner.

"You're back." She turns around. "That was qui—"

She stares at me for a beat, then another. It's like she's not quite sure who she's seeing.

I reach up and touch my hair again. "I thought I'd try a new style. Do you like it?"

"I suppose it's been a while since you changed things up." Mom turns back to the stove. Her tone was light, but she didn't answer my question.

My mouth tastes sour. I turn to Tamar. "Let's look at your Intermediate Moves clips."

She nods. We head toward my bed.

"Oh, Ana-Marie, I almost forgot," Mom calls over one shoulder. "Alex messaged while you were gone. He wants you to bring your new free-skate costume to the rink tomorrow."

"Okay." I can't quite keep the frown off my face. I know what this means. We do a run-through every year before my first competition so I know what it feels like to perform my program in costume.

Tamar stops halfway to my bed. "You didn't tell me you got your new costume."

"It just came in Friday. I can show it to you if you want."

Tamar loves all things fashion, but she shakes her

head and takes a few steps in the opposite direction. "I should probably get going. Mom said she'd be here by seven."

I glance at the digital clock on Mom's bedside table. It's six forty-five and it only takes two minutes to get back downstairs. Three, tops.

"What about your Intermediate Moves?" I ask.

"I'll text them. You can send me suggestions or tell me what you think the next time we hang out." She speaks fast with her back to me.

"It was good seeing you." Mom waves as Tamar turns the doorknob. "Please say hello to your mother."

"I will." Tamar looks back at me with an expression I can't read. "See you, Ana."

"See you," I echo. I step forward for our goodbye hug, but the door clicks closed. Tamar's already gone.

Chapter Eighteen

On Monday morning, I wait for the Parks while Mom and Samuel chat in front of her office.

Soon, their SUV appears, and I hug the garment bag in my arms tighter. When I open the trunk, voices drift back from the front, a rise and fall of words I can't quite make out.

In goes my duffel. Two garment bags already hang under the back seat headrests. I hook mine beside them.

"...don't get why you won't just let me skip—" Faith clamps her mouth shut as soon as I open the door.

I take my usual seat beside Hope.

At first, no one says anything. Faith crosses her arms. The rearview mirror reflects Mrs. Park's face. Her jaw clenches and relaxes, then clenches again.

It's Hope who finally breaks the silence.

"You got your hair cut!" She sounds overly excited, like she's trying to shift the focus away from Faith.

"Yep."

"It's super short."

"Hope." Mrs. Park shoots her a warning look in the rearview mirror, but Hope keeps her eyes on me.

"You kind of look like this boy who was in my class last year."

"*Hope!*" Faith's voice joins her mom's.

"What? It was a compliment! He was nice—for a boy."

Mrs. Park shakes her head and says something in Korean. Hope slumps in her seat.

"Sorry, Ana," she mumbles.

"It's fine."

Hope's comment didn't bother me. She just said what other people probably think when they see me—short hair is usually for boys, long hair for girls. I run a hand over the top of my head, wishing there was a third option.

Hope puffs out her cheeks and turns toward the window. Up front, Faith's head tilts down, eyes on her iPad. Everyone's gone quiet.

I pull out my phone. There are no new messages, probably because Hayden's still asleep and Tamar hasn't texted since we hung out yesterday. I'm not sure if she's upset that I didn't tell her about my dress, mad about me choosing a different hairstyle than the ones she picked out, or something else. I fiddle with my seatbelt strap, pulling it up and down.

I pull out my phone. Maybe things will be better the next time we see each other.

7:38 a.m.: Want to hang out next weekend?

7:38 a.m.: Saturday or Sunday, I can do either.

7:39 a.m.: And don't forget to send me your Moves clips!

I switch over to Hayden's texts.

7:39 a.m.: You're lucky you get to sleep in. I'm sooooo tired today. 😭

We file out in front of the rink. I wish I could "forget" my garment bag, but it's hanging on top of two other dresses.

Hope soars through the doors, the argument in the car already forgotten. "Today's going to be so much fun, like an ice show with all of us in costume!" I grimace, imagining Hayden watching me perform in my new dress. Hope stops at a table, unzips her bag, and peeks inside. "I wish we could put on our costumes and skate right now."

"She would've worn hers straight to the rink if Mom

had let her," Faith tells me. She turns to Hope. "Come on. We don't want to be late. You only have to wait an hour until freestyle."

"An hour and *fifteen minutes*." Hope sighs but scoops up her bag and follows Faith toward the stairs. This doesn't stop her from making silly faces the moment Faith turns away. On any other day, I'd struggle to hold back laughter. But right now, my throat feels too tight to make a sound. I can't even smile.

Hope and I fidget during stretching and off-ice dance. I bet she can't wait for us to be done so she can change into her new dress.

I can.

She shoots out the door the second class ends. I check my phone before following a few steps behind Faith. No texts from Tamar yet, which is a little weird. I send her another text in case she missed my last three.

9:16 a.m.: Up yet? Or sleeping in because summer is awesome?

By the time we get downstairs, Hope's already inside the bathroom. Faith enters next, leaving me alone at the entrance. I look over to the boys' side, wondering if I'd feel more comfortable in there. But too many people here know me as Ana-Marie Jin, Juvenile girls champion. I enter the ladies' room, choose a stall, and change into my costume.

This isn't the first time I've worn my new dress. Mom had me try it on the day I got it. But that was quick, just to confirm it fit.

As I exit the bathroom stall, my gaze drifts to the mirror on the opposite wall. I don't want to look, but I can't help myself.

From the neck up, everything's fine. My hair is shorter and spikes at new angles, but I'm still me. Everything below, though? From the sweetheart neckline to the long flowy skirt that tapers short in the front, it's all wrong.

Now I see the missing piece of the puzzle. It's not my body that makes me uncomfortable, or the shimmering, sparkling costume. It's what other people will think when they see me wearing it: *girl*, *princess*, *Intermediate lady*.

Skin prickly and hot, I look away from the mirror and hurry out of the bathroom.

I sit down on the bench across from Faith as she stands,

skates already laced. I slip into my warm-up coat and try to control my shallow breathing as I tie my laces.

I start my warm-up, shoulders rounded, trying to make myself smaller. I head for a corner of the ice to work on my footwork while Hope starts her lesson with Alex. She skates off in her new costume, chin up and confident. It's dip-dyed pink with hints of white at the ends of long bell sleeves.

She smiles wide enough to reach the top row of her imaginary audience. Her music is a traditional Korean song with plucky string instruments.

I perform a turn, the tip of my skirt flitting and fluttering with every movement, and attempt to lose myself in the music.

This time last year, I practiced in my Nationals costume for the first time. I flew across the ice, adjusting to the feel of performing jumps in the black head-to-toe fabric. Mom had sewn strips of lightweight chiffon to my costume's arms and legs. During spins, I was a blur of sleek black with red and gold accents. My run-through wasn't perfect. I forgot a few steps that I hadn't totally memorized yet, but I didn't feel like fleeing the ice and hiding every time another skater looked at me.

Hope's program ends, and another song begins. This one's stronger, with piano chords that build on one another. A tall skater whips past me on his way toward one corner of the rink. He lands a huge double lutz right on the music's crescendo.

Normally, I'd feel the song deep in my bones and let its rhythm carry me through my jumps. Now I hover by the boards, only venturing out to spin or jump when it looks like no one's watching.

Once Hope's lesson is done, Alex calls me over.

"How does your dress feel? I know you said wearing a skirt for your choreography lessons was an adjustment."

"It's fine." I'm not lying. It's a perfect fit. My discomfort is all in my head.

Alex stares—I can't tell if he believes me, but it doesn't matter. My competition is in less than two weeks. It's too late to change anything.

"It's fine," I say again. "Easy to move in."

"We'll get started, then." Alex doesn't look fully convinced, but he gestures toward the music box. "Ready to do this?"

"Sure..."

Three minutes. It'll be done before I know it.

Alex extends his hand. "Jacket off."

I puff my cheeks, copying Hope, but shrug out of my coat. I shiver a little as my skin meets the chilly air. Time to get this over with.

I lift my arms, just the way Miss Lydia taught, as the first quiet notes of my music filter down from the speakers. It should be easier to *feel* the music and *become* the princess in this costume.

But that's the problem. I glide down the ice for my salchow, thinking about how much I look like someone I'm not.

I turn fast, swing through, and launch, but my timing is rushed. Both feet hit the ice at once, blades skidding as I fight to stay upright.

Alex watches from the boards. I know I need to keep going. You don't get a do-over at a competition.

I steady my breaths and start my footwork. More mistakes. A stumble. Shallow edges. Twizzles scraped and spun in place instead of traveling across the ice.

The music cuts out before my next jump.

Despite the cold, my face burns.

Alex doesn't look mad as I glide back to him, just

thoughtful. "You seem to be getting stuck in your head today, Bean."

All summer, actually.

I shrug and look down. My costume's crystals reflect the ceiling lights like they're mocking me. "Should I start over?"

"Yes, but I want to try something different and have you skate without the music."

I look up. "No music?"

Alex nods. "You're getting used to this program, plus performing in your new costume, so let's break it down and focus on one thing at a time. Run it all the way through. Don't stop, no matter what happens."

I return to my opening pose as another coach takes over the music box. It must look strange for me to be wearing this glittery dress with my arms lifted gracefully as the staccato beats of a different skater's music fill the rink.

I glide toward one end of the ice for my triple salchow. Taking my time, I rotate fast and strong. No two-foot flub this time around. I'm midway through my footwork when I finally start feeling the music. The only problem? It's someone else's. My rhythm is all wrong, movements sharp instead of soft.

At least I'm centering my spins and landing my jumps.

I finish my final spin, hold the ending pose, and wait for the usual rush of excitement that comes after skating a clean program.

Nothing.

So what if I can nail everything without music? The judges won't be impressed.

The Zamboni appears at one side of the rink. Faith, Hope, and the other skaters head for the exit as I glide back to Alex.

"I knew you had it in you." He pats my back. "You look like the full package with that costume, too. A real Intermediate skater."

"Really?" I'm able to hide my frown but there's no question I sound doubtful.

"It's coming along." Alex gives me an encouraging smile. "Now go ahead and enjoy your lunch."

I step off the ice, wondering if Alex is right. Maybe I'm overthinking things, or getting stuck in my head.

He seemed to believe skating a clean run-through should be something to celebrate, even without music.

I dig out my phone on the way to the bathroom. Still nothing from Tamar. I'll call her over lunch.

My whole body seems to breathe a sigh of relief once I'm back in my leggings. As I head toward the coaches' lounge, my phone finally buzzes.

It's Hayden.

11:35 a.m.: Sorry ur tired

11:36 a.m.: If it makes u feel better, M and E wake up super early

11:36 a.m.: And they're LOUD

I smile for the first time today. After last Saturday, I can totally imagine them making tons of noise. Especially Mattie.

Hayden sends another text.

11:37 a.m.: Hey do u want to hang out again next Saturday?

Yes, I text back. Totally.

Another Hayden text comes in fast.

11:38 a.m.: Cool!

11:38 a.m.: I was thinking u could come to my house

11:38 a.m.: Call when u can and we'll figure out what time works best

I head to the second rink, away from the chatter in the lobby. The lights are dim. No hockey players are around yet, but a voice floats down from the stands.

"...first two weeks in August. Same as the Rising Stars camp. I can't do both."

It's Faith. There's a beat of silence, followed by a heavy sigh.

"I already asked, but I'll keep trying. I want to do the musical, but Mom thinks skating's more important."

I had no idea Faith acts. Or sings, even. No wonder she's so good at performing on ice.

I step out into the open.

"I'll call you back later." Faith slips the phone into her coat and eyes me cautiously. "Hi."

"Hey." I climb a couple of steps. "Sorry, I didn't know anyone was up here."

"I was actually just leaving for lunch." Faith takes a few steps down. We pass each other, and that should be it. She'll go eat while I call Hayden.

Except she looks upset, and I can definitely relate after my disastrous practice.

I whirl around. "Is everything okay?"

She pauses at the bottom step and nods. It looks like

she's about to say something, but I rush on. "It's just, I heard you and your mom arguing in the car."

"Oh. Yeah." Her shoulders slump. "It's not a huge deal, though."

I inch closer. "It kind of sounded like one."

"I got asked to help out with my church's musical. The sound designer said I could be her assistant."

"That'd be cool."

"Yeah." She looks down. "Except I can't do it. Hope and I always go to a skating camp in August. I don't know why I bothered to even ask Mom if I could skip it."

I've never been to a training camp, but I know that skaters who attend can get lessons from top US coaches. They also cost thousands of dollars.

"Oh." I hop down another few steps, until I'm just two above her. "The camp sounds great, too, though."

"It is." But she sighs again. "Do you ever just..."

"What?"

"Just hate skating, I guess. Like, not all the time, but..."

I think back on my program run-through, about how I felt in my new costume. How I can usually land all my jumps, no problem—until I have to perform them. "Sometimes it can be frustrating?"

"Yeah, but not even that. It's more like skating gets in the way of things you want to do instead, if that makes sense?"

I blink. The rink is like a second home to me. Usually I'm daydreaming about when I can go back, not wishing I could skip practice. "So, you want to do the musical instead of the camp, but your mom said no?"

"Well—I mean, Mom doesn't know I got asked to help with the musical. I just told her I didn't want to do the camp."

"Oh."

"She just thinks I should focus on getting good at one thing," Faith bursts out. "Dad, too. But I *really* want to do the musical. I could learn so much, and it wouldn't even interfere with any skating competitions."

I take another step down, until we're only one apart. We stand eye-to-eye because Faith's taller. "Maybe you should ask again, but tell her about the musical this time."

"You think that'd work?"

"It could." I nod a little. Her situation is different,

but it feels a lot like me trying to figure out how to tell Mom I want a new free program. "Whenever I need to ask my mom for something, I make sure she's in a really good mood first. Then I tell her why it's important to me, so she knows I'm serious. Maybe you could do something like that with your parents?"

"Maybe." Faith says the word slowly, like she's thinking it through. Below us, the lobby doors swing open to reveal Hope.

"I'm coming," Faith calls, before Hope can say anything. She looks back at me. "I'll think about telling them. Thanks for the ideas."

"Sure."

She takes a step away, then turns back. "Did you want to come get ramen with us?"

Faith hasn't invited me to lunch since the day Miss Lydia revealed my free-skate music, and I don't blame her. I wouldn't keep trying if someone always turned me down, either. It feels like she's offering me another chance to hang out, maybe the last.

But Hayden's waiting for me.

"I want to, but I have to make a call." I hold up my phone with an apologetic shrug.

"Oh, okay." Faith turns to go.

"But hey." I wave. "I really do want to have lunch sometime. I just usually bring my own. Maybe we could hang out together here at the rink? Or I could bring my food wherever you're going to eat."

"Cool." She waves back, then disappears into the lobby.

Climbing back into the stands, I text Tamar to let her know I'm actually not free on Saturday. Hopefully she'll understand, then text back to let me know that Sunday's still an option.

I call Hayden's number, and he answers on the first ring.

"Hey! So, here's what I was thinking...."

I settle into a seat in the stands. Hayden hasn't even told me his plans yet, but I'm already smiling.

Chapter Nineteen

I don't know what to expect when I arrive at Hayden's home on Saturday, but it's not a three-story building that looks like a huge treehouse built right into the Berkeley Hills.

As Mrs. Lubeck locks the van, Hayden leads me up a set of uneven wood stairs. Metal tracks snake toward the house, parallel to the steps.

"What's that?"

"A tram elevator," Hayden says over one shoulder. "There's a road that stops near the house, but Dad says you're taking your life into your own hands to park up there, because it's all loose gravel."

"You can ride that all the way up to your house?"

"Yeah. Except Mom and Dad told us we can't use it."

"We said you can't use it *yet*," Mrs. Lubeck calls a few steps below us. "We want to have someone come out and make sure it's safe first."

This makes sense to me, but Hayden rolls his eyes. "It'll be cool to ride," he says, "but it's not all that great for a family of six. It only fits two at a time. Maybe three if you're small like Mattie."

"Or one, if you're an elephant." A man looks down at us from the ledge of the Lubecks' front porch. Mattie and Elliot peer out from behind him. "You must be A."

I have just enough time to nod before the man lowers his hand. Hayden reaches out and is hoisted up.

My turn. The man's fingers wrap around my wrist, gentle but firm. For a moment, I'm airborne and weightless. I wonder if this is how it feels to be a pairs skater.

He sets me down beside Hayden, who turns to me. "It's probably obvious, but this is my dad."

"Call me Dan." I'm treated to a wide smile.

I've never called a friend's parent by their first name before. Even though my father isn't around, I still think of him as *Dad* in my head, not *Jacob*. I've never seen someone who looks quite like Dan. I wouldn't call him an elephant, but he has broad shoulders and a thick wiry beard, blond with a red tinge.

"Come on in." Dan waits until everyone enters,

then shuts the door. "And excuse the mess. We haven't finished unpacking yet."

The house is cool with dim lighting and window shades drawn tight against the afternoon sun.

"Shoes go there." Mattie points to a nearby rack.

"Mom doesn't want us tracking in dirt." Hayden shrugs a little, like this is another annoyance. It feels normal to me. What's weird is keeping my shoes on when I visit Tamar.

A faint smell tickles my nose as we head farther into the house. It's a mix of hickory, grass, and something smoky.

"Make yourself at home. Lunch'll be ready soon." Dan disappears into another room, along with the rest of the Lubecks, except for Hayden.

"Dad makes the best barbecue," Hayden says with a hint of pride.

Dan's voice reaches us from the next room. "There'll be chicken, but I'm trying my hand at some veggie dishes, too."

I glance at Hayden. "I'm guessing my mom told your parents we don't eat meat?"

"Yeah, probably. Let's go upstairs while we wait."

I wonder what else our parents talked about, but Hayden doesn't say.

We pass a living room with a sunken center. Two pairs of feline eyes follow our movements from an old sectional.

Upstairs, my feet sink into shaggy orange carpet. Wood panels line the hallway walls. This house is huge like Tamar's, but it feels more like a home than a castle.

Hayden pushes open a creaky door. I can't wait to see what his room looks like. I've never been invited into a boy's room, although I've caught glimpses of Eli's before. Eli's bookshelves overflow with graphic novels and collector's edition comics.

Moving boxes litter Hayden's floor, just like downstairs, but they're easy to miss. Because from a desk in one corner to a bed in the other, large pieces of fabric cover every surface. Most of the fabric is a patchwork of white and black. I also spot shades of red.

The walls are weirder. They're the same paneling from the hallway, but a dictionary's worth of cut-out letters hang in various places, spelling out short words. I recognize *él* and *ella* from last year's Spanish class. They mean "he" and "she," but I'm not sure about the others.

"I would've cleaned before you came over, but I'm behind on this cosplay." Hayden sidesteps the clutter. He grabs swatches of fabric from the desk chair and waves me over. A tall bolt of pea-green cloth tumbles to the floor, giving him a place to sit on the bed.

"What's cosplay?"

Hayden's eyes widen. "You mean you don't know?"

I shake my head.

"Okay, wow. It's like…" He trails off, looking thoughtful. "Well, who's your favorite character from a TV show? Or a movie or video game?"

I don't play video games or watch much TV. Between skating and homework during the school year, there's no time. The only recent movies I've seen are sports-themed.

One thing I know for sure: My least favorite character is Princess Aurora from *Sleeping Beauty*.

"I really like Kenny from *Mighty Ducks 2*. Have you seen it?"

Hayden shakes his head.

"It's an old movie, but it's funny and about a hockey team so you might like it. I think it's even set in Minnesota."

"Sounds cool."

I take in all the fabric scattered around his room. "What do movie characters have to do with all this, though?"

Hayden leans forward. "With cosplay, you choose a character, make a costume, and then meet up with other people and take pictures."

"So, you're dressing up to play a character in front of other people?" This sounds a little like skating, except without jumps and spins and blades strapped to your feet.

"Yeah! People go all out with costumes and makeup. Some create props. I'm working on a Keyblade for my *Kingdom Hearts* costume. That's why I got behind on the actual outfit."

"Do you need help?"

"As much as I can get." Hayden grins. "Do you know how to sew?"

I hesitate, swiveling a full circle in his desk chair before answering. Sewing feels a little girly. When I imagined hanging out with Hayden, I figured we'd do boy things. Now I realize I don't even know what that means. Does watching football and soccer on TV count as a "boy thing"? Reading comics? I know girls who do both.

And Hayden's a boy who likes to sew costumes.

"A bit. Sometimes Mom has me help with my skating outfits."

"That's awesome. You're probably better than me, then."

"Maybe."

My eyes drift up to Hayden's walls.

I point to the cutouts. "What are all those words for?"

Hayden follows the line of my finger.

"Nothing, really. They're pronouns in different languages, and other random stuff."

I immediately perk up. "They're all pronouns?"

"Most of them. Cyn wanted to be a linguist or a translator or something when she was younger, so she collected all these words. She wanted to throw them away when we moved, but I rescued them."

He waves toward a spot behind me, at yellow construction paper with *E-L-L-E* written on it. "That one, there? *Elle* is the word *she* in French."

"Oh, neat. That's pretty close to *ella* in Spanish."

My gaze shifts to a pair of words by Hayden's window. They're in a script I recognize from temple, but I'm curious if he knows them. "What about those?"

"Hebrew. They write it backward, from right to left. *Hu* means 'he.'"

"Who means he?" I already knew this, but it sounds too silly not to repeat.

Hayden throws me a grin. "Yeah. So, *hu* means 'he,' but it gets better. *He* means 'she.' Weird, right?"

"So weird." I play along. "So, what's *me* mean?"

"It's who—hey." Hayden studies me as I try to hold back a grin. "You attend a synagogue with your friend. Tamar, right? You know this stuff already."

I can't help giggling. "Tamar and I know some Hebrew, yeah." I pull out my charm necklace from under my shirt. "This means 'life' in Hebrew. My dad gave it to me."

"Your dad?" Hayden eyes my charm necklace. "I thought you said you live with your mom."

"I do, but my dad still sends me letters sometimes. Or used to, I guess. This is the last thing he sent, for my eighth birthday. He's not very good at remembering important dates."

"Yeah, my dad, either," Hayden says. "He likes to do fun things and celebrate when he feels like it. Mom has to remind him about anniversaries and other stuff."

I nod.

"That's not the same as your dad not being around, though. Sorry."

"It's okay." Now I'm curious. "But your dad does lots of things with you? And he cooks, too?"

"Yep. Mom's more into baking sweet stuff. Trust me, you wouldn't want to eat anything she cooks for lunch." Hayden makes a face. "But yeah, Dad hasn't found a job yet, so he spends lots of time hanging out with us and cooking while Mom's at work."

I try to imagine what my dad and I would do together for even one afternoon. But all I have is his graduation picture, which doesn't tell me anything about his interests.

I tuck the charm back under my collar, then point to another group of words that looks like backward cursive. "What do those mean?"

"I think they're Arabic. Hold on, I don't have everything memorized." Hayden gets up. He digs through his desk, pushing aside strips of tan fabric to unearth a notepad and pen. "Yeah, they're Arabic. Those two are *anta* and *anti*, which are male and female versions of 'you.'" He points the pen to another word on the notepad. "And this one's *ana*, which means 'I.' You can use that if you're a girl or a boy."

I stare at him. "*Ana* means 'I'?"

"Mm-hmm. I think Arabic and Hebrew have lots of close-sounding words." He looks up. "What's 'I' in Hebrew?"

"*Ani*," I say, but I'm in a daze. Hayden just said my name, and he doesn't even know it.

Ana means "I" in another language.

"Another weird thing Cyn told me is that lots of languages have male and female nouns," Hayden continues. "That makes no sense to me. Like, why do they have to say a room is male or a table's female?"

"Mandarin doesn't. I mean, the words for 'he,' 'she,' and 'it' sound the same whether you're a boy or a girl. They just look different in writing."

I bite the inside of my cheek to stop myself from rambling.

"Huh." Hayden hands me his notepad. "Can you write those down? It'd be cool to know them."

The door creaks open, and Cyn pokes her head in. "Hey, you guys. Lunch is ready. I'd hurry. Mattie's already loading his plate."

She's gone in a flash.

"We should probably go. Mattie's appetite is epic." I pass the notepad back to Hayden, whose eyes linger on it, like he's disappointed.

"I'll write them down after lunch," I promise. "Then we can work on your costume."

I stand up, and my gaze flickers past another set of words. They're taped to the front of his closet.

Zie, zir, zirs.

"Hey, what language are those?"

Hayden takes a few steps back to look where I'm pointing.

"That's not a foreign language. They're gender-neutral pronouns. C'mon, I'm starving."

Gender-neutral? Like Mandarin? I look at the words again, sounding them out in my head. I want to know more.

But food is ready. People are waiting. I'll have to save my questions for later.

Chapter Twenty

Zie, zir, zirs.

The words buzz between my ears all through lunch. Gender-neutral.

I repeat them to myself, through a first course of salad and coleslaw, then a second of noodle casserole. I want to ask Hayden more questions, but not in front of his family. Mattie and Elliot shovel food into their mouths across the table, while Mrs. Lubeck holds a napkin out and reminds them to wipe their faces. Cyn sits beside her, eyes fixed on her phone. Dan, Hayden, and I eat on the opposite side of the table.

When we get to the main course, Dan passes me a plateful of messy-looking sandwiches.

"May I present? Meatless sloppy joes." I take one and thank him as Dan passes the plate on. "Thank *you*, actually, for giving me the chance to try a new recipe."

"Dad loves to cook," Elliot informs me as he leans

across the table to pull a serving plate of chicken toward himself.

"That I do." Dan's voice naturally booms. "It's just a shame I'm the only member of this family who likes experimenting with food."

My sandwich has a nice smoky taste to it. Across from us, Mattie stuffs a big piece of chicken into his mouth, then looks at me. "How come you don't eat meat?"

"My grandma is Buddhist and didn't cook meat when my mom was growing up."

"Wait." Hayden takes a quick swig of his drink. "I thought you're Jewish."

"I am. My dad's Jewish. He and Mom dated in high school and then moved to San Francisco for college. Mom decided to become Jewish before she had me. She jokes that it's a lot easier to keep kosher if you don't eat meat."

"I bet it is." Mrs. Lubeck scoops another spoonful of coleslaw onto Mattie's plate.

"I would probably die if I couldn't eat cheeseburgers," Mattie says. Beside him, Elliot solemnly nods.

"Cyn used to be a vegan," says Hayden. "For, like, a week before she gave up."

"Oh, hush." Cyn shoots him an annoyed look. "Veganism just wasn't for me. That's all."

Hayden leans toward me. "Because she loves cheeseburgers too much, just like Mattie and Elliot."

I half snort, then cover my mouth. Cyn rolls her eyes and looks back down at her phone. I wait for someone to tell her to put it away, but they don't seem to mind like Mom would.

I sneak a quick look at my own phone. Except for a k that came in after I went to bed on Monday, Tamar hasn't sent any other texts. Is she free to hang out tomorrow? I asked again yesterday but haven't heard back.

"So." Dan clears his throat. "Did you two have fun before lunch?"

Hayden nods. "A knows how to sew, so he's going to help me with my Roxas cosplay after lunch."

I chew on the inside of my cheek. Boy pronouns feel just as weird as girl pronouns now.

"Sounds like fun." Dan turns to me, beaming with pride. "I may be at my best in the kitchen, but Hayden has all the talent when it comes to cosplay."

"Dad, stop." Hayden shakes his head, hair falling into his face, but not before I see his cheeks turn rosy.

Mrs. Lubeck stands and begins to collect our plates. She stops beside Dan. "Don't embarrass him, darling."

"What? It's true!" Dan throws his arms up like he's exasperated, but the proud smile never leaves his face.

I try to imagine Dad talking about my skating the same way but come up empty.

Mrs. Lubeck starts clearing the table.

"Can I help?" I ask, but she shakes her head.

"No, no. You're our guest. You and Hayden go enjoy yourselves."

As she bustles in and out of the dining room, I turn back to Hayden. "You never actually told me who Roxas is."

"Oh, he's a character from *Kingdom Hearts II*. It's a video game. I'll explain more when we get upstairs. I wish I could show you on my PlayStation, but it's still buried in a box somewhere."

"It's in the family room."

We both look over at Dan.

"I spotted it in a box with some of my old DVDs. Want me to set it up?"

"Yes!" Hayden hops up from his seat. "I'll show A my cosplay stuff while you do that."

Dan gives us a thumbs-up.

This time when we head upstairs, Hayden takes the steps two at a time. I glance at the *zie*, *zir*, and *zirs* cutouts as we enter his room, but Hayden starts talking before I can ask anything.

"How much do you know about *Kingdom Hearts*?" He grabs a sheet of creamy white fabric off a tower of boxes. It looks like a crudely shaped jacket.

"Not much." My eyes dart from the wall to the floor. "Okay, nothing."

"It's cool. Not everyone's into the same things." Hayden sits on the floor. "So, Roxas is a part of this other character, Sora, but he doesn't have a heart, which is why he's a Nobody."

"A...nobody?"

"Yeah." Hayden's gaze drops, like he's suddenly self-conscious. "It's complicated, but the main point is that Roxas has to discover who he is and who his real friends are."

I join him on the shaggy orange floor as Dan enters with the PlayStation and a stack of games. He slides a sheet of fabric off a TV on Hayden's desk, then plugs in a cord, and it flickers to life.

I watch Hayden as he slides a plastic container out from under his bed. I think I get why he'd want to portray a character like this. Roxas has to figure out who he is in the game and maybe Hayden had to do the same thing in real life.

I wish I could relate to Princess Aurora so I could skate my program better, but all I know is she gets cursed and then a prince comes to her rescue. I'd rather be the brave hero instead of the person who needs saving.

"Voilà!" Dan straightens. He passes Hayden a controller.

"Thanks, Dad."

"Thanks, Mr.—" I catch myself. "Dan."

"You're both very welcome." Dan heads for the door. "And I'm off. My work here is done, but I'm afraid the dishes are not."

Hayden scoots closer to the TV. It looks like he's fast-forwarding through an animated movie. "Okay, check this out." He hits pause. "That's Roxas."

I lean forward to study the image. With his tousled blond hair, Roxas looks a lot like Hayden. I point to the top of the fabric pile. "You're making his jacket out of this?"

"Right. I still need to sew on the checkered pattern, plus attach the zipper to the red fabric. There's this Square Enix fan event coming up that I want to get it done for." Hayden must notice my confusion. "That's a video game maker. They created the *Kingdom Hearts* games, which Roxas is a character in, plus *Final Fantasy* and a bunch of other awesome stuff."

I take another look at the boy frozen in place on Hayden's TV. The pattern that runs along Roxas's chest repeats along the seam of his shoulders. "We can totally get this done before your meetup. I'll work on the checkerboard pieces."

"Here." Hayden opens the container he pulled out from under his bed. I choose a spool of black thread and a needle.

While he starts connecting his silver zipper to the red fabric, I tackle the checkerboard pattern. It's detailed work, requiring sharp eyes and careful hands, just like when I helped Mom bead my Nationals costume last year. We work in silence, totally focused.

When something slams against the door, my whole body jerks. My fingers fumble the needle. It slips from my grip, disappearing into the carpet.

"Got you!" The door hardly muffles Mattie's voice at all. "Now you're it!"

"You got my *shirt*. You're not supposed to grab clothes!" That sounds like Elliot.

Beside me, Hayden lets out a heavy sigh. "Hold on." He gets up, moves to the door, and sticks his head out into the hall.

"Hey, you two. Play somewhere else."

"We were just—" Mattie starts, but Hayden cuts him off.

"Playing tag in the house? Mom won't like that if she finds out."

The hall becomes silent. Hayden shuts the door and turns back to me. "Sorry."

"It's okay." I feel my way carefully through the carpet for my lost needle. "Are they always like that?"

"Like, annoying?" Hayden sits down beside me. "All the time, morning to night. I almost can't wait for school to start. Even if there're a thousand people in my grade, it'll still be calmer."

"Or you can just come over to my house sometime on a quest for quiet," I say, leaning over to peer at his carpet a little closer. "Mom's so busy with work she's almost never—oh!"

A quick flash of movement. Bright going dark and then bright again under Hayden's bed.

I sit back with a quiet gasp.

Hayden follows my gaze. "That's just Fisk. Sorry if she scared you. You saw the cats downstairs, right?" I nod, pulse slowing. "Fisk came with us from Minnesota and the other two already lived here with Aunt Becca. Dad says it'll take time for them to get used to one another. Until then, I guess Fisk's just going to hide in my room."

"Poor kitty." I remember my first days at the Oakland rink, when everyone knew everyone else, except me. "I hope she gets comfortable soon."

"Me too. She used to be really friendly." Hayden glances back at me. "What did you say before you saw her? Something about a quiet...quest?"

"A quest for quiet." When he doesn't say anything, I explain. "You know, like in a video game where everyone is always going on missions and stuff?"

"That's a perfect name for it." Hayden drops his

fabric. "Want to play *Kingdom Hearts*? My fingers need a break from sewing."

"Oh, I'm okay." I pretend to concentrate on my needle and thread. "I honestly don't even know how. I'd probably be awful."

"Like I was on my first day of skating?" He reaches for the controller. "Gotta start somewhere, right?"

He has a point.

Hayden presses a button, and the screen flickers to a start menu. "I wish we could play all the way to the end, but this game takes, like, a million years to finish." He sets the difficulty level to beginner and passes me a controller with tons of buttons.

"Which one does what?"

"It'll tell you when you start playing. You'll get the hang of it fast."

The game starts. As promised, pop-up messages tell me which buttons to use. The problem is remembering everything in time to fight my first opponent.

I die in under five seconds. "Told you I was bad!"

"It's your first try. You're fine!" Hayden laughs. "Start again."

It takes me four attempts to figure it out. Then I'm

off on another mission, running Roxas through Twilight Town. I glance at Hayden during a lull in the game. "What grade are you going into this fall?"

"Eighth. What about you?"

So Hayden is a year older than me. I press a button, and Roxas hops onto his skateboard. "Seventh. When do you start?"

"The last week in August, which feels so early. My Minnesota school didn't start until after Labor Day. How about you?"

"Around then, too." I run Roxas straight off a building roof, but he bounces back to his feet without any kind of injury. "I can start whenever I want because I'm in an online program, but I like to get ahead on homework. That way, I stay caught up when I'm gone for competitions."

"Do you travel a lot for skating?"

"Not a ton." I shrug. "Usually, I do local events as practice before traveling to wherever Regionals is." I don't tell him I'm hoping to skip it this year. The closer I get to Los Angeles, the less I want to jinx it.

Hayden fiddles with his costume's half-attached zipper. "It's cool you get to visit other places and don't have to go to an actual school."

"Well, I just started homeschooling last year," I explain. "I went to regular elementary school in San Francisco." I go quiet, eyes on the screen. Roxas is caught between two buildings. I've been so focused on Hayden, I'm not even sure how he ended up there. "I think I might be stuck."

Hayden takes my controller and gets Roxas back on track in a matter of seconds. He pauses the game to give it back to me, but I shake my head. "Keep going. I just want to watch."

Hayden guides Roxas into a dark forest, in pursuit of a mysterious enemy. Roxas attacks the creature, but it doesn't seem to have any effect at first.

"Watch this," Hayden says as the screen switches to a movie cut-scene. A weapon appears in Roxas's hand out of nowhere. It looks like a huge key, but he swings it like a sword, easily defeating the enemy. "That's the Keyblade I'm trying to design. Dad said he'll help me cut it when I'm ready."

"That sounds like something I did in my fourth-grade art class," I say. "Except it was a mask, made out of papier-mâché."

"Maybe I'll take art this year." Hayden looks thoughtful. "My new school lets you choose a focus, like science or performing arts and stuff."

Performing arts. As Hayden quickly completes Roxas's current mission and moves on to the next, my gaze shifts to the fabric strewn around his room. "Maybe you could focus on theater."

Roxas stops moving on the TV screen as Hayden looks at me. "How come?"

"Well, you like dressing up as characters and—"

"Yeah, for cosplay," he cuts me off. He looks tense, knuckles clenched around the controller. I meet his gaze, and his cheeks flush a little. "Sorry. It's just, I like getting to choose, not having someone tell me who I have to be. Maybe that doesn't make sense to you, but it's different for me."

I think about my free program, about how things were different before Miss Lydia chose my princess music. "I think I get it, actually."

"Okay." Hayden doesn't say anything else, but Roxas starts moving again. By the time Mrs. Lubeck comes upstairs to take me home, things feel back to normal.

Hayden fills me in on more of Roxas's story during the drive back to the BART station, and as we talk, it feels like we've known each other forever. But when I step off the train back in San Francisco, reality sets in.

Ana might mean "I" in another language, but the Lubecks only know me as a boy named A. Then there's Mom, Tamar, and Alex, who know me as Ana, but don't know how I truly feel.

I'm still hiding who I am from all the people who matter.

Chapter Twenty-One

Before I can pack for next week's competition, Mom and I take a trip to the laundromat down the street. We load clothes into a big washing machine, then Mom leaves to pick up toiletries while I keep an eye on our clothes from my perch on a folding table.

I could text Hayden while I wait, or even Tamar. Part of me wants to ask Hayden about those gender-neutral pronouns, but I'm not sure exactly what I want to know that I can't look up online on my own. It's not like he uses them himself.

I pull out my phone. Although we didn't meet up last Sunday, Tamar finally sent me the videos of her Intermediate Moves. I click on the first clip, hoping it'll be a good distraction.

Tamar appears on my screen, standing at one end of the San Francisco rink. Turning backward, she starts the back double three-turn pattern. Her edges look steady, turns controlled, although she could work on extending her free leg more.

I click to the spiral sequence clip. This doesn't look bad, either. Tamar isn't super flexible, but her leg is at hip level for all but her last back inside spiral. I make a mental note, then move on to the video of her bracket turns.

A woman steps in front of my table, arms full of clothes. I slide over to give her space and return to my video. Tamar's brackets are scratchy. Her blade wobbles before and after each turn. I watch the clip again, but my washing machine dings before I get past her first set.

I feed quarters into the dryer, then return to my seat just as my phone buzzes in my pocket.

12:20 p.m.: Roxas's jacket is DONE. 🧵 Onward, pants!

12:20 p.m.: Also look at this!

Hayden's attached two pictures. The first is a selfie, highlighting the checker pattern lining his shoulders and chest. The second is harder to figure out. I zoom in until a little white face with glowing eyes stares back at me from under his bed. I text him back, swinging my legs like a pendulum.

12:22 p.m.: That looks really good!!

12:22 p.m.: And is this Fisk?

I should get back to watching Tamar's videos, but I look back at Hayden's selfie instead, then google *Kingdom Hearts* Roxas cosplay images. I scroll through colorful outfits and people with makeup covering their entire faces. For every costumed boy, there's a page full of girls.

My legs go still. If these girls dress up as boy characters on purpose, why is it so hard for me to skate as a princess?

I type in another search term: *boys versus girls*. All I get is a list of internet parenting articles.

Next, I try *the difference between boys and girls*. That gives me lots of links about brain science.

"Is the laundry done, Ana-Marie?"

I click my phone off fast and look up at Mom. The empty tote bag she grabbed on her way out the door now brims with items from the corner store. I glance past her to the dryer.

"Yep. I'll get it."

We head home to pack. I climb the ladder up to my bed with an armful of clothes and get to work deciding what to take to Los Angeles.

My clothes are half-sorted when Hayden texts again.

3:04 p.m.: Yes it's Fisk! She came out of hiding today for like 3 minutes!

3:05 p.m.: M and E were out with Mom. Q4Q achieved for both of us

3:05 p.m.: (That's quest 4 quiet if ur wondering)

3:06 p.m.: And guess what

His next message is in Chinese characters. After I jotted down the promised list of pronouns last weekend, Hayden installed a special keyboard app. He's been sending me new words as he learns them.

Today, he's advanced to simple sentences.

His latest text declares, *I am a cat.* Laughter bubbles up. I bite the inside of my cheek so Mom doesn't come investigate.

I send Hayden a pair of cat emojis and finish folding my clothes. We'll only be gone for a couple of days, but my skates and other competition supplies take up lots of space. I have to choose my non-skating clothes carefully so everything fits. Alex calls it "suitcase Tetris."

I grab the clothes I've chosen and climb down the ladder. Mom set out my suitcase on her bed. Now she's in the kitchen, back on her laptop. Laying my folded clothes beside the suitcase, I grab my duffel bag and remove anything not coming with us to LA.

I try to focus on packing, but my thoughts circle back to Hayden. His *I am a cat* text seemed silly at first, but now I can't get it out of my head.

I am a ____.

Girl? No, I don't think so.

Boy? Maybe, but it's not that simple.

Why is that blank so hard to fill?

I try again.

I am Ana-Marie Jin? True, but that means the same as *girl* to most people. The Marie part of my name still tells the wrong story.

Skater still works, at least.

But when I head to the closet and pull out my free-skate costume, even that word turns against me. Now I have to deal with a glittery dress. It may be the perfect size for me, but it definitely doesn't feel like a good fit.

I return to Mom's bed and slide the costume inside a garment bag, zipping it out of sight as fast as I can.

Sitting on the edge of her bed, I pull out my phone again and find the picture of Hayden and his Roxas jacket. This time, I study the wall over his shoulder, zooming in until I can make out the blurry *zie*, *zir*, and *zirs* cutouts.

I open another browser tab and search *gender-neutral pronouns*, chest fluttering as I skim the links.

How to use gender-neutral pronouns
Respecting people's gender-neutral pronouns
Five reasons people use gender-neutral pronouns

I click on the third link, skipping past the list's first header about not knowing the gender of the person you're talking about, then the second that focuses on *Limitations of the English Language.* My eyes pause on the next header: *Identifies as Nonbinary.*

The short paragraph says gender-neutral pronouns can be used by people who don't identify as the gender they were assigned at birth. I guess for me that would be a girl. But then wouldn't I prefer boy pronouns like Hayden does?

I tuck my legs under me and open a new tab, searching for only one word this time. My first result is a dictionary definition.

The fluttering in my chest intensifies, like a spin

picking up speed when I pull my arms in closer to my body.

Nonbinary: not relating to, composed of, or involving just two things.

That's totally me.

I study Mom at the kitchen table, then look down again. There's no time to google more stuff, but I wonder how I would explain this to her. Alex once told me that "coming out" is when a boy says he likes a boy, or when a girl shares that she likes another girl. Maybe it's similar to explain that you *are* a boy or girl.

Or nonbinary.

My legs are falling asleep, so I shift positions. The mattress squeaks, but Mom doesn't turn around.

How did Hayden come out to his parents? When he told them he's a boy, did they believe him immediately? Or did they think he was lying?

Each time I try to imagine the conversation, I see Mom shaking her head at me. Definitely confused. Probably disappointed.

Hayden hasn't really talked about his past to me. Maybe it's too private. Or maybe it's because he thinks we're both boys. My stomach clenches, but I have to know. I'll never be able to figure out how to talk to Mom if I don't.

4:09 p.m.: Can I ask u a question?

Across the room, Mom sighs. She doesn't turn around, but I still delete *u* and replace it with *you*.

4:09 p.m.: Can I ask you a question?

That gives me time to figure out the rest.

I tap send. Hold my breath.

4:10 p.m.: Go for it

"All packed?"

I jump, nearly dropping my phone at Mom's feet.

"Almost," I mumble.

"It looks like you're texting when you should be packing." Mom smiles. She knows she's caught me.

"I—um." The phone is still warm in my clammy hands. "Sorry."

I slide it into my pocket, then stare at the pile of unpacked clothes.

"Use a smaller bag to separate the street clothes from your skating outfits," Mom prompts.

Whoops. I travel for competitions enough that I should've already done this. "Sorry," I say again, before sprinting back to the closet.

"Is everything all right?" The lines in Mom's forehead deepen.

"Yes." I look down. "Why?"

"You seem distracted lately—and always on your phone."

True. But what else could I possibly say? *I'm sorry you spent thousands of dollars to get me the best choreography and costume, but I just found out I'm not a girl and don't want to perform my princess program?*

Not happening. I have to wait until after the competition. Maybe Mom will be so happy if I skate well enough to skip Regionals that it'll be easier to tell her.

Her eyes stay on me as I return with a second bag. I swipe a pair of practice pants off the bed and shove them into my suitcase, still imagining that conversation between Hayden and his parents. All I can see is Dan. Smiling down at me from the porch in Berkeley. Looking so proud when Hayden talked about his cosplay costume.

"I think I left a pair of tights on my bed." I climb a few rungs of my ladder. "I'll start packing my suitcase after I grab them."

"All right, then." Mom doesn't look convinced, but

she nods and heads back toward the kitchen. "Let me know when you're done, and I'll start dinner."

It's no fun lying to Mom, but I tell myself it's only for another few days as I look up at my Michelle Kwan poster. Michelle technically lied to her parents when she was my age, too, telling them her coach gave her permission to take the Senior free-skate test when he hadn't.

When they found out, Michelle moved up a level, even though her coach didn't think she was ready. But then she medaled at Nationals and became an alternate skater for the Olympic team.

I grab my tights, but my eyes keep drifting back to Michelle. I know lying is never okay, but maybe sometimes it's necessary. Plus, now that I know there's a word for how I feel, I should be able to perform my free program better. After LA, everything will be easier.

My gaze drops to my parents' graduation photo, still pinned to the poster's bottom left corner. Before I realize what I'm doing, I crawl across my bed and pluck it off its pin. I pull out my hongbao and slip the photo between my emergency money.

I still need to figure out some stuff before I ask Hayden coming-out questions.

I shoot him a text before climbing down my ladder to finish packing.

4:19 p.m.: Never mind! Mom started talking and I forgot what I wanted to ask.

I'll get to the bottom of this on my own—after I skate well enough next week to skip Regionals.

Chapter Twenty-Two

"Ana-Marie Jin." The announcer's voice trills over the sound system. "Your program music will start in thirty seconds."

My name feels like a burn that stings long after the announcer goes quiet. I breathe in, then press my shoulders down and exhale as I skate to my starting position.

I'm in first place after this morning's Intermediate short program. Tonight, skaters are allowed to run through their free programs once on practice ice. Tomorrow is the real deal. After the scores from both of my programs get added together, I'll know if I performed well enough to skip Regionals.

I rise up on my toe picks. My shoulders are tense, arms rigid as I strain to hold the position.

My feet used to cramp in my skates when I was younger. We went through pair after pair, but nothing felt right. Our last resort was to buy expensive, custom-made boots. Mom started staying at the office later to work on extra projects and save up for them.

The first day I wore those skates, it was like inhaling deeply after holding my breath for a whole program. My jumps soared. My spins were fast, centered, and better than ever. All because I found something that finally fit.

That's the exact way I feel about knowing I'm nonbinary. I'm already imagining how it'll feel to come out to Mom and Alex, like finally stepping into the light after hiding someplace dark. I'm ready.

But first, I have to qualify for Sectionals.

My ears ring as my program's first notes blare through the speaker. My throat vibrates. I glare in the direction of the music box, wishing they'd turn the volume down.

I force myself to smile as I set up my triple salchow. Turning backward, knee bent, I ride a steady inside edge, and prepare to—

Schwick.

For a split second, my arms flail, legs wide apart instead of tightly crossed. I land on two feet after a single rotation. The smile drops from my face.

I fly past Alex, knowing what he'd say: *Don't stop. Put it behind you.*

My first spin feels slower than normal. The judges aren't here tonight, but I imagine them taking away a ton of points. First, the popped salchow, then my sloppy spin, and now my footwork sequence. My edges are too shallow. My turns scratch and scrape.

I raise my arms as the music changes. The chorus of old voices drones over the speaker. Still too loud.

It's hard to bend my knees with so much tension in my legs. This is no way to set up a triple jump. I turn but I don't launch off my blade like usual. No rotation.

A hot surge of frustration fills my chest. My eyes water as I skip my next two solo jumps, then another jump combo. I refuse to look over at Alex.

One last spin is all that stands between me and the end of three minutes of embarrassment. I pivot hard.

Even this feels off. My positions aren't crisp and my revolutions seem sluggish. I'm barely breathing hard when I hit my final pose.

Now there's nothing left to do but face the music with Alex. I glide over and take a sip of water.

"What's up, kiddo?"

His voice is quiet. Unlike Miss Lydia, Alex doesn't believe in negative comments. If I were him, I'd definitely yell at me. I deserve it.

I thought discovering that I'm nonbinary would make it easier to skate my program, but I was so wrong. *I* might know who I am, but everyone else still believes I'm a girl—especially when my music's on. This program doesn't fit any better than my old skates.

I shrug, a sharp up and down of my shoulders.

"Are you tired from your short program this morning?"

"Yeah. Just tired."

Alex squeezes my shoulder. "Let's call it a day, then, so you can get plenty of rest."

I trail behind him as he gestures to Faith. Our eyes meet. Her expression is hard to read but hot embarrassment sparks in my chest again. I duck my head and hop off the ice fast.

She follows me to the bench where we left our skate bags. Glancing toward the stands, she leans over to untie her skates. "I guess our moms are still up there talking."

"Probably."

"Are you nervous about tomorrow?"

I keep my eyes down. "A little."

"Me too. I've been thinking about what you said back in the hockey rink. About telling my parents how I feel about the musical."

I finally look up. "Oh yeah?"

She nods. "I think that's why I'm so freaked out. I want to skate well so they're in a good mood when I try to talk to them."

I get that, even though Faith doesn't know it. I want Mom to be in a super good mood when I come out to her and tell her I need a new free-skate program.

Hope appears at the bottom of the stands. Mom and Mrs. Park come next. I turn to Faith and give her the advice I hope to use myself. "Just focus on one thing at a time. First, skate awesome tomorrow. Then, figure out how you'll tell your parents."

She gives me a quick smile before heading off with Hope and her mom.

Mom and I meet Alex in the rink lobby. He uses his phone to hail a rideshare back to the hotel. When the car arrives, Alex sits behind the passenger seat. Mom

· 234 ·

waits for me to slide into the center, then takes the seat behind the driver.

We buckle up, and she reaches out to squeeze my hand. "We'll get some dinner at the hotel, shower, and have an early night."

"Okay." I don't look at her, don't even feel like checking my phone. Mom rubs small, soothing circles in my palm with her thumb, but it only makes me feel worse.

"Are you upset about your practice?" she asks.

"No." There's no point telling her I'm worried about scoring well enough to qualify for Sectionals. She and Alex told me that's not supposed to be my goal.

"It's been an intense day." Alex nudges my shoulder. "But you skated a stellar short program this morning."

"It was wonderful, wasn't it?" I can hear the warmth in Mom's voice. "I'm glad you kept that music for one more season. It brought back so many good memories from Nationals."

My fingers twitch. So much depends on me skating well tomorrow.

The car pulls up in front of our hotel.

"More great memories to come. Right, Ana?" Alex

winks at me before getting out. I smile, but my face falls the moment he turns away.

We say goodbye to Alex in the hallway between our hotel rooms. I make a beeline for my bed, dropping my duffel on the floor next to it.

Mom sets her purse on the desk, then reaches for a leather folder with the word *Menu* printed across it in gold letters. "How would you feel about ordering room service tonight?"

She looks so hopeful that I force myself to say something. "That'd be good."

We choose our food, and Mom calls in our order. "Do you want to take the first shower?"

"You can." Now that I'm lying down, my legs feel impossibly heavy.

Mom heads for the bathroom. "Dinner should be here around the time I'm done."

Twisting onto my stomach, I exhale hard through closed lips. My phone pokes my ribs through the pocket of my warm-up jacket. I pull it out, then sit up fast when I see Tamar's text. We haven't talked in ages.

8:39 p.m.: Hey, how'd your short go today?

No exclamation marks or emojis, but any text is better than nothing.

A wave of cold loneliness washes over me. If she can't be here, at least I can call to hear her voice.

She picks up fast. "Hi."

"Hey." I sigh. "We just got back to the hotel. I can't talk for long, but I wanted to say hi."

"That's okay. How'd you do?"

I switch to speakerphone. "First, by a couple of points."

"Oh, congrats. That's awesome."

"Thanks." My lips scrunch up to keep from frowning. Something feels off. Maybe it's because I don't feel like giving her a play-by-play of my short program. "What's up with you?"

"Not a ton. Lots of skating and synchro practice."

A new text pings in, with a picture attached to it. "Has synchro season officially started, or is that in August?"

"August," Tamar says as I tap on the new message.

8:52 p.m.: I brought in reinforcements!

Hayden's snapped a picture of Dan in the middle of his bedroom. He holds a needle and thread, along

· 237 ·

with a strip of pant-shaped fabric. The waist looks half-hemmed, but Dan seems pretty pleased with himself.

My dad never even calls anymore.

"Ana?"

I startle, knocking a pillow onto the floor with my elbow. "Yeah?"

"Okay, you *are* still there. I thought the call dropped."

"No, I'm here. Sorry." I keep staring at Hayden's photo. "What'd you say?"

"I was just wondering if you had a chance to look at my Intermediate Moves yet? I'm testing really soon."

"Oh, yeah! I mean, some of them. I started looking at the first few clips and then got busy packing for this trip."

"What'd you think of the ones you watched?"

I slide off the bed and snatch the pillow from the floor. My eyes return to Hayden's photo. I can't help thinking about how much time Dan spends with his family. My dad hasn't sent me a letter in years. What would it be like if he came to my competitions? Maybe cosplay isn't Dan's thing, but he's still there for Hayden. My hand reaches up, fingers tugging at the chain on my charm necklace.

"Hey, Tamar. I have to go. Mom's done with her shower. Is it okay if I text you later?"

The line goes quiet. Now it's my turn to wonder if the call dropped. Another beat of silence, then Tamar says, "Sure. Good luck tomorrow." She hangs up.

I crouch down and grab my hongbao from my duffel bag, then pause, eyes darting toward the bathroom.

The shower's still running.

I slip a finger between two bills, pulling out Mom and Dad's graduation photo.

I'm not sure why I dug out this picture from a box at the back of our closet a couple of years ago. Maybe I was curious even back then. Mom doesn't talk much about Dad. I don't know what he's like at all. Didn't think I cared, either. It's been Mom and me for as long as I can remember, and that never used to bother me.

All it took was one afternoon with the Lubecks.

Hayden's whole family seems to support him. I wonder if this is always the way it's been, or if there was a time when they struggled to accept him as a boy.

I sit on my bed, still studying the photo. I don't have the kind of relationship with my dad that Hayden does with Dan. It's Mom I'm most worried about telling I'm nonbinary. I know she loves me, but I can't guess how she'll react. One more day, and I'll find out. My stomach lurches.

The bathroom door clicks open. I stuff the photo back into my hongbao as fast as possible as Mom pokes her head out.

"No food yet?"

"Not yet."

She steps into the room, twisting a towel into place on her head. "Well, I'm sure it'll get here soo—" She stops at her bed. "What's wrong?"

"Nothing," I say quickly. The sick feeling in my stomach must also show on my face.

"Something seems to be bothering you." She takes a seat on the edge of her bed, across from me. "Was it your practice this evening?"

I shake my head and look down, toward the hongbao still clutched in my hands. I rub it, feeling the thick edge of the photo inside.

"Do you think Dad is proud of me?"

"Pardon?" Mom's voice is higher than it was a second ago. Her towel tilts precariously on her head. She reaches up to steady it, then glances back at me with a puzzled expression.

"Dad," I say again. "Does he know about my skating? Or care how I'm doing?"

A sharp series of knocks makes both of us jump.

"Room service!" a man calls through the door.

Mom looks at me a moment longer, then moves to open it. She trades a tip for a serving tray. My eyes follow her across the room to the desk. She turns and passes me a plate, plus utensils wrapped in a cloth napkin.

"Your grandmother tells Jake about your competition results when she sees him." Mom's reply is slow and careful. "Is that what you're asking?"

But how much does Grandma Goldie even see him? She's Mom's mom, not Dad's. She and my dad just happen to live in the same town. I look up at Mom, ready to ask. She sounds as unsteady as I feel when I rise to my toe picks at the start of my free program.

Swallowing down my question, I manage a quiet "Yes, thanks."

I reach for my plate, stabbing a piece of lettuce with my fork. Mom sits at the desk and starts buttering a roll, occasionally glancing at me.

Twenty-four hours, I tell myself. Just one more day.

Chapter Twenty-Three

When I was little I had a pre-competition plan: Instead of anxiously waiting in the locker room for my event to begin, I'd make a beeline for the bathroom. My competitors would fill the locker room, sizing one another up with narrowed eyes and serious faces under layers of makeup. But safe inside the bathroom, I'd put the finishing touches on my hair and makeup, then chew a tab of ginger to calm my nerves.

Now that it's almost time to perform my free program, I pause in front of the competition rink's bathrooms. I don't want to use the girls' room, but the boys' isn't an option, either. I tug down the hem of my dress and decide to skip it. I don't want to see myself in the mirror, looking like someone I'm not.

I head for the locker room, but that's also sorted by gender. There's no avoiding it.

Inside, two girls sit on a bench, removing their skates

across from Faith, who has her headphones on. She looks up when I enter.

"Hi," I mouth as I sit and spread out my supplies nearby. Across the room, one girl recaps her program for the other while she wipes slush from her blades. I try to ignore them. My only job is to visualize a clean program.

I close my eyes and run through every element, imagining each controlled takeoff, fast rotation, and solid landing. In my mind, I'm skating in silence. No music. Leggings instead of a dress and tights.

The girls change topics to which famous skaters they've spotted coaching up-and-comers. Normally, I love talking to other skaters, especially those I haven't met before. But today is different. I need to stay completely focused if I want to score high.

I look down. Flesh-colored over-the-boot tights cover my feet instead of yesterday's glossy black fabric. One side of my leg glitters with a sprinkle of crystals. Everything I'm wearing right now screams "girl."

"Hellooooo!"

Hope appears with a flourish of sparkles and bouncy curls. The Pre-Juvenile girls skated hours ago, but her competition dress peeks out from under her jacket. She's still wearing a yellow ribbon that displays her fourth-place medal. Two large fake flowers rest in her arms, the floral equivalent of stuffed animals.

Hope tosses Faith an oversize fabric rose, then skips her way to my bench.

"Milady." Hope bows, offering me a blue flower. The word echoes in my head. I accept the gift but look away fast.

"You know we haven't skated yet, right?" Faith's headphones rest on her shoulders now.

"Duh." Hope rolls her eyes. "But now you won't have to wonder which one is from me when people throw them after your program, because you'll already have it. You're welcome."

The two girls stand, eyeing Hope like she's an alien before exiting the room. Hope whirls back to me, a tiny hurricane of glitter and hairspray. "*Anyway.* I just wanted to say good luck. Go, Team SF!"

Faith exchanges a look with me. "Team what?" she asks.

"SF! San Francisco. Alex said we're a team, remember? We never picked out a name."

"We've been a little busy with training," Faith points out.

"So, I picked one for us. Unless you have a better idea."

We both stay silent.

"Thought so." Hope grins. "Have a great skate. Smile, sparkle, shine!"

She flits off, and a flurry of nerves shoots into my stomach. I lean down and pop a tab of ginger into my mouth. A spicy jolt tickles the back of my throat when I swallow.

When I look back up, Faith's eyes are on me.

"Want one?" I hold out my supply.

"What is it?"

"Ginger tabs. They help settle your stomach when you're nervous."

Faith nods, then comes and sits beside me on my bench. "I feel like I need a whole bag of those today."

"Me too." I stand. "Let's warm up. Maybe that'll help."

For the next ten minutes, we run in place, then move on to stretches. Faith leans forward, extending her leg into a spiral position. I reach for it, raising it high behind her. We switch, and I stretch while Faith lifts.

With only five minutes left before our on-ice warm-up, we sit down again and tie our skates. I wrap special tape around the top of my boots so my laces don't come undone on the ice, while Faith does the same with her own roll.

"You ready?" she asks.

I nod. My skirt sways as I stand and I tug at it again.

We make our way from the locker area to the rink, where Alex waits. I check in with a volunteer, then take the ice.

Background music plays over the speakers, but I tune it out. Six minutes isn't a long time to get my feet under me.

I turn backward and launch into a big, airy waltz jump. Faith and I whiz past each other as I run through my double jumps, then triples.

"Skaters," the announcer's voice booms over the speaker. "You have one minute remaining in your warm-up."

I head back to Alex, who offers small corrections. Chin up. Right side strong. Check my left arm as I land each jump.

The warm-up ends. Skaters file off the ice.

"You look good." Alex offers me water. "Calm."

I am. This is the one part of my routine that's always the same. The taste of ginger lingers in my mouth. My stomach no longer flip-flops.

The announcer welcomes the first skater. Keeping my back to the ice, I bounce my knees to keep limber.

I shrug out of my warm-up jacket and hand it to Alex as the girl finishes. A volunteer nods at me to take the ice. Gliding in little half circles by the door, I wait for the announcer to introduce me. Cold air prickles up my bare arms.

"She comes to us from San Francisco, California. Please give a warm welcome to Ana-Marie Jin."

Between the "she" and "Marie," two parts of that introduction feel wrong, but I paste on a wide smile. I head for center ice, arms raised to acknowledge the judges, then the audience.

I take my opening pose.

The first quiet notes tell me the music technician fixed the volume. This should calm me, but my legs still shake as I perform my opening choreography. Air whips against my thin tights as I pick up speed. People are watching.

This never used to bother me.

Come on. Focus.

I take a deep breath in through my nose. Release it out of my mouth. Three-turn with shoulders in position. Chin up. Ride my blade to a straight takeoff.

One, two, three rotations—

My left arm flies back on my landing. I flip forward, salchow over-rotated.

Tiny mistake. Keep going.

I sit low in my first spin. Glancing at the ice when I'm done, I spot the tight, coiled mark.

Good. Now, ankles loose on the step sequence.

I bend my knees, blades carving deep edges. My turns are crisp and controlled.

The violins fade out. For the last ninety seconds, it's just me and my mortal enemies, the choir.

In the stands, a flash of short blond hair snags my gaze. It's probably someone's brother, maybe a competitor from one of the men's events. But my mind transforms him into Hayden as I turn backward for my triple toe.

Hayden in the stands, watching. Hayden seeing me in a dress, discovering my lie.

There's no time to second-guess my technique as my blade taps into the ice.

It's only a split-second hesitation, but I tilt in the air, one shoulder higher than the other. I come down sideways, hip smacking against the unforgiving ice. The sting travels down the rest of my leg.

I push up, rushing to get back on time with my music. My double flip comes next. Simple. Steady inside edge. Right leg behind my left before vaulting off my toe.

Thoughts of Hayden linger as I launch into the air. I pull in too tight for a double, too loose for a triple. Landing forward after two and a half rotations, I stumble onto my knees.

My breath hitches, the wind knocked out of me. The crystals on my dress twinkle under the overhead lights as the audience watches. A few offer claps of encouragement, but I know what they see: a princess, dethroned and weak.

I rise again and throw myself into a double axel. My landing leg quivers, and I turn into my final spin, finishing with a stiff arm position.

The audience applauds politely. No one stands up for me like they did at Nationals or throws stuffed animals.

I give the judges a quick bow, then leave the ice, neck hot. There's a wet spot on my hip from one failed jump.

My knees throb from my over-rotated flip. I brush past Alex before he can say anything. He has to stay for Faith's program, anyway. I don't bother grabbing my blade guards or stopping for a sip of water.

Mom appears, just as I pass the stairs that lead up into the stands. I pause and we lock eyes. Then I pick up my pace.

"Wait." The rubber soles of Mom's shoes squeak against the floor, but I don't slow down. "Please, Ana-Marie—"

It's all too much. My dress. Hope's comment. My full name feels like a slap in the face. I whirl around.

"*Don't* call me that." The words burst out before I can stop myself.

Mom freezes, mouth half-open. I turn away fast, rushing into the locker room.

I drop onto my bench and wrap my arms around myself. Time passes by the changing of my competitors' program music, first a dramatic ballad, then Faith's elegant violin piece. The announcer calls the end of my event, but I don't get up, not even when the Zamboni rumbles to life to resurface the ice.

When the door creaks open, I look up, expecting Mom.

"Ana?" Faith peeks in. "You forgot your blade guards. And your warm-up jacket." She makes her way over and hands them to me.

"Thanks." As Faith heads to the bench where she left her roller bag, I ask, "How'd you skate?"

"Okay, I think." She doesn't ask how my program went, probably because she saw how bad it was. "We should go. The scores will be posted soon."

I want to get this dress off as fast as possible, but I push myself up. Faith and I head out of the rink and into the lobby, where a podium is set up. Printer paper flutters on the wall. At big competitions like Sectionals and Nationals, the announcer calls out your score in the Kiss and Cry area. At other events like this one, they get posted in writing. Faith and I squeeze through a crowd of skaters, coaches, and parents.

"Look." Faith points as a volunteer tapes a new sheet to the wall. We inch closer.

"Congrats," Faith says before I even spot my name. I scan the results.

Third. I dropped two places from the short program to my free skate. Faith moved up one, from sixth to fifth, just off the podium.

"Ana! Faith!" I turn and see Alex waving as he heads our way. Mrs. Park, Hope, and Mom follow him.

They read the results. Mom turns my way, but she doesn't pull me into a hug like she usually does. "Are you all right?" She keeps her voice low, meant only for me. Her face pinches with concern.

"I'm fine." I look away, cheeks burning, as Alex turns to Faith.

"Great job. I'm so proud of how much improvement you've shown this summer.

"And Ana." He turns to me. "I know this wasn't the performance you wanted, but you rotated your jumps and fought through your stumbles. A bronze at a new level during preseason is a fantastic accomplishment."

Out of the corner of my eye, I see Mom nod.

I don't say anything, because I know they're wrong.

"Congrats, Ana!" Hope skips with us as Alex guides me toward the medal podium. "Now we'll both have medals."

I glance back at Faith, but she doesn't seem bothered

by Hope's comment. Stepping up onto my spot at the podium beside the girls in glittery dresses, I accept my award with a strained smile. For the second day in a row, my eyes water.

There's no way my score will hold up and let me qualify directly for Sectionals. That means there's not enough time to change my program, because I'm going to have to work twice as hard to get it ready for Regionals.

The camera flashes. I blink and find Mom in the crowd. She claps along with everyone else, but her jaw looks tight. I can relate. My jaw hurts, too, from all my fake smiles.

Chapter Twenty-Four

We hail a car to the airport just a few minutes after I hop off the podium. Alex sits up front. Mom and I take seats on opposite sides in the back of the car. She doesn't reach for my hand this time, and I don't offer it. I stare out the window as we zip across on the freeway, not seeing anything.

"Aside from the step-out on your salchow, the first half of your program looked strong," Alex tells me. "There were just a few hiccups in the second part. Actually, your flip just looked like you were planning a triple and bailed out at the last minute."

"Yeah."

"That might've been my fault, since I've been focusing so much on it in the harness. You're so close to landing it on your own, though. Let's consider adding it into your program when we get back."

"Okay." I should be excited. Nailing a triple flip would be a huge deal at Intermediate. It'll definitely make me a contender for the national training camp if I land it at Sectionals.

If I qualify for Sectionals. I still have to get through Regionals now.

We hop out of the car and head into the airport, make it through security, then settle into seats in front of our gate. Mom pulls out her laptop, while Alex calls Myles to tell him when to pick us up from the San Francisco airport later tonight. I think about grabbing my phone, too, but I can't imagine texting with Tamar or Hayden right now.

"Ana!"

I twist in my seat as Hope dashes in front of Mrs. Park and Faith, her pewter medal bouncing against her chest. She looks so proud wearing it around her neck. My bronze medal feels like a failure. It's already packed deep in my suitcase.

Hope rubs her medal between both hands. "Are you on this flight, too?"

"Of course she is," Faith answers. "Why else would she be at the same gate?"

Hope ignores her. "Want to come get snacks?"

I turn to Mom. "Is it okay if I go with them?"

"Of course." Her voice sounds tired. "You still have some money left after your haircut, right?"

"And from Grandma Goldie." I still haven't spent my Chinese New Year money.

We check out a nearby kiosk, where Hope flits around, trying to convince Mrs. Park to buy her everything from gummy bears to Cracker Jacks. Meanwhile, I can't help thinking about how I snapped at Mom. As Faith and I browse a magazine rack, I realize Mom and I didn't even take a picture together. There'll be nothing new to add to our collection on the refrigerator.

"Are you okay?" Faith keeps her eyes on a magazine featuring a celebrity wedding, but she doesn't seem to be reading the headline. "You've been really quiet today."

I could say *yes, I'm fine*, like I told Mom. She'd probably believe me if I said I was tired.

But, the only thing I'm tired of is lying.

"Did you see my performance?"

"Some of it. Your double axel was huge." Her face fills with sympathy, which means she probably saw enough to know my axel was one of my only good elements.

We turn toward a wall of packaged snacks. Faith

chooses a bag of nuts and dried cranberries while I grab the cheapest chewing gum I can find. This doesn't feel like a good time to be spending all my money.

"The rest of my jumps were pretty terrible."

"But you still medaled."

"My short program score held me up," I blurt out before I can stop myself.

I remember that Faith placed fifth and look away, wishing I could disappear. I can't say anything right today.

Passengers have started boarding by the time we return to the gate. We get in line with Mom and Alex. Hope turns to Mrs. Park. "Can Ana sit with me and Faith? Please?"

Mrs. Park looks at Mom, who nods and says, "It's fine with me, if you don't mind switching seats."

"Yay! Now we can figure out a team name." Hope bounces in place. "I call the window seat!"

As the gate agent scans Hope's ticket, Faith turns to me. "I'll sit in the middle so I can tell Hope to be quiet if she gets annoying."

I smile a little. Hope really doesn't bother me.

We find our seats, and Hope begins chattering immediately.

"Okay, so, I still think Team SF is the best choice, but if you *really* don't like it, how about Team Regionals? Because we'll all be competing there in October."

I swallow hard. Every word Hope says drives the dagger of my failure deeper. Faith glances at me, then back at Hope. She shakes her head, and Hope's mouth turns down in a pout.

"Why not?"

"Because it's just one competition." I'm glad Faith is explaining this, because I can't form a single word. "Are you still going to want to be called Team Regionals once it's over?"

"Oh." Hope's frown relaxes. "Well, I can't think of anything else. I need some help."

"We will help." This time when Faith looks at me, I nod. "It's just hard to come up with good names when we're exhausted."

The flight attendant's voice crackles over the intercom. As I listen to the safety instructions, Hope yawns. By the time we take off, her eyelids droop.

I scroll through the entertainment options on the screen in front of me, but our flight's not long enough to watch a full movie. I click on the trailers instead, not really watching any of them. Eventually, Faith turns on her overhead light, then leans forward and pulls a sheet of paper out of her bag. It looks like a list of jumps and spins with a breakdown of the judges' marks.

I can't help looking. "Is that your free-program protocol?"

She nods. "I landed my triple toe."

"You did?" I lean over as she points to an element a few lines down the list. It reads *3T<*.

"It got called for under-rotation." Her finger stops at the less-than sign. "But I landed it. First time in a competition."

"That's amazing."

"Thanks." Hope turns in her seat, lashes fluttering, but her eyes stay closed. Faith clicks off the overhead light and our row floods with darkness. It wraps around me like a blanket, safe and comforting.

I wish I could be as happy about my medal as Faith is with her triple toe.

But earning a medal means nothing if I didn't skate my best. It's not even about a flawless program. I've skated imperfect programs that I'm still proud of. This time, I got distracted and made silly mistakes. Even if I had won, I'd still feel disappointed.

But Faith? She tried hard and landed her first triple toe in competition. Maybe fifth is great for her.

"Did you buy a video of your free skate?" I ask.

"Mom ordered one. They said they'd email us a link when it's ready, probably after the Rising Stars camp."

"I'd love to watch, when you get it."

"Yeah?" She smiles shyly.

"Definitely. And speaking of the camp, have you decided if you're going to tell your parents you want to do the musical instead?"

"I think I will, yeah." Her fingers curl around the edges of her protocol sheet. "Mom's happy with how Hope and I skated, and Dad seemed excited when we texted him about our results. You said the best time to talk to them is when they're in a good mood, right?"

I can still imagine the conversation I was going to have with Mom after I nailed my free program and secured my spot at Sectionals. That's completely ruined now, but maybe Faith still has a chance. "That usually works for me, yep. What are you going to say?"

"I'm still figuring that out. I know they already paid for the camp, but there are skaters on the waitlist, so they can get their money back if I don't go."

I nod. "That's good. Plus, it shows that you don't want to waste their money."

"Yeah. And I'll be applying to private high schools next spring. Right now, all I have is skating and church youth group as activities to put on my application. If I did the musical, I bet I could get the sound designer to write me a letter of recommendation."

"See? You've already figured a lot out. I'll keep my fingers crossed for you." I hold up both hands, crossing my middle and index fingers, then my ring fingers and pinkies for good measure.

Faith grins.

We say our goodbyes once we land. The tension comes back fast when it's just Mom and me, plus Alex.

"Did you have a nice time with Faith and Hope?" Mom asks. Everything she says sounds cautious.

As Alex calls Myles to let him know we've made it

down to the pickup area, all I can do is nod at Mom. There's an invisible barrier that feels as thick as a wall between us.

A sporty red car parks at the curb. The passenger-side window rolls down, and I catch a glimpse of Myles as Alex helps Mom put our bags in the tiny trunk.

"Welcome home, Bean." Myles smiles at me, but I can't get myself to smile back. Mom and I settle into the back seat, Alex in the front. Myles leans over and gives him a quick kiss. It lasts less than a second, but it reminds me that both of them can freely be who they are. I'm still hiding in the dark.

"Thank you for picking us up," Mom says as Myles merges onto the freeway that'll take us north to San Francisco.

"No problem at all, ma'am. We have to go through the city to get home to Oakland. You're along the way."

I sit back in my seat as he continues talking with Alex and Mom. My muscles ache. It's hard to even think. Soon, the smooth drawl of Myles's voice lulls me to sleep.

I wake to Mom's soft touch on my shoulder. Alex and Mom get our bags from the trunk as I rub my eyes from my spot on the sidewalk.

"Rest up this weekend." Alex gives me a quick hug. "We'll ease back into training and have you running your program again by midweek."

The climb to the fourth floor takes forever. Alex's words echo like a threat, even though I know he didn't mean them like that.

I drag my feet in the hallway, eyes on the floor as I enter our apartment.

Back to training. More free-program run-throughs.

Mom and I leave our suitcases by the door, taking turns in the bathroom. This almost seems normal.

Except, there's no talking as we get ready for bed.

"Good night." Mom finally breaks the silence. Her voice drifts up to my top bunk where I'm curled into a ball, knees to my chest. "Sleep well."

"Night," I murmur, but sleep doesn't come. My thoughts tilt and swirl like an off-center spin.

No skipping Regionals or asking for a new program. Definitely no coming out. My plan completely failed.

AUGUST

Chapter Twenty-Five

Mom and I make an unspoken pact over the weekend: We act like the competition never happened.

Even without talking about my performance, we exist in awkward silence. When Mom tries to talk to me, I answer in one or two words. Our eyes play tag. I steal glances at Mom when she's distracted. If she looks up, my gaze skitters away.

I don't even feel like texting Tamar or Hayden at first, even though both asked me how I skated at the competition.

I want to tell them the whole truth, but it feels like I've waited too long. I've known Tamar since we were little kids. What if she doesn't believe me if I tell her I'm nonbinary? What if she thinks it's weird?

Hayden is a different story, because I've been lying to him since the first day we met. I could barely look his way during skate-school yesterday. I even waited to put my name tag on until I'd skated to the far side of the ice.

I snapped at Mom. Bombed my free program. I don't know how to tell Tamar, and I'm still lying to Hayden.

What a mess.

I stand alone in front of Mom's office Wednesday morning, waiting for Mrs. Park. Mom kisses the top of my head quickly, then heads upstairs for an early meeting. She leaves me out front with Samuel promising to keep watch.

"Hello, Miss Ana-Marie!"

"Hi, Samuel." The curb is nothing special, but I study it like I'm about to be quizzed.

"How do you like your new rink?"

"It's fine."

Neither of us speaks for a moment. A nearby streetlight turns from green to red. Bus brakes whistle.

"It takes time to settle," Samuel says. "Especially when the reality is different from your expectations."

My head jerks up. I wonder if Mom told him something, but Samuel's gaze travels toward Market Street. He doesn't look at me.

"That was how it was for me, at least. I came here because of a war in the country where I was born. When I

· 268 ·

first learned I would be living in San Francisco, California, I had preconceptions. I assumed there would be palm trees and beaches, with celebrities walking on every street."

"That's mostly just Los Angeles."

"I know that now, yes." Samuel smiles ruefully. "But ten years ago? I had no idea! I arrived in July, and imagine my surprise—so much fog. Also, no celebrities."

I can imagine Samuel in shorts, flip-flops, and a T-shirt, even though I've only ever seen him in the suit he wears to work. Plus, his bewildered look as he steps off the ferry, shivering in the city's infamous summer cold. It's a small one, but I smile.

Mrs. Park's SUV appears. I take a step toward it, then stop. Maybe Samuel has a preconception about me I can help change.

"Hey, Samuel?"

He looks at me expectantly.

"Can you please call me Ana? Not 'Miss' or 'Marie.' "

"Just Ana?"

I nod.

"Of course...Ana." He says my name slowly, like he's trying to get used to something new.

I smile a little bigger. *Ana* means "I." Asking people

to call me that feels like I'm telling them, "I am me."
If they want to know more, they can ask. I wish I had
explained that to Mom instead of snapping at her.

Waving to Samuel, I hop into my usual seat. It's not
until I buckle myself in that I realize I have new company sitting next to me.

"Hey," Faith says.

"Hi." I look toward the front seat, but it's empty.
"Does this mean what I think it does?"

Faith breaks out in the biggest grin I've ever seen
from her. "Hope left last night for the Rising Stars
camp in Colorado Springs."

"So you get to be an assistant to that sound person?"

"Sound designer." Faith lowers her voice so only I
can hear. "I spoke to Mom and Dad and told them how
I felt, just like we talked about."

"That's awesome," I whisper back.

I wish I could do the same with Mom, Alex, Tamar,
and Hayden.

"Yeah. I've only been to two meetings, but I've
already learned so much. The musical is in September.
Would you maybe want to come?"

"Um, *yes*." Like she even has to ask! "That'd be cool. Just let me know the dates, and I'll ask Mom."

"Okay." The grin still hasn't left her face.

As Mrs. Park turns onto a ramp that leads up to the Bay Bridge, Faith glances down at her iPad. I check my phone, even though I doubt I have new messages. Hayden isn't awake yet, and Tamar's been pretty quiet.

"Are you competing in Salt Lake City next month?" she asks.

I shake my head. "We'll probably just focus on training for Regionals."

"That makes sense. Especially since you already got a medal at your first event."

"Right..."

My phone buzzes. I reach for it, relieved to have a way out of this conversation.

7:30 a.m.: ARRRG! Mattie woke me up for NO reason 😤😤😤

7:31 a.m.: Be glad u don't have sibs

I reply back fast.

7:31 a.m.: Oh noooo. Boo to Mattie!

I look over at Faith, who's tapping away on her iPad. "What is that app? Does it make music?"

"It can." Behind her, the freeway disappears as we exit near the rink. "Some people make music on it, but I use it to edit song files."

"Edit, like"—I imagine how someone would use it for skating-program music—"shortening a song or something?"

Faith nods. "Or combining pieces together and changing the volume in a specific place."

The car stops, and we get out. I slide the strap of my duffel up onto my shoulder and wait while she grabs her roller bag. Side by side, we walk upstairs to the yoga studio for off-ice class. She unrolls her yoga mat next to mine. The instructor greets us, and we sink into our first stretch.

By the afternoon, a weight feels like it's lifted off my shoulders. Competitions use up a lot of energy, so Alex and I always take a break the week after an event. I only have to skate half my sessions today. Alex gives another student an extra lesson during his usual time with me, so I grab my supplies and head off to eat an early lunch.

I open the door to the coaches' lounge, pausing

when I see a familiar face I didn't expect to see—not today, anyway.

"Corinne?"

She turns. "Well, hello there!"

"Hi." I tilt my head, wondering why she's here on a Wednesday. She holds a rolled-up poster in her hands.

"This was going to be a surprise." She lifts the poster. "But since you're here, would you like to take a look?"

I don't know what she means but step closer.

She unrolls it, and—

My jaw drops.

"Isn't it wonderful?"

Corinne must mistake my shock for excitement as I stare at a picture of myself in my free-skate costume. I'm balanced on my toe picks in my opening pose, the boards of the Los Angeles rink blurred out behind me. The top of the poster has text announcing the skate-school's upcoming recital.

It stars none other than *Ana-Marie Jin, US Juvenile Girls Champion*.

"One of my colleagues teaches in Los Angeles. She was at your competition last week and sent me this picture," Corinne explains. "Normally, we just hand out small flyers to remind everyone about the end-of-session recital, but I thought your performance called for something extra special to ensure as many people attend as possible."

I look at the seats under the row of skate-school jackets, at the jack-o'-lantern name tag bucket. Anywhere but the poster Corinne holds out so proudly.

"Where will you put this up?" I manage to ask.

"All over. I had several made," Corinne chirps. My stomach drops like a rock at the thought of Hayden and Cyn seeing it as they enter the rink. "They'll stay up until the day of the recital."

I thought I had another week to figure out how to explain things to Hayden. Maybe two.

Now he'll know I lied to him the moment he arrives for skate-school next Tuesday.

Chapter Twenty-Six

The next day, one of Corinne's posters stares back from the off-ice studio door.

Faith pauses in front of it. "Hope loves your dress. She's been talking about it almost nonstop since the seamstress sent it to us."

Awesome.

Now everyone who hasn't seen my dress yet can talk about it, too. I take a deep breath and try not to think about it at the beginning of stretching class. For a little over an hour, I push the poster out of my mind, focusing on the yoga mats, the instructor, and other skaters. My muscles relax as I sink into a deep stretch.

That's the only break I get. Back downstairs after dance, I notice the posters everywhere, demanding my attention:

SKATE-SCHOOL RECITAL NIGHT
FEATURED PERFORMER: ANA-MARIE JIN
US JUVENILE GIRLS CHAMPION

Everywhere I look, there I am, stuck to walls and doors. There's even a postcard-sized ad taped to the side of the concession stand's napkin dispenser. In each picture I'm frozen in my opening pose with my chin lifted, eyes scanning a blurry crowd.

The photographer captured me moments before I choked. I still had a chance to qualify for Sectionals in that photo. Now I don't. I keep my head down and lace up my skates next to Faith. We take the ice.

One of the posters hangs from the plexiglass by the rink entrance. It faces the benches, but my eyes still drift to the silhouette in the shape of my free-program dress every time I skate past.

I only have a few days left to figure out what to say to Hayden. Each passing freestyle session takes me closer to the moment when he'll know I lied to him.

I flex my head from side to side. The muscles in my neck twinge in protest.

If Tamar were here, she'd roll her eyes and tell me

I'm overreacting. *Chill, Ana. It's only a bit of boy trouble.* Suddenly, Tamar's absence is a physical ache.

I cast a quick glance toward Alex—he's busy with another skater. I leave the ice five minutes before my freestyle session is supposed to end.

The second rink is quiet, lights dimmed. Hockey practice hasn't started yet, and the smell of sweat mingles with disinfectant. I find a spot near the bottom steps of the bleachers and pull out my phone.

It takes her four rings to answer.

"Hi." When Tamar doesn't immediately reply, I lower the phone from my ear to check the signal. All good. "...It's Ana."

"Hey." The word is flat.

"How're you?" I ask, even though we usually skip questions like this.

"Fine."

I wait for her to ask why I called, or at least say something about how I should be training right now.

She stays quiet, and a shiver climbs my spine. I balance my phone on my shoulder, pressing it against my ear. Mist rises to the ceiling from the rink surface.

"So, what's up?" Tamar finally asks.

"A ton." My thoughts immediately turn to Hayden. One thing at a time, though. I need to start from the beginning. "I totally bombed my free program at the LA competition. It dropped me from first to third."

I wait for her to say something, but the line stays silent.

"Still there?"

"Yes." There's an edge to the word, a sharpness in her tone.

"The choreography's all wrong for me." I need to figure out the best way to tell her I'm nonbinary. First, she has to understand how miserable the last two months have been. "The dress is pretty, but it's not right for me, either. Same for the music. It makes people think I'm a—um." I try to swallow again and cough a little.

Just say it.

Another beat of silence.

"Is that all?" She didn't even ask what I was going to say. It's like she's not even listening.

"Not really..."

"Well, that sucks."

That's it. No extra questions or helpful suggestions. This isn't like Tamar.

"Is everything okay?"

"Oh, now you care?"

I shiver again, unsure if this chill is coming from the ice or through my phone.

"Yes?" I'm not sure what she's getting at.

"Could've fooled me," Tamar shoots back. "You've been flaky all summer."

"*What?*"

"You heard me."

I shake my head. What is Tamar even talking about? "Okay, I know it's been hard with me training in Oakland, but we've still met up. We still text and call each other to talk."

"About what?"

I blink. "What do you mean?"

"I mean, *what* do we always talk about every time we meet up, and text, and call?"

The question throws me off. "Just...stuff. Skating, usually."

Tamar scoffs. "Yeah, *your* skating."

The line goes quiet again, but this time I know it's not dead. My next words are softer, more timid. "And movies."

"Yeah, like, once. You've been so focused on your new friends, working with a famous choreographer, chopping all your hair off, and whatever. But every time I try to talk to you about my life, you barely say a word. Or you promise to do something, and you don't. You know what that makes you, Ana? *Selfish*."

I open my mouth, but no sound comes out. Is this how Mom felt when I snapped at her last week? My breath mists in front of me, but I don't feel the rink's chill anymore.

Tamar hangs up.

I return to the other side of the building in a daze. My eyes don't snag on the recital posters for the first time all day.

It's not my fault I've been busy. And I'm *not* selfish. Or flaky. My program is a huge problem. It's not selfish to ask your best friend to listen when you need to talk.

Is it?

My temples throb as I spot Alex leaving the ice.

He mentions something about lunch. I nod, but it feels like someone else is in control of my motions.

We enter the coaches' lounge. Alex talks some more, but his words don't make sense.

Selfish, selfish, selfish.

The weight of his gaze finally jolts me out of my thoughts.

"Sorry, what?"

Alex opens his salad container. "You seem distracted today, Bean."

Eyes down, I run my fingers along my duffel bag's zipper but don't open it. "Tamar's mad at me."

"I doubt it." Alex spears a tomato with his fork. "She's been having a rough week, but I don't think that has anything to do with you."

I look up, my mind clearing a little. Maybe Tamar's mood isn't completely my fault.

Alex meets my gaze, then takes a sip of water. "Tamar's nerves got the best of her at the test session a couple of days back. Her new coach told me she didn't have the skate she was hoping for."

Test session. A couple of days ago?

My pulse pounds, full-out drums at both temples. The lounge swirls out of focus, then back again, like a badly centered spin. I never sent her notes about those video clips, didn't even finish watching them.

"Ana?"

I look up. My vision shimmers.

Alex rises, and I close my eyes. Shake my head.

A cool hand presses against my forehead. My eyes flutter open as Alex stands over me.

"Is everything all right?"

I start to nod but stop.

I'm so tired of lying.

"I don't feel good," I whisper.

"I can see that." Alex lifts his hand from my head and studies me. "Let's skip your afternoon training. Rest here until Mrs. Park arrives. I'll text your mom so she knows what's up."

"Okay." Relief tingles through my arms and legs at knowing I won't have to skate more today.

Soon, Alex heads out to teach his afternoon lessons. My talk with Tamar replays in my head.

First, I lied to Hayden, then yelled at Mom. Now I've let Tamar down.

I pull out my phone. Maybe I can fix this before I go home.

11:20 a.m.: I am so sorry. Can I call you?

The read receipt appears, then an ellipsis. I wait for her to text back a yes.

· 282 ·

The ellipsis vanishes.

Guilt burrows deep into my stomach. I wait three minutes and ten seconds, just a bit longer than my free-skate program, but it feels like years. I text her again.

11:25 a.m.: I'm calling

It rings once. Twice. Three times.

The line clicks and my heart leaps into my throat.

"Heyyy, you've reached...me!" Tamar's recorded voice chirps in my ear. "I never check my messages so text, please!"

I slump in my seat, my pulse returning to its normal beat. Now my stomach's churning.

I didn't feel sick when Alex was here, but I sure do now.

Chapter Twenty-Seven

The Parks drop me off at Mom's office. She insists we can't walk home if I feel sick, so we board the Number 5 bus. I watch Mom count out change for two fares. Every choice I make costs something.

We walk from the bus stop to our apartment in silence. Climb three flights of stairs. Slip off our shoes by the rack inside our apartment. Rung by rung, I climb the ladder to my bed. Mom's hand is on my back, keeping me balanced.

I curl up under the sheets. I'm not cold, but my shoulders tremble as she tucks me in. There's comfort in her warm hand on my face, in her fingers gently combing through my hair.

I want her to get in bed with me. I'd tuck my knees to my chest, my back against her stomach. I used to do that when I was little, listening to the low hum of her voice reading stories I'd chosen at the library. When she got too tired to read out loud, she'd dim the lights.

Pressing her lips against the back of my head, she'd murmur my name until I fell asleep.

She hasn't said my name in days. Not since the competition, I think.

"Tea?"

I nod, and Mom disappears under the bed rail. The moment she heads to the kitchen, I pull out my phone. No new texts. I tap into my messages, just to be sure. My last texts to Tamar stare back at me, unanswered.

The hiss of a kettle comes to me first, then the flowery scent of chamomile. I slide my phone under my pillow and sink into my mattress.

My eyelids are heavy by the time Mom returns. I want to tell her everything, but I barely have enough energy to sip my tea. I hand the cup back to her, then pull my blanket up over my head, letting the world disappear.

I open my eyes to a hint of morning light. Water's running in the bathroom.

Everything comes back fast. Tamar snapping at me. Corinne hanging recital ads. Hayden about to discover I lied to him, if I don't think of something quick.

I make a grab for my phone, but it's not in its usual spot. It takes me a second to remember it's under my pillow. I slide it out, hold my breath, click it on.

No new messages from anyone.

Not a shocker. Hayden's probably not up yet, and Tamar's still mad. I sigh and put it away again.

The water turns off and the bathroom door clicks open.

"You're awake." Mom walks toward my bed. "How are you feeling?"

I bury my face in my pillow. The next thing I know, Mom's fingers coax me to face her.

She checks my temperature with the back of her hand. "You don't seem to be running a fever."

"I still don't feel good," I mumble.

I open one eye a sliver as Mom studies me. "You don't think you can skate?"

I shake my head, squeezing my eyes shut.

There's a long pause before Mom finally says something. "Okay. One more day off. I'll text Alex and let Mrs. Park know not to stop by the office. Mrs. Lee is down the hall if you need anything. I'll tell her you'll be at home."

I wish Mom could stay here with me. I wish for a lot of things, actually. But what I want most right now is to tell Mom how I feel without her being mad or disappointed that I'm not the person she thinks I am.

My eyes follow her around our apartment, until she heads out.

One more day off, then the weekend. I close my eyes, trying to pretend yesterday never happened.

I spend the weekend in bed, but not much time actually sleeping. Mom checks in on me both mornings. She leaves jook porridge and tea on the table before heading out to tutor kids who've returned from their vacations.

Mom makes jook whenever I'm sick, mixing in soy sauce to give it more flavor. It settles my stomach like ginger. I don't feel like I deserve it now since I'm not actually sick.

I lie in bed, sheets pulled up to my chin, until the hollow ache in my stomach grows fangs. Eventually, I push the sheets back, grab my phone, and drag myself to the kitchen table.

Yesterday, I got up after Mom left and ate a tiny bite of jook before pouring the rest into the sink. Now

I sit down and reach for the spoon. I take a bite, swallowing a whole mouthful of creamy porridge. Another spoonful. One more, then a sip of tea before checking my phone.

There's nothing new from Tamar, but Hayden's texted me a ton the last few days.

Thursday—4:02 p.m.: I am SO close to done with my cosplay! 👟

Friday—3:20 p.m.: Closerrrr

Saturday—7:10 p.m.: D.O.N.E. 🎉

I click on the attached photo. Hayden stands on his porch dressed as Roxas from head to toe. The checkered pattern wraps around his chest and shoulders, and the collar is layered red over black, just like video game Roxas's jacket.

I tap back into his texts.

Sunday—9:12 a.m.: Hey are u OK?

I had a feeling that was coming. I type up a quick message.

11:30 a.m.: I'm fine. I didn't feel good so I stayed home the last few days.

11:30 a.m.: PS Your Roxas cosplay looks really great.

Hayden responds fast with a trio of barf-face emojis,

and I almost snort tea. At least he didn't ask me what I was sick with.

Then more messages.

11:31 a.m.: Hey so I asked Cyn if I could come watch u skate next week

11:32 a.m.: And she was cool with it but can't take me til Thursday

11:33 a.m.: Will u be back by then?

The jook churns in my stomach, but I remind myself that Hayden coming to watch me skate on Thursday isn't my biggest concern. I have to figure out how to talk to him on Tuesday first.

11:34 a.m.: I'm going back tomorrow. Thursday totally works.

There's just enough of a pause for me to take another sip of tea before Hayden responds.

11:35 a.m.: COOL! I'll tell Cyn

11:35 a.m.: Time to work on my keyblade. BBL!

11:36 a.m.: PS I'm sad I can't say "onward, pants!" anymore cuz they're done

Normally, that'd make me smile. Now I set my phone down and try to think of anything other than telling Hayden I lied to him. I reach for my spoon and force myself to eat the rest of my porridge. It brings back memories of eating jook on cold mornings before heading out to meet Tamar at the rink. For more than half my life, we were there for each other.

On the very first day of skate-school, I chickened out the second Mom left me with my class and headed into the stands. My legs teetered, unsteady on thin blades and rickety rental skates.

It was Tamar who caught my hand and kept me from falling. She cheered loudest when I landed my first axel.

I finish my last spoonful of jook, letting the warmth settle in my stomach. I'm still thinking about Tamar as I carry my empty bowl to the sink.

I know what I have to do.

I settle onto Mom's bed and pull up a list of recent calls. Seeing Tamar's name reminds me of the last thing she said to me. How can I prove I'm not selfish when I'm at home, hiding from all my problems?

I stare at the call button, throat dry. Holding my breath, I tap it.

It rings once, then sends me straight to her voice mail.

The last hint of warmth vanishes, and a trickle of cold settles deep in my bones.

I push up from Mom's bed, feeling defeated, then slip my phone back under my pillow.

Back in the kitchen, I finish my tea, but the cold lingers when I think about returning to the rink on Monday, then seeing Hayden on Tuesday.

I won't be able to hide from my problems for much longer.

Chapter Twenty-Eight

Monday morning, Faith sits in the SUV's back seat again, but she doesn't slide her headphones off. "Sorry, I can't talk today. I have to finish these sound edits."

That's fine by me. My nerves were a soft hum this morning. Tomorrow, my stomach will probably be doing handsprings by the time Hayden arrives for skate-school.

I reach for my phone, but the pocket of my warm-up jacket is empty. I try to remember if I put it in my duffel bag this morning instead, but the closer we get to Oakland, the more I'm convinced I left it at home. It's been hidden under my pillow all weekend. I slouch back against the seat.

Without anything else to do, I steal glances at Faith. She's using the same app I've seen all summer, with several rows of what look like music files. Each has its own zigzaggy line that seems to show the rises and falls of the song. Faith drags and drops a track into the row above it. She merges one over the other, then presses the play button. Her eyes rise to the SUV's ceiling. Then she looks down and makes another adjustment.

She tucks her iPad under one arm when Mrs. Park drops us off.

"How far did you get?" I ask as we make our way into the rink.

"I'm almost done. There's just this one section where I'm trying to blend two tracks that's giving me problems."

Her shoulders don't look tense. She doesn't frown like she does during freestyle practice. She looks like she knows she's doing something hard but it's still worth the effort.

That's how I used to feel about skating.

My recital poster still hangs from the off-ice studio's door, reminding me I've *got* to figure out how to tell Hayden my secret before he gets to the rink tomorrow.

Faith holds the studio door open for me. I slip past her, trying to ignore how much my skin prickles every time I'm near that poster.

We unroll our yoga mats. Around us, other skaters chat about Regionals and famous skaters' coaching changes. Faith pulls out her iPad and makes more tweaks while we wait for the instructor to arrive. A couple of minutes later, she looks up at me, eyes sparkling.

"Got it!"

"Yeah?"

"I'll have to listen to it with my headphones later, but I'm pretty sure."

I wish I had as much control over my free-program music as Faith has over her sound clips. I sit on my mat, knees tucked up to my chest, while she stows her iPad back in her bag.

"Hey, Faith?" She looks over her shoulder at me. "Was it you or Miss Lydia who cut the music for your program?"

"Me." Faith settles into a cross-legged position on her mat. "She sent me a few tracks before her visit. I picked the ones I liked and blended them so they sounded good together. Miss Lydia still had to approve them when she arrived, but yeah."

An idea takes shape. I might be stuck with a program I hate this season, but maybe that could change next year.

"How hard was it to learn how to cut your music?"

"It takes a little time to learn how to use the app. And sometimes tracks don't sound good together no matter how well you blend them. But it's fun once you figure out how everything fits together." As the instructor enters the room, Faith looks at me. "I could show you sometime. If you want."

"That'd be awesome."

"Okay." She seems surprised but happy. "I'll send you info on the app I use. What's your number?"

"I actually forgot my phone at home today. Is it cool if I just add my number to your contacts? Then you can text me so I have yours."

In the moments before stretching class starts, I add myself to her phone before passing it back to her. Then, I spend the next hour and fifteen minutes planning how I'll tell Hayden the truth tomorrow.

There are recital posters everywhere. In the lobby. At concessions. All around the rink, from the vending machines to the plexiglass overlooking the ice. I can't just wait for him to arrive and hope I catch him before he sees one.

But I could invite him to the diner across the street before his class and tell him everything.

Off-ice classes end, and I meet Alex on the ice. He runs me through my usual warm-up, then works on jumps for most of my lesson. I almost think I'm going to slide by without having to skate my program when he waves me toward the music box.

"I'm glad to see you're feeling better. Ready to get back on the horse?"

Nope. But running a program I hate seems like nothing compared to the talk I'm about to have with Hayden. Before a competition, Alex always says to imagine a positive outcome by visualizing myself skating a clean program. I imagine Hayden with me at the diner now, forgiving me after I tell him my secret. I picture us laughing at how silly I look wearing a dress in the recital posters.

It's a small, fluttering hope that I hold on to as I take my opening position.

The music starts. At least after a month of run-throughs, I have the choreography memorized, even if I'll never be a fan of Miss Lydia's arm flourishes.

I'm still imagining positive outcomes with Hayden as I glide into my triple salchow. I turn backward, bend my left knee, then snap it straight. My right leg swings through to help me rotate. Three quick twists in the air, and I return to the ice on a strong edge.

Finally, something done right.

I picture Hayden grinning as I enter my first spin. I whirl perfectly in place. Ankles loose and knees bent deep, my step sequence is controlled and edgy. I fly across the ice, timing my arm movements with the music.

I also sail through both jumps in my triple toe combo. Launch and land, launch and land. *Take that!* Lifting my chin, I feel more defiant than graceful.

One after another, I breeze through my elements. I complete my final blur of a spin, one arm rising as the music fades.

I skated a perfect free program to music for the first time all season. This is everything I've worked for since moving to Oakland.

My chest heaves as I try to catch my breath. As Alex claps from the music box, I feel a surge of warm triumph.

"That was fantastic," Alex calls as I glide over to him. "Everything in its own time, right? Keep this up and you'll be hard to beat at Regionals."

Regionals, the competition I was supposed to be

good enough to skip. My stomach twinges but I ignore it. Imagining a positive outcome with Hayden helped me skate a clean program. That has to be a good sign.

As Alex glides off to his next lesson, I return to my starting position, determined to nail it again. I take a breath and close my eyes, pretending I'm about to skate in front of an audience of royal subjects.

When I open them, aquamarine hair catches my eye.

I blink, eyes fixed on Cyn by the rink entrance.

Then I see Hayden.

My arms drop to my sides, sending a vibration up my shoulders. It travels into my neck before settling in my chest. Instead of dwindling as the seconds tick by, it thrums harder.

Why is he here *today*? He said he was coming to watch me skate on Thursday.

Hayden waves at me, then freezes as his gaze shifts away from the ice, toward the plexiglass where a poster hangs. His hand hovers in the air, then drops. The smile falls from his face.

My body goes hot, then cold.

Hayden turns back toward the exit with Cyn on his heels.

I sprint on my toe picks, hopping off the ice without my blade guards.

"Hayden!"

He pauses at the door but doesn't turn around. Cyn catches up, and they enter the lobby together.

I'm only a few feet behind. It's tricky to run in skates, but I have to catch up to him.

"Please, wait!" Rink workers stare as I burst into the lobby, but my attention is completely on Hayden.

"*What?*" He shoots me a look that's icier than the coldest rink. It roots me in place. Cyn stands behind him, her hand on the door that leads out onto the street. Her eyes dart between me and the nearest recital poster.

"Just—" I stop. Look down at my skates. Without my black boot covers, the white leather seems blinding. "I was planning to tell you...."

"When? You could've said something at Fairyland. Or at my house or even skate-school. You didn't." His words are clipped, sharper than Miss Lydia's at her most irritated. I open my mouth, then close it.

Hayden's eyes flicker from an ad on the concession stand napkin dispenser to a larger poster above the front desk cash register. They return to me, unforgiving. "Was this some sort of game? A prank?"

"No! I—"

"Am I a joke to you, *Ana-Marie*?"

I flinch like I've been hit.

"I can't believe you lied to my whole family." Hayden's face twists into a grimace. He shakes his head, not bothering to brush the hair out of his eyes as he turns to Cyn. "I thought—I want to go home." His voice catches.

Wait!

It's too late. Cyn holds the door open and Hayden heads onto the concrete sidewalk where I can't follow. She glances back at me. For a second, I think she might say something.

The moment's over in one stuttering quick heartbeat. Without a word, Cyn follows Hayden out the door.

Chapter Twenty-Nine

All night, I had dreams about what happened, imagining what I could have done differently. In one, I didn't forget my phone. I saw the texts Hayden sent Monday morning telling me that Cyn was driving him to the rink four days early. Dream-me tore down the posters before he arrived, ripped apart every glossy copy, until I was unrecognizable to anyone. Even myself.

Mom and I walk hand in hand toward her office. I look up at the streetlights, but no rainbow flags wave above me. Pride month is over until next summer. There's nothing left to celebrate.

"We should think about spending some time outside if this weather holds up through the weekend." Mom squeezes my hand. "We could go to Golden Gate Park again, or change things up. The beach could be nice."

"Okay." I feel like a zombie.

"I'll give Mrs. Naftali a call and see if she and Tamar would like to come."

My hand jerks out of Mom's fast. She turns to me, a question in her eyes.

"Sorry." I raise my hand to the back of my neck. "I had an itch."

Another lie. I don't know how to tell Mom that Tamar and I aren't talking.

Each step I take feels heavier as we approach Mom's office. Around us, people rush to work or file into line at coffee kiosks. Cars honk.

I watch and listen in a daze. The only thing that matters is that I ruined everything, first with Tamar, then with Hayden. Aside from Faith, no one my own age is talking to me.

Mom has been trying. I'm the one with the one-word replies. I didn't even tell her about skating a clean free program yesterday.

I should be thrilled about my progress. But all I can see is the look of anger on Hayden's face, and the hurt that followed. I caused both.

I can't imagine how he'll act when he sees me at skate-school tonight. Will he yell again? Let me explain?

Maybe he'll completely ignore me.

"Good morning, Ms. Jin." Samuel smiles by the front door of Mom's building. He turns to me. "Hello, Ana."

Mom glances between the two of us, brows rising.

I can barely manage a halfhearted smile. Mom and Samuel talk while we wait. My duffel digs into my shoulder and a skate blade pokes my hip through its cloth cover. Mom hasn't said my name in over a week, Alex believes I'm over my issues with my free-skate program, and Hayden and Tamar both hate me. Who's next? Faith? Other skaters at the rink? What about the members of my temple?

How long will I have to keep pretending if I never speak up?

The Parks' SUV appears at the street corner and my breakfast churns in my stomach. The sensation rises, tightening into an uncomfortable ball in my chest. It expands as Faith and Mrs. Park stop at a light one block over. By the time the light turns, cracks form. Mrs. Park slows to a stop in front of us, and I split apart more.

There's no way I can act strong all day knowing I'll see Hayden at skate-school tonight.

My vision blurs. I sniffle but the tears don't come.

Something must look off when Samuel glances over. "Ana?"

This time, the word stings. It prickles against my skin. I want it to be Mom who says my name.

"What's wrong?" Mom's forehead creases. She takes a step toward me, then stops.

Where to start? My program, the choreo, and the costume are nightmares. All I know is I'm tired of lying to people I care about.

"I don't want to do this."

The words catch me by surprise, but now that they're out, they make complete sense. My eyes stay fixed on my feet. I can't see Mom or Samuel, but their gazes burn deep.

"What did you say?"

I steal a glance at Mom. Is she mad?

I want to tell her: *I'm not a girl.*

Just four simple words.

They lodge in my throat. In their place, my frantic hope from yesterday returns. My thoughts scatter, then patch themselves haphazardly back together.

The seconds tick past. As the Parks wait for me to hop in, I look up for real.

"I can't go to practice today." I set my jaw the way Mom does when she makes a decision. If I skip skating today, at least I won't run into Hayden for another week.

She studies me, and I suddenly know this is all wishful thinking. There's no way she'll let me skip more days of training. I'm obviously not sick.

To my surprise, Mom walks toward the SUV. Mrs. Park rolls down her window, but their conversation is too quiet to hear. I imagine Faith in her seat staring out at me through the tinted window.

As Mom walks back to the sidewalk, the SUV pulls away.

Unsure what's happening, I look up at Mom, who's stopped in front of me.

"Come."

I follow her through the door Samuel holds open. Mom stays quiet until we enter the empty elevator. When the doors slide shut, I feel her eyes on me again, then her hand rubbing small circles on my back. "I'll call Alex once we get to my office. If something's going on that makes you want to miss practice, it would be good to discuss it with him."

A cold chill travels through me. I'm not scared of Alex, but Mom and him asking me questions together?

I take a deep breath as the elevator opens, then release it in one heavy word that expresses all my feelings of failure.

"Okay."

Chapter Thirty

Half an hour later, Mom requests a rideshare from her office to the San Francisco rink where Alex is currently coaching.

The whole way to the rink, I try to come up with a good reason for wanting to skip practice, but my mind stays as blank as the ice after a Zamboni resurface.

Alex is on the ice with two other coaches when we arrive. A group of girls stands in front of him in matching pants and jackets. I stop fast, eyes darting from synchro skater to synchro skater until I see Tamar. She's between two girls with hair in identical blond buns.

Mom beckons to me. I walk toward her, eyes never leaving Tamar as she lifts her arms and connects with the girl on either side of her. Alex calls out, "Five-six-seven-eight," and they're off on the next count of one. Their back crossovers carve identical marks into the ice.

Mom and I walk to the stands, finding seats half-way up. As Alex makes his way off the ice, Tamar's line stops on the opposite side of the rink. Her eyes follow Alex from the exit to the steps to the stands.

She sees me.

Our entire fight comes back all at once.

I clasp my hands tight. She looks away just as Alex reaches us.

"Hi, you two."

Mom greets him quietly. "Thanks for meeting with us. We're sorry to bother you."

"It's no problem at all. The team won't miss me for a few minutes. In fact, they'll probably be glad to move on from line drills."

He offers a small smile, which neither of us returns.

"Your mom said you were upset this morning, and you don't want to go to practice today?"

Below us, Tamar hooks arms with her partner, then skates toward another pair of girls, releasing her hold as they intersect. That move has improved since the video she showed me at the beginning of summer.

I've never been on a synchro team because of the high monthly fees. But Tamar and I always felt like a pair. We practiced together. Celebrated competition wins. Hung out, listening to music or watching movies on her iPad.

Things changed a lot this summer, and not just for me. Tamar got a new coach, she failed her Intermediate Moves test, and her parents have been fighting. And I've been too stuck in my head to remember to be a good friend and listen.

"Ana?" Alex's voice is soft.

Tension makes my chest clench. I don't want to skip practice for weeks on end, not even to avoid Hayden. I just want to love skating again, like I used to before things got complicated.

"I can't do my free program anymore," I blurt out. "It makes me feel awful."

Mom and Alex exchange bewildered looks. They wait for me to continue, but I press my lips together.

"Why?" Mom finally asks. The word sounds high and sharp. It reminds me of Miss Lydia.

Alex leans in closer. "No one's mad about how you skated at the competition, if that's what you're worried about."

That's not even *close* to what's wrong.

I shake my head, but Alex doesn't seem to notice. I squeeze my hands together in my lap so tightly the tips of my fingers turn red and my knuckles go white.

"You've been doing so well getting used to more challenging choreography, a longer program, harder jumps...."

My head starts to pound. I can recite the definition of nonbinary by heart, but saying it out loud makes it real. What if this feeling changes after I've come out to everyone?

"Plus, a new training environment with a whole group of different skaters—"

Mom nods along with his words.

No, no, no! My breaths become shallow.

"I'm not a girl." The words tumble out and the tension releases its grip, letting me breathe again.

Alex goes quiet. Beside him, Mom just looks confused. I've thrown them both for a loop.

"What do you mean?" Mom asks slowly.

"I'm not a girl," I say again. The words come easier this time. "I'm nonbinary."

Alex's brows rise, but Mom's expression doesn't change. "I'm not sure I understand," she says.

I take a long, deep breath. "Some people feel like girls and others feel like boys. Usually, I don't feel like either. I was going to say something weeks ago. To both of you." I glance at Alex before turning back to Mom. "But I wanted to qualify for Sectionals first."

"What? Why?" Her gaze moves past me. Out of the corner of my eye, I see Alex shake his head. He looks just as confused as Mom.

"Because I wanted to change my free-skate program, and I thought we'd have more time if I got to skip Regionals. Plus, it'd save you money." My voice gets quieter. "And I hoped you'd be so happy about saving money on Regionals you maybe wouldn't be mad about me asking for a new program. Or being nonbinary."

Mom sucks in a shaky breath. "But how can you be something other than a boy or a girl? What else is there?"

I can't tell if she's asking me or Alex, but I bite my lip. Didn't I already answer that?

"I was there when you were born. I know what you are." I flinch and her gaze lands on me. Her voice drops low. "Or I thought I did."

Alex looks at me. "Does this have something to do with your internal identity?"

I nod, but my eyes stay on Mom. "It's not about how my body looks," I tell her. "It's how I feel and what people think I am when they see me. That's why I cut my hair shorter and wear the clothes I do. I don't want them to think *girl*." I scrunch up my lips, thoughts on Hayden. "But I don't want people to think *boy*, either. It's tricky."

"Because you're something in between?" Mom seems to pick her words carefully.

"Yeah. Or neither. I'm not sure yet. I just know how I feel. Not a boy, and not a girl."

Mom blinks. A look passes across her face, like she's seeing me as who I really am for the first time.

"Come here." Her voice catches. She pulls me to her before I can move.

I hug her back.

"I know you and Alex told me not to focus on qualifying for Sectionals, but it's all I could think about." Mom's shirt muffles my words a little. "I should've said something earlier."

"And I should've asked," Mom murmurs into my hair. Her voice still sounds shaky. "I should've known something was off, that you weren't just upset about those competition results."

"You can't always know these things." Alex keeps his voice low and soothing as Mom and I pull apart. "My mother and I were particularly close, but I never said a word to her until I came out to my whole family during college."

He looks directly at me. "I'm sorry if you felt put on the spot here. I think I speak for both of us when I say that wasn't our intention."

"It absolutely wasn't," Mom agrees.

"It's okay. I know you were just worried."

"It's definitely not like you to ask to skip practice." Alex smiles a little, then glances at Mom. "Remember when she had that stomachache before her Juvenile Moves test, but she insisted on skating anyway?"

A moment later, a spark of something that might be understanding flickers in his eyes. "I just realized we haven't asked what the right pronouns are for you."

The corners of Mom's mouth quiver.

"I don't know yet," I say quickly.

"That's completely fair. And it's good that we know

what's going on now." Alex turns to Mom. "Would you mind if I speak to Ana alone for a moment?"

She glances at him, then me. "I'll be downstairs."

I wait until she's out of sight, crossing my arms tight over my chest as I look up at Alex. "Do you think she's mad?"

"It doesn't seem that way to me. Maybe surprised. Possibly upset."

My whole body trembles. I hug myself tighter.

"But hey." Alex reaches out. He squeezes my arm, just like he did at Nationals. "That's not on you. Sometimes the people we love form ideas about who we are that don't fit with the reality they've just discovered."

My arms loosen. "A preconception?"

"Yes, exactly. It took me a long time to realize that my family's negative reaction wasn't my fault. I left my whole life back in Iowa to tour with that European ice show before moving to San Francisco."

"But then you met Myles?"

"Then I met Myles. That was a couple of years after I moved here, and several after I stopped talking to my family. It was Myles who convinced me to reach out to them. It took time, but things are a lot better now."

I knew Alex grew up in Iowa. I've seen the video of him performing in Europe. But I had no idea he'd struggled with who he was, too. My arms uncross, hands lowering to rest on either side of the bench.

Below us, one of the coaches glides to the music box. A song from the *La La Land* soundtrack plays over the speakers. My eyes drift back to the group of skaters, but Alex leans in before I can find Tamar.

"Your mom might be confused right now, even upset. But it's clear that she cares about you and wants you to be happy. Help her see what happy means for you."

I think about this as he stands, offering me a hand. "I should get back to the team. Under the circumstances, I'm going to text your mom that it makes sense for you to take the rest of the week off from skating. We'll figure out a game plan for your free program next week."

"Okay."

Alex heads back onto the ice, and I meet Mom downstairs. She looks small, her shoulders rounding just like mine when I get tense.

"Alex wants me to take the rest of the week off." I look up at her. "He said he'll text you later."

Mom looks at me, toward the exit, then back again. She nods without a word. My heart twinges, but I remember what Alex told me she might be feeling. I slip my hand into hers, and we make our way to the door together.

I take one final look at the ice before we exit. Tamar looks back and our eyes meet again. Her head tilts like she's unsure of something.

I hold the door open for Mom, then step outside with her. Tamar and Hayden will have to wait. First, I need to make sure everything's okay between Mom and me.

Chapter Thirty-One

The bus stop is empty except for us. It's still too early for the afternoon rush.

Mom and I stand next to each other. Our eyes play a game, meeting only to dance away.

It feels like an eternity before a bus rolls up. Mom holds her hair away from her face between curled fingers. I try to copy her, but my hair's too short and my hand hovers awkwardly.

We sit quietly for the four blocks to Market Street. As passengers exit and board at a stop, Mom's hand settles on my knee.

"I love you."

The words flood my chest with unexpected warmth.

I'm not sure what made Mom say this, but I place my hand over hers. "I love you, too."

"I still don't understand—" Mom stops mid-sentence when I squeeze her hand gently. She breathes in through her nose and lets out a long breath from her mouth.

The same way I do before a skating event to ground myself.

"I don't understand what you're going through, but I love you. I don't want you to feel miserable or hate skating."

"I don't hate skating." Mom waits as I search for the right words. "My free program just isn't right for me. The costume isn't, either."

"This is all very new for me, but I want to understand." She turns her hand over, fingers twining through mine.

The bus moves on. It climbs a small hill just past downtown, then Mom and I get off.

Once we're back on the sidewalk, Mom turns to me. "If you don't like your program, we'll find something different. Same for your costume."

"Mom, that's not..." I pause. "It'll cost a ton."

"Yes," Mom says as we turn a corner. "It will be expensive to start over. But there are things that are more important."

She looks at me until it sinks in. Deep down, I think I always knew things like my happiness and health are more important than saving Mom money. The extra training costs were just easier to worry about.

We pass old brick buildings and familiar side streets, unlock the heavy metal gate into our building, and take the stairs up to our apartment.

My thoughts keep returning to the conversation with Mom and Alex. To what Mom said on the way home after. I come to a stop near our kitchen table and turn back to her.

"Hey, Mom? You always say to focus on training and not worry about money. But just because we don't talk about the cost doesn't mean I don't think about it."

She blinks fast, like she's trying to hold back tears. "I thought it was best to let you enjoy skating and be a kid."

"It was a good idea, when I was younger. I could just have fun on the ice." I pull some tissues out of my duffel and hand them to her. "But I'm twelve now. I'm old enough to work as a skate-school assistant, so maybe it's time for me to help choose what I'll be skating to for a whole season, too."

"This all feels like it happened so fast." Mom dabs

her eyes. "One day you were tottering around in rental skates, the next you're landing double axels and winning Nationals. No one tells you what to do when your daughter"—she swallows hard at the end of the word—"when your *child* has this kind of talent.

"Then Alex decided to move to Oakland and told me about that famous choreographer. It came right after I got my bonus at work, and I thought, here's my chance to finally give you everything skaters with two parents already have."

I open my mouth, then close it. I don't understand how I can feel happy and sad all at once.

"I wish I'd known how you were feeling earlier." Mom looks at me. "You can always talk to me if there's something you're unhappy about. Anything at all. You know that now, right?"

"Yes." I smile a little.

Mom lets out a sigh as she glances at her watch. "I'm afraid I have to go back to work." The corners of her mouth turn down. My expression matches hers.

Right now, I know what *happy* means to me more than anything. I take Alex's advice and tell her. "I wish you could stay."

"I wish I could, too, but I didn't even leave with my laptop this morning. They're expecting me back." She looks so defeated.

I hide my disappointment by looking toward the window. I had a feeling she'd say that.

"But I have an idea," Mom continues. "Let's spend Friday together, just the two of us. We can have a longer conversation, without work interrupting. I'll put in the time-off request when I get back to the office. What do you think?"

It looks like Mom's holding her breath, like she's not sure I'll want to spend a whole day with her.

I don't take long. Reaching out, I wrap my arms around her waist. She hugs me back.

There's no need for words. Mom knows my answer.

After Mom leaves, my thoughts turn to Tamar and Hayden. Those are two friendships I still need to fix, if it's even possible.

I have to start somewhere, though. I climb the ladder to my bed, determined to come up with a plan. It's time to take matters into my own hands instead of sitting around waiting for people to text me back.

Chapter Thirty-Two

The next day is cold and foggy: typical for San Francisco in August. Zipping my coat up under my chin, I brace myself for the walk ahead.

I know what I need to do, but I'm still not sure how. I run through ideas as I walk. By the time I ring Tamar's doorbell, I still haven't totally figured it out.

The familiar yappy sounds of Pix and Ponch precede a patter of canine feet. When the door cracks open, Eli looks down at me.

"Hey." He shoos the dogs away. "Haven't seen you in a while."

I try not to flinch. It's probably just small talk, but Eli's comment still feels like an accusation.

"I've been busy with skating," I explain. "Is Tamar home?"

I should've let her know I was coming, but I deleted every text I tried to write to her this morning. There's too much to say to send over the phone. It kept turning into a novel.

Eli nods. "She's in her room."

He saunters off. I stare at my feet for a second, slide my shoes off, then head for the stairs.

I take them two at a time. Even after being gone most of the summer, I remember which creaky steps to avoid.

I pause in front of her door. What I do next will determine whether Tamar and I stay friends. My eyes drift up to the crown molding that snakes across the hallway ceiling.

Or *she* might decide she never wants to talk to me again.

No more stalling. I force my eyes away from the ceiling, then knock.

"Yeah?"

I crack the door a sliver, then push it open a little more. Tamar's in bed on her stomach. Her eyes are fixed on her phone, legs crossed at the ankles.

"Hi," I say, but don't enter. My eyes travel her bedroom, coming to a stop on a new movie poster for *A*

League of Their Own. I don't even know when she got it.

Tamar goes still when she sees me. She glances at her phone again. "Did I miss a text about you coming over?"

"No." Normally, I'd plop down in her purple armchair. I can't imagine doing that now when I feel like an intruder. "I was in the neighborhood and wanted to say hi."

Tamar raises an eyebrow. "Unless you're a lost tourist, no one's ever just 'in the neighborhood.'"

It's true. The hills keep most people away. I've barely started talking and already made a mistake.

"You looked good with your synchro team yesterday," I try again. My voice quivers.

Tamar's expression doesn't change, but she sits up. She slides her legs off the edge of her bed. "What were you doing there, anyway?"

Posture stiff, her eyes narrow.

"I...um." My gaze moves away, toward her closet, her desk, the window. I stop at the bulletin board covered in synchro photos. There's a picture I never noticed before, nestled between two others.

My hair was longer then, held back with an elastic

band. Tamar stood beside me, in front of Alex. We were both so short, he had to crouch to stay in the frame.

"I told Mom I wanted to skip skating practice, for the second week in a row. That's why we were at the rink yesterday." My words sound like they're being said by someone else. And I can't take my eyes off that photo.

"Why would you do that?"

"Because Mom wanted to discuss it with Alex."

"That's not what I was—" She stops, but I stay quiet. I remember watching the Winter Olympics together and the determined look on Tamar's face when she told her parents she wanted to learn to skate. If she hadn't insisted I go with her, I might not be a skater at all now. No national title. No pic of us grinning with Alex. When I started improving faster than her, Tamar never even got jealous. She was as excited about each new jump as I was.

That final thought buries itself deep in my chest. It pulses like a second heartbeat.

Selfish.

My eyes fill with tears.

"Sorry," I whisper. Tamar doesn't say anything. I drag my eyes away from the photo, but my vision's too blurred to see her. I blink once. Twice. Tears trickle down my cheeks. "About being flaky all summer, and never giving you notes on your Moves videos. I'm so, *so* sorry about that. And about everything else."

When Tamar stays quiet, I keep going. "I've been so busy training in Oakland and hating my program that I didn't even notice how much I was ignoring you until you told me. I thought texting you and hanging out once in a while would be enough, but I was still distracted and focused on myself."

"Just a little, yeah." Tamar gives me a stiff nod.

"No, a lot. Almost every time you tried to talk to me, I blew you off." I take a deep, shuddering breath. "You didn't deserve that, no matter how much I had going on."

"Come here." Tamar pats her mattress.

I take a small step toward her, then another, until I'm close enough to sit at the edge of her bed. Her arms wrap around my shoulders. She pulls me closer.

"Why are you skipping so much practice?"

I sniffle, remembering the first day I missed freestyle. It was right after our last phone call, but that wasn't Tamar's fault. "I've just been really confused lately."

"About…" Tamar leans back to look at me. "…your free program?"

"Yes. Kind of?"

Tamar waits for me to continue, but I can't. "I know you said you didn't like it, right?"

I wipe my eyes, then nod.

"So, what's up? Is the choreography too hard, or what?"

I rub at tear streaks with the back of my hand but shake my head. "No, it's bigger than that. I…told Mom I don't think I'm a girl."

Tamar's eyes go wide.

"And Alex," I add.

"But, what do you mean by that? Do you want to be a boy? Or…?"

"No." I shake my head. "I think I'm somewhere in between a boy and a girl. Or neither, maybe?"

"So *that's* why you didn't want to skate to *Sleeping Beauty* music. One sec." Tamar swipes a tissue box from her desk and hands it over. "And this is what's been bothering you all summer?"

Dabbing the corners of my eyes with a tissue, I nod again. She fiddles with a curly strand of hair.

"Why didn't you tell me?"

"I didn't tell anyone, but..." I hesitate. "Remember the day you showed me your team's intersection video?"

Tamar looks at me blankly.

"We were eating cupcakes, and you said it'd be weird for someone to throw a party to let people know they're a boy or a girl." I look down.

"Oh, Ana." Her voice drops to a whisper.

"Plus, I was so excited about getting to train in Oakland, and I didn't want to seem ungrateful. I actually told *you* I didn't like my program before I told Mom or Alex."

"You didn't tell me why, though," Tamar points out. "Because you thought I'd think you're weird?"

I shrug but don't look up.

"I don't think that. Promise. But just so I understand, you didn't like your program because you don't feel like a girl—or aren't one?"

"Or a boy. Right."

Tamar still looks confused.

I ball up the tissue in my hand, then grab a second. "You know those Venn diagrams? The ones where the two circles intersect at the center?"

"Yeah, kind of."

"It's like that. One circle is for boys, the other's for girls. I'm the part that overlaps. Or maybe I'm outside both circles."

Her brows rise a little.

"And I did try to tell you last week, but you were upset. Probably about your Moves test." I look down into my lap. "Why didn't you tell me you failed it? I found out from Alex."

"Because it felt like you were keeping secrets. I knew you didn't like your free program, but it felt like there was something else you weren't telling me."

I swallow hard, knowing I danced around my real problem all summer, with Tamar and everyone.

"So, I guess I wanted to keep something from you, too, like failing my Moves." Tamar shrugs. "I didn't mean to fight with you like that. I was mad and you were only a small part of it. But it just built up and up. On the day you called, I couldn't hold it in anymore."

I scoot a little closer. "Why were you mad? Because of your test?"

Tamar sighs in a way I would've called dramatic in the past. Now it makes her seem tired and vulnerable.

"This summer's just sucked since you switched

rinks. Completely. Most of my friends are gone until fall, the synchro coaches have been tough on us because they want to move the team up a level—so I *really* need to stop freaking out in front of the judges and failing my Moves—and we didn't even go on vacation like usual."

Tamar's family usually visits someplace cool each summer. "You're not going anywhere before school starts?"

"Dad's been too busy with work, and Mom's never home, either. Then they fight about dumb stuff whenever they're together. Walking the dogs. Who has to take me to practice." Tamar acts like it's no big deal, but her tense shoulders rise to her ears. "It's fine. I wouldn't want to spend two weeks in a hotel somewhere listening to them argue all the time, anyway."

I brush my shoulder against hers. "What does Eli think?"

Another shrug. "He says they'll get over themselves eventually and pretends he doesn't care at all. Typical." She hugs her knees to her chest. "I guess I've just been feeling kind of lonely lately. Kell's a cool coach, but practice isn't the same without you."

"I want to be there for you," I tell her, "to hang out and

help you with your Moves, for sure, but also so you've got someone to talk to when your parents fight." Tamar still looks doubtful, and I know why. Even when we do hang out, I've been off in my own world lately. "It's been hard to juggle training in Oakland and doing stuff together with you, too, so I thought of something that might work."

I pull out my phone and show her the new calendar I set up before leaving home. "If you download the same app, we can share our schedules so we'll know when we're both free. You can even make edits to my calendar if there's a specific day you want to meet."

"You are such a dork sometimes," Tamar says with a small smile, but she pulls out her phone. A few seconds later, the calendar app appears on her screen, fully downloaded. "But now I can call you out when your new friends are taking up too much of your time. I'll send you screenshot evidence."

I know she's joking, but I can't help focusing on one part of her sentence. "My new friends?" I shake my head. "Who are you even talking about?"

"You know." She flops onto her back. "Faith Park, all the other Oakland skaters, and your millions of adoring fans, of course."

I snort.

"Plus, that boy you keep ghosting me for. Him, too."

"Um?" I look back at Tamar over my shoulder.

"Blond hair. Tallish. Purple eyes for all I know since you never reported back to me."

"So..." I groan. "About that."

I drop down beside her. We lie next to each other without saying anything for a moment, eyes on her light fixture.

"Okay, first: I barely have any friends in Oakland. Faith seems cool, but we're both busy with our own things and still getting to know each other. Second: I *definitely* don't have fans, unless you count an adoring nine-year-old. Third: Hayden and I were friends, but I'm not sure we are anymore."

Tamar waits for me to continue.

"Remember how I told you I mixed up my name tag and Alex's when I helped with Hayden's class?"

"Sure. But that was, like, over a month ago."

A lump forms in my throat. I try to swallow it down, but it stubbornly stays put.

"He thought you were a boy." Tamar props herself up on an elbow. "You didn't correct him, did you?"

Squeezing my eyes shut, I shake my head and remember the look on Hayden's face when he discovered I'd lied to him.

"Why don't you tell him now?"

"It's too late. The skate-school has a recital coming up and I agreed to perform in it. The school director put up posters showing me at my last competition in my free-program costume. I didn't get to talk to Hayden before he saw them."

Tamar mutters a word that'd get me grounded for a month.

"Right?" I sigh and rub my knuckles into my eyes. "She used this huge text for my name. And it says I'm the Juvenile *girls* champion, which I know I am. But Hayden was *so* mad when he saw it, and I don't blame him. I lied to him and his whole family."

"Yeah, I'd be hecka mad, too. What a hot mess." Tamar rolls over and swipes a small packet from her bedside table. "Gum?"

I shake my head. Tamar unwraps a square and pops it into her mouth. "Anyway, I still think you should talk to him."

"I would! But he won't text me back."

"So? Text him again. Don't harass him or anything, but let him know you want to talk. People mess up. If he doesn't get that, maybe he's not as awesome as I am."

She's trying to cheer me up, but this feels like it'll take a lot more than a simple text to fix. "I will. I'm not sure how much it'll help, though."

"That's all you can do. It's up to him to decide if he wants to forgive you."

"Okay." I make up my mind. "I'll text him again."

"Good." Tamar blows a big pink bubble, then looks over at me with a serious expression. "Do you want me to use 'she' when I talk about you to other people, or something else?"

Is it weird to be thrilled when I don't even know the answer to her question? It makes me want to grab her hands and twirl in a big circle.

" 'She' is fine, for now. I still have a ton of stuff to figure out. Like, is there a way for me to have a nonbinary mitzvah ceremony? I don't even know."

Tamar sits up straighter. "That *is* a really good question."

"Yeah. I'll probably have to find someone to talk to at temple."

"Let me know if I can help. Or if you want me to make a Venn diagram for anyone. I'll do it, no problem."

That's the Tamar I know and love.

"I'll for sure ask."

I push myself up from the bed. "I should get home before Mom's off work." I meet Tamar's eyes. "But if you do need to talk, about Moves or your parents or anything, I'm here. I mean it."

Tamar nods. Her bubble pops. "Got it."

"See you soon?"

"You'd better." Tamar types something into her phone, then waves it at me. "I've already picked a date on our calendar."

My phone pings with the new entry as I head for the door. "Got it!"

"Hey, Ana?"

I stop, looking back at her. "Yeah?"

"Aren't you forgetting something?"

"What?"

"Our goodbye hug." Tamar stands and heads to me, rolling her eyes. "Duh."

I've never wrapped my arms around her faster.

Chapter Thirty-Three

I wake up before Mom on Friday. Even though we agreed not to set an alarm, the sun shines through our window. It teams up with my internal clock, coaxing my eyes open on my normal weekday schedule.

Mom's soft, measured breaths tell me she's still asleep. Now would be a good time to follow Tamar's advice and text Hayden. I reach for my phone—

—and totally chicken out.

Not ready yet. Nope.

There are plenty of other messages to respond to. Tamar's texts flood my front screen, full of emojis. I skim through them and reply back.

Faith also texted me a couple of days ago, asking if I was okay after Mom told Mrs. Park to leave for the rink without me. I didn't know what to say then. Explaining myself feels simpler now, even if I'm not ready to share all the details.

6:27 a.m.: Hi! Yeah, I'm fine.

6:27 a.m.: Just got stressed about my program.

Her replies arrive fast.

6:29 a.m.: If you ever want to talk, I'll listen.

6:29 a.m.: (I promise not to tell people at the rink.)

Mom would totally approve of her properly punctuated sentences.

6:30 a.m.: Thanks. I hated my free program and finally told my mom, that's all.

6:30 a.m.: Now I have to figure out what to do with my new costume because I don't like skating in dresses!

Her next texts pop up right after mine.

6:31 a.m.: And I'd rather choreograph & cut music than skate to it. What a combo. 😆

6:31 a.m.: I might have an idea about your costume, but I have to get dressed. Text you later!

That brings me back to having to figure out what to say to Hayden. It's been days since we've talked or texted. For the last two months, we've sent each other a steady stream of texts, most silly, a couple serious. Now I can't find the right words. It's like I'm at center ice, waiting for the music to start without having a clue what my first steps are.

I type out a long message, then copy and send each line individually.

6:36 a.m.: I'm really (really, really) sorry I didn't tell you my real name.

6:36 a.m.: Or warn you about the posters.

6:37 a.m.: Do you know what nonbinary means?

6:37 a.m.: Actually, can we talk before your class next week? I'll explain everything.

I hit send as fast as possible. Hayden probably isn't awake, unless Mattie got him up early again. I shut off my phone anyway. I'm finally trying to make things right, but that doesn't mean I want to read an angry response if Hayden decides to tell me off.

Carefully, I climb down the ladder. Mom shifts as I step onto a creaky rung but doesn't open her eyes. The lines on her forehead are smooth.

Today is supposed to be about us, but I want this morning to be all about Mom. She works so hard to pay for everything. She makes sure I keep up with my homework and prepares meals for me, even when she's exhausted. Now I want to do something for her.

Opening a cabinet, I scan each shelf. Special

occasions call for special meals. My thoughts move immediately to pancakes.

I don't want to make just any pancakes. I love the fluffy, syrupy kind, but Mom's favorite comes from a traditional recipe Grandma Goldie taught her when she was my age.

I stack ingredients into my arms. Soy, salt, oil, and flour all get placed gently on the counter.

Chopsticks and a mixing bowl come next before I stop dead in front of the refrigerator. We usually go grocery shopping on the weekend. I open the door and scan the shelves, but it's just as I suspected. No chives or eggs.

I stare at the items on the counter. They're useless without the main ingredients.

I sulk to the bathroom and wash my hands, still trying to think up a solution. The mattress squeaks as Mom sits up in her bed. I scurry back out.

She rubs her eyes, then looks from the kitchen counter to me. "What is all this?"

"I was going to make breakfast so you could sleep in. Chive pancakes." I purse my lips. "But I didn't have all the ingredients I needed."

Realization washes across her face. Mom heads to the window. Sun streams into the room as she draws back the curtain.

"How would you feel about a trip to the beach instead? We can get food on the way to take with us, then stop at the grocery store when we head back."

It takes me a second to remember the last time we went to the beach. We bought samosas from a food truck with Tamar and her family, watching bursts of glittering fireworks as we perched on a concrete ledge that separated the sidewalk from the sand.

That was over a year ago. There hasn't been time to go back between my training and Mom's work, even though she loves the beach. It reminds her of Hawaii.

I look up at Mom and nod. "Okay."

She gestures toward the counter. "Let's put this away together and get dressed. We'll make the most of this nice weather while we have it."

The underground train takes us from our home to a forested, foggy neighborhood behind Mount Sutro. We board a bus at street level that rolls through more neighborhoods on the western side of San Francisco.

A few blocks from the beach, Mom nods to me and I pull the stop cord above my head.

We stop at a deli, then a bakery. At both shops, I pull out my hongbao, refusing to let Mom pay. Surprise passes across her face as I order us sandwiches from the deli, handing over Grandma Goldie's Chinese New Year money. By the time I order some bao at the bakery, she's smiling.

The sun rises like a hazy disk through the fog in this part of town. Only swimmers willing to brave the icy Pacific Ocean venture past the shoreline and into the water. This may remind Mom of Hawaii, but it's definitely not as warm.

I shiver and zip my coat up to my neck. At first, Mom and I eat our sandwiches in silence. A whoosh of salty wind tickles my face as seagulls screech overhead, searching for crumbs.

"How was your time off from practice?"

"Good." I set what's left of my sandwich on my lap. "I helped Mrs. Lee with some chores after I got back from Tamar's house." That gets me an approving nod. "And I'm still thinking about what to do with my free program. But I was wondering..." I hesitate as Mom looks at me. "I mean, I noticed that you haven't been calling me by my name lately."

I hold my breath, waiting for Mom's response.

She sighs. A soft release of breath. "I wasn't sure if you wanted me to call you that anymore."

My chest gets hot. The heat creeps up my neck toward my face. "Because of what I said at the competition?"

Mom nods. "And because of my phone conversation with Mrs. Lubeck. She called you A instead of Ana-Marie."

I look down. I never used to keep secrets. Not from anyone, but especially Mom. I have nothing left to hide, but guilt still twists tight, knowing she learned about my identity from someone else.

"I should've told you before you called." I stare at the half-eaten sandwich in my lap.

"Perhaps," Mom says. "Or I should've asked. Mrs. Lubeck only confirmed something I'd noticed much earlier." This makes me look up. "You've always been a bit different from other children. Talented, of course, but there was something else. I couldn't put my finger on what it was, though. I wasn't sure how to bring it up with you—your grandmother and I didn't have the kind of relationship where we could talk about these things."

"You didn't?"

"No." Mom shakes her head. "We didn't see eye to eye often, and it only got worse when your father and I moved to San Francisco right after high school. The distance made it easier to hide things from each other. It was years before I told her I'd converted to Judaism. I even put off telling her it hadn't worked out between your father and me until he'd already returned to Hawaii. I didn't want to upset her, so it was simpler to avoid certain subjects."

That last part sounds familiar. Tiptoeing around topics is something I got good at this summer. It's the only time I'm dainty.

Mom looks me straight in the eye. "I don't want that to be the same for us, but change can be scary. Even for adults. When you didn't mention anything to me, I convinced myself I was imagining things."

"I guess we both could've done stuff differently."

"Yes."

"I miss talking to you, like we used to after skating and school." This isn't something I'd planned to tell her, but I'm tired of keeping secrets. Even small ones.

"I know you have lots of work to do, but it feels like we barely talk anymore."

"That wasn't my intention. Not at all." Her voice catches, eyes shining like the sun's reflections on waves.

I move my sandwich to a napkin and shift to my knees, wrapping my arms around Mom's shoulders before she can say anything else. "I know."

"I miss our chats, too." Mom's voice sounds muffled against my neck.

"Do you think maybe we can switch our schedule?" I ask. "Cook first on weeknights when you get home, then extra work projects after I go to bed? I'll help with the dishes."

She nods against me, hair swishing.

Mom wipes her eyes with one hand as I sit back and grab my phone. "Want me to add it to our calendar?"

"I think that's a wonderful idea." Her smile reaches all the way to her eyes. "Now, if it's all right, I have a question for you."

"Sure."

Mom looks out toward the ocean for a second, and I reach down to take another bite of my sandwich.

"Is there anything you'd like to know about your father?"

"Um." I frown and look down at my charm necklace, then back up at Mom. "I don't know?"

"You seemed interested recently, during the competition last month. I don't know much about his life anymore, but your grandma Goldie might since she sees him around town from time to time."

I take the final bite of my sandwich and wonder what knowing more about my dad will accomplish. I'd like him to tell me why he left, why he doesn't write or video-chat with us, even on holidays. I'd like to know if he'd accept me for who I am, even if I'm not the daughter he thought he had.

I guess there are things I want to know after all.

Eventually.

"I think I want to talk to him, to see what he's like. Someday. Is it okay to wait until after I've figured out my program stuff?"

"Of course." Mom reaches for her sandwich, tearing off a piece of baguette bread. "If you decide you want to get to know your father, I'll reach out to him.

I want you to feel comfortable coming to me in the future, no matter what."

More talking, fewer secrets. I like that.

We finish the sandwiches, then grab our stuff. This feels like a perfect end to our day, but I still haven't told her about the decision I've made.

"Mom?" I squint up at her, one hand over my eyes to block the sun. "I haven't figured out if I want to try different pronouns yet, so you can keep using 'she' for now. And it's okay to call me by my name. But just use Ana, please."

For me, this is just like getting a new skating program. I learn the choreography, then practice it in segments, only putting it all together once every step feels right. I learned what nonbinary means, so asking to be called just Ana is my first segment. Pronouns will come later.

"Okay." Mom nods as I hand over her purse. "I'll do my best to honor that."

The knot in my stomach loosens, evaporating like fog in the summer sun. My phone vibrates, and the knot threatens to return. As we wait for the streetlight to turn green, I take a quick peek at my phone.

It's not Hayden.

I read Faith's message and have to fight the urge to dance in the street.

"What is it, Ana?"

The light turns. "This isn't for sure yet," I tell Mom as we cross the street. "But I think I've figured out what to do about my free-skate costume."

Chapter Thirty-Four

By Monday morning, I know what I have to do with my program, except I'll need help. I wave to Mom and Samuel and head toward the Parks' SUV, stomach fluttering.

"Welcome back." Faith watches me buckle in.

"Thanks!" For the first time in weeks, I can't wait to get to the rink. As Mrs. Park pulls away from the curb, I finally notice that Faith's lap is empty for the first time this summer. The fluttering stops. Maybe I should've texted her before assuming she'd have her iPad. "No music edits today?"

"Nope. I finished last week."

My heart sinks.

"Is something wrong?"

"No. I mean, not really. I was just hoping you could help me cut music at lunch today." I shake my head. "But no big deal if you don't have your iPad. I should've texted to let you know what I was thinking. You might not even be free for lunch, and that's fine, too. I'm just being—"

"Ana." Faith looks amused now. "I brought my iPad with me. It's in my bag."

"Oh."

"And yeah, I'm free for lunch. I can teach you."

It's impossible to hold back my grin. This day just got a frajillion times better.

"Do you have anything you want to edit?" Faith asks. "It's okay if you don't. I have sample clips."

I pull out my phone. Still no text from Hayden, but that's not what I'm looking for right now. "I'll text them to you."

As Mrs. Park rolls to a stop in front of the rink, I send Faith two music files. The grin doesn't leave my face all through stretch class and off-ice dance. After I persuade Alex to focus on jump technique for our morning lesson, promising to run my programs in the afternoon, I'm convinced my smile might be permanent. He hooks me up to the pole harness, and I rotate flip after triple flip with hardly any assistance.

After freestyle, Faith and I unlace our skates on the bench next to each other.

"Is it okay if I go grab some ramen?" she asks. "I didn't bring lunch today."

I stand up, swinging my duffel over one shoulder. "Only if I can come with."

We exit the building side by side. She orders at the ramen restaurant, and we sit in a row of chairs by the front window while we wait.

I turn to her. "Has your mom decided anything about my costume?"

"Oh yeah! She said she'd call your mom this week." Faith crosses her fingers and I copy her with both hands.

Once her food is ready, we head back down the block. We make a beeline for the hockey rink, climbing the stairs into the stands. Faith pulls out her iPad, then opens the lid on her ramen container. Steam rises between us in a slow spiral.

"What do you want to do with these two clips?" Faith asks as she transfers them from phone to iPad. "Just paste one after the other with some blending?"

"Kind of." Faith and I haven't talked much about how uncomfortable my free program makes me, just my costume. "Have you ever seen *Sleeping Beauty*, the Disney movie?"

"Maybe a long time ago." She looks at me closely. "Is one of these clips your program music?"

I nod.

"Not a fan?"

"Good guess." I laugh. "I thought about picking something else, but Hope was kind of right about Miss Lydia's choreography. It's hard, but the judges seem to like it."

The steps are starting to grow on me, too. It's just the program's theme that needs some tweaking. I explain my idea to Faith, giving her as much detail as possible. "Do you think that'd work?"

She's already tapping on her music app, uploading the files. "Won't know unless we try it, but it's a cool idea."

For the rest of lunch, she cuts and blends, explaining what she's doing as she works. She puts on her headphones, listens, then does it again. Occasionally, I remind her to eat some ramen.

Finally, she sits back and passes me her headphones.

For three minutes, I listen, eyes closed. When the last note fades out, I slowly open them. Faith keeps her eyes on me. "What do you think?"

"It's totally perfect."

She beams.

"I also think we should come up with a new team name."

Faith tilts her head. "Oh, you mean for Hope, you, and me?"

I nod. "Team SF doesn't really work. We all live in San Francisco, but Alex moved to Oakland, you know?"

"Yeah."

"I couldn't think of anything skating related, either, because we're all good at different things." Faith takes a sip of her ramen broth. "But that makes us special. I can help you with triple toe loops because that's what I'm good at, and you can help me with choreography poses and feeling the music. And we can both teach Hope how to land her double axel when she gets back from camp. So, I was thinking we should call ourselves Team Unique."

"Okay, I *love* that." Faith snaps the lid onto her ramen container. "We can double-check when Hope's back, but I bet she will, too."

Team Unique. Because we're all good at different things.

We head downstairs to the freestyle rink and lace up for our afternoon session.

"Oh, Faith, I was thinking. Would you maybe want to come see the skate-school recital next week?"

She nods just like Hope when she's excited. "I'll check with Mom to see if we're free. If the skate-school needs help with setup, I'm really good at that, too. Or music, obviously."

I knot one skate, then the other. "I'll check with Corinne tomorrow and let you know."

We take the ice, stroking toward the boards to drop off our bags together. Faith skates off to warm up. I look around until I spot Alex.

"I've made a decision about my free program," I announce as I glide to a stop in front of him. "I'm going to keep part of the music Miss Lydia chose and use a different piece for the end. But I want to change the program's theme."

"Okay," Alex says. "Can you break that down for me?"

I can do better. I head to the music box and plug in my phone. The track starts with the same soft flute sounds. I skate back to Alex.

"You know the Disney version of *Sleeping Beauty*?" It'd been years since I last saw that movie, but Tamar watched it with me on Saturday while I took notes and we both munched on popcorn. I wait until Alex nods. "This part of the music plays when Princess Aurora is waltzing in the forest. And this"—I hold up a finger; the music switches to livelier brass instruments—"is when Prince Phillip enters the forest and first sees her."

I study Alex's face, but he gives nothing away, just nods again.

"I want to be Aurora in the first half of my program and then portray Prince Phillip after. That way, I can still use a lot of Miss Lydia's choreography. We can change the arm movements to look stronger in the second half and more—you know—like a prince. What do you think?"

Alex takes his time, listening all the way through to the song's final brassy *pah-pah-pa-rahs*. "Honestly? I wish I'd thought of this. It's a solid idea, with a cohesive theme, and it's something you can relate to, which will make your performance meaningful. With these tweaks, you'll learn to perform as an actress—or actor—and not just a technically proficient skater."

"I have ideas about the costume, too," I continue.

"Mom and I ordered some fabric online yesterday. We'll start working on it soon, then I'll show you."

"You know I'm fine with whatever you wear, as long as it adheres to the rules."

"Okay, and…" I hesitate on this one. "I decided I'm okay skating as an Intermediate lady this season with all these program changes. But I'd like to propose a meeting with you, me, and Mom after the national training camp—if I qualify, obviously—to talk about how I'm feeling and what I want to do next year."

He's quiet. I rehearsed what to say so many times over the weekend, but I never practiced how I'd react if Alex didn't say anything.

"About if I want to stay competing with the girls or switch to boys' events," I rush on. "I don't know if that's even possible, but we should talk—I mean, I'd like to discuss it, if that's okay?"

"You're just full of good ideas today." Now Alex smiles. "I think keeping the lines of communication open is crucial. If you decide you don't want to compete in ladies' events anymore, you should definitely say something. We'll cross that bridge when we get to it as a team. All three of us."

Perfect.

Our lesson comes to an end. I skate back to the music box and grab my phone. As I glide toward the exit, I stare at a pair of new texts.

Hayden's name appears at the top of each message, but I can't bring myself to read them in such a public place. I zip off the ice and into the hockey rink.

It's been three days since I texted him to ask if we could meet before class. Now that I have a response, my stomach swoops up into my throat.

1:43 p.m.: Ok

1:45 p.m.: Be there at 5:30 tomorrow

I reread them once, twice, three times but they don't change. They're short—and no emojis.

I type a reply, but the only word I can manage is a copy of Hayden's *Ok*.

My phone's clock blinks from 2:02 to 2:03.

A little over twenty-four hours, and I'll be able to tell Hayden how sorry I am.

For now, all I can do is wait—and hope he's willing to forgive me.

Chapter Thirty-Five

I don't know if I want time to move faster or slow down on Tuesday. Morning off-ice classes drag by, but my afternoon freestyle sessions are over in the blink of an eye.

Faith leaves with her mom. The rink empties out. Suddenly, it's five o'clock.

I walk toward the coaches' lounge. It'd be so easy to hide there until Corinne announces the start of classes.

I make myself turn back toward the rink, settling down on a bench. Avoiding Hayden won't solve anything. My eyes move from skaters working on single jumps to adults practicing edges. I bounce my legs, then stop and look at the clock.

5:25.

My face gets hot. It's hard to swallow. I need to think about something else—like next week, when things'll be back to normal. Skaters will return from the Rising Stars camp. Hope will be here, chattering like usual, and skate-school will be over until the fall. After tonight, all that's left is Saturday's recital.

The clock flickers from 5:29 to 5:30. Skaters exit the ice, but my eyes stay glued to the rink entrance.

5:33.

I check my phone, but there are no new messages. I want to call Tamar, but she can't help me now. Even if she could, I don't really deserve to be bailed out.

5:36.

5:37.

This feels like Nationals—I'm at the boards alone, waiting for my name to be announced.

Skate-school students start arriving with their parents. Some people stop to look at the recital posters. My breaths come fast and shallow.

What if he lied to me? Maybe this is payback.

A flash of blue green snags my gaze. I squint through the crowd. Cyn holds open the door for Hayden. She points my way, then nudges him toward me.

Hayden doesn't smile. His posture is rigid as he stops in front of my bench. "Hey."

"Hi." I look up but he avoids my eyes.

"Sorry I didn't make it sooner. Cyn drives like a turtle covered in syrup."

"That's okay."

Say something! I don't know if I'm ordering myself to speak, or silently asking Hayden to help me.

His eyes travel the space. They pause on one of Corinne's recital posters, before dropping to his feet. "Is there somewhere more private we can talk?"

I lead him to the second rink. Hockey players warm up by skating circuits around the ice, but the stands are mostly empty.

Halfway up, we sit. I force myself to swallow, clammy hands tightly clasped in my lap. I've already gone through this with Tamar, Alex, and Mom. I don't know why this feels harder with Hayden.

Okay, I do. Hayden and his family are the only people I outright lied to.

"I know what nonbinary means." Hayden looks at me, and my stomach flutters like a desperate butterfly. "But I have some questions I need you to answer honestly."

"All right." My voice is barely above a whisper.

"You know about me, right? That I used to have a different name and pronouns?" He looks at me until I nod. The *pap-pap-pap* of hockey shots rings in my ears. "Did you just cut your hair shorter and pretend to be a boy so you and Tamar could make fun of me, or what?"

I shake my head, eyes on my lap. It's always been easier to express myself on ice than in words, especially when I'm nervous.

"Okay, great. Thanks, or whatever. That's all I wanted to know."

The metal bench creaks as Hayden rises.

"Wait!" I stand up fast, forcing myself to look at him. "I didn't know I was nonbinary when you met me."

Hayden turns back to me with narrowed eyes.

I need him to understand, even if we don't stay friends. "Was there ever a time when you weren't sure who you were?"

"No." I flinch at the harshness in his tone. It feels like a door's about to slam in my face, and there's nothing I can do to step out of the way.

But then, he seems to waver. The door stays open a sliver. He glances around the stands, like he's checking for anyone listening. "People kept calling me a girl. I knew they were wrong, even when I was little, so I told them. But my teachers wouldn't listen, and my friends stopped being my friends because they didn't believe me, either. Then we moved to California, and I thought people were done making fun of me." His jaw tenses, hands clenched into fists by his side. "Until I met you."

"It's not like that, I swear." My voice sounds shaky, but I force myself to keep going. "I never told Tamar. Or anyone."

Breathe in, breathe out. It's time to tell the truth.

"I'm not a boy."

His look of distrust makes my stomach turn inside out.

"But I'm not a girl, either. I'm nonbinary, but I only learned that word a couple of weeks ago, after we met."

"Okay, then why did you tell me your name was Alex?"

"I didn't! You read it off my name tag, but I was wearing the wrong one. I grabbed my coach's badge by accident that day."

Hayden doesn't look convinced, but now that I've started to talk, the words flood out.

"You know that recital poster? The dress I'm wearing? That was supposed to be the costume for my new program, where I'm portraying a princess. I'd just found out before the first skate-school class, and I already hated the idea, even if I didn't know why yet.

"Then I met you, and no one has ever used boy pronouns for me before. I liked how they sounded, at first." I look down, studying my hands.

"I guess I was afraid you'd start thinking I'm a girl if I told you my real name. It took meeting you and seeing those gender-neutral pronouns in your room to realize there was a better option. I'm sorry I lied and made you feel like I was making fun of you. I don't care that you're trans, and I wouldn't joke about it. Never ever, squared."

A quiet laugh meets my ears. I glance up. It's not a full grin, but Hayden half smiles at me.

"What?"

"This is probably the most you've said all summer. You're usually so quiet." His smile levels out. "The first thing I thought when I saw those posters was that you were pranking me. Some of my classmates made fun of me back in Minnesota when I started school with a new name and pronouns. That's why I didn't respond to your texts right away." He shrugs, but there's hurt in his voice, just like after he saw the recital posters.

"And I lied to you and your family," I add.

"I mean, I get why you did, but yeah."

For a breathless second, neither of us speaks. Below us, a hockey coach splits up players into two teams and a match begins.

"So, should I use 'zie' and 'zir' now with you?"

"I—no." I look at Hayden out of the corner of my eye, suddenly shy. "I told my mom she could keep calling me Ana and use girl pronouns for now. You can call me Ana, too. But I was thinking"—I take a breath, trying to be brave—"it'd be cool if you and your family wanted to keep using boy pronouns. Just until I figure things out. Then I'll tell everyone what I've decided all at once."

"Sure."

It's the simplest word in the universe, but it makes my heart soar.

"I can do that. Anyway, it kinda sounds like we should start over."

"Start over?"

"You know, with correct names, ages, and stuff like that. Whatever you want me to know."

The tension I've been holding on to all day—all

summer—releases. In skating, there are no do-overs at competitions, but Hayden is offering one for the two of us.

"Hey, guys! You're going to be late if you don't put these on, like, yesterday." We both turn. Cyn waves a pair of rental skates, but her eyes are on Hayden. A quick look passes between them.

"We'll be there in a sec," Hayden calls, waving her away.

He turns back to me. I make a mental note to tell Tamar his eyes are blue.

"Hi. I'm Hayden." He extends his hand. "I'm thirteen, about to start eighth grade, into cosplay, and just moved here from a small town in Minnesota you've definitely never heard of."

I reach out and shake his hand.

"I'm Ana Jin. Twelve years old, and this year's US Juvenile champion in the girls' division. I'll be in seventh grade soon, I'm homeschooled in San Francisco, and I definitely *won't* be skating in a dress for the skate-school recital."

"Cool. Let me know if you need help with a new costume?"

I nod as Hayden gets up. He takes a few steps down the stands, then turns back with a mischievous expression. "Hey, did you know *ana* means 'I' in another language?"

"Yes." I'm all smiles now. "And *someone* even told me it's gender-neutral." I hop down a couple of steps and glance back at him. "Come on. Let's go get our skates on."

Breathe Out

"Those were your level five and six graduates, folks. Give them a round of applause for that fun number."

Coach Jen's voice booms over the loudspeaker as I tuck a lace into the tongue of my left skate. I hook an elastic stirrup strap, sewn to a pair of black pants, under my boot. The fabric's a little long and bunches at my ankle, but I don't mind. This makeshift costume wouldn't exist at all without the help of three awesome people.

Applause filters to me through a velvety thick curtain. Corinne went all-out for the recital, with this curtain on one end of the rink, Jen's announcing, and even spotlights. I'm glad she didn't seem to mind my last-minute costume change. My new look isn't anything close to what her posters advertised.

"Now, we have a special treat for you this evening. A local celebrity, who's not just a talented athlete but also one of our very own skate-school assistants."

My hands move to my waist, adjusting the belt that holds a boy's dress shirt in place. It's not the tunic I envisioned. That'll come later, when the fabric Mom ordered arrives. For now, I'm grateful to Tamar for lending me a belt, and to Hayden and Dan for their quick sewing work. They modified one of Hayden's old cosplay outfits for this performance. The shirt's flaps look like a skirt under my belt—boy and girl clothes blended together. A perfect fit for my new program.

If anyone wants to see my princess costume, they only have to look for Hope. She scampers between the stands and curtain in a shimmer of powder blue, while Faith helps out Jen in the sound booth. I never would've thought to ask Mrs. Park if she wanted to buy my dress for Hope without Faith's help. I can't wait to attend Faith's church musical next month and hear the songs she edited all summer on our drives to and from Oakland.

"We are thrilled to welcome..."

A hand on my back. I glance up and see Alex. We share an amused look. Jen is really drawing this out.

"...this year's US Juvenile champion. The last one ever, in fact—"

I grin. That final part came straight from Tamar.

Gliding out from behind the curtain, I raise my arms to the audience. I lift my leg in a one-foot glide, a skill Hayden nailed in his own group number only a few performances ago. We've both come a long way this summer.

"—Ana Jin!"

No "Miss" or gendered-anything tonight. Someday soon, I'll find pronouns that feel right. Until then, Jen's wording is perfect.

I slide to a stop at center ice. The spotlights obscure my view of the stands, but I know Mom, Tamar, and the Parks are out there. Same for Hayden, Cyn, and the rest of the Lubecks.

I take a breath and rise to my toes. Applause fades to a buzz of hushed voices. Arms out and gracefully rounded, I lift my chin like the princess I'm about to become. The flute's soft, lilting notes still represent someone I don't identify with, but that's okay. Acting like a girl on the ice doesn't say anything about me after I take my skates off. It's just a fun performance.

I set up my triple salchow with a flourish of arms and a three-turn. Shoulders check, legs snap together. I'm an airborne blur for three full rotations. The crowd cheers the second I land. My smile reaches my ears, no fighting it back. I'll always be alone when I perform on the ice, but there are people all around who love and support me.

I'm not sure when I'll absolutely know if I fall in between a boy and a girl, or outside that binary entirely. No clue if I'll make it to the national training camp, either, and that's fine. Uncertainty feels like less of a burden and more of an opportunity.

I am Ana and Ana is I.

I'm done being anyone but me.

AUTHOR'S NOTE

When I was Ana's age, I didn't know what it meant to be transgender. Nonbinary was an even bigger mystery. Neither word was part of my small-town vocabulary. What I knew was how different I felt from everyone else. Like Ana, I was a young figure skater and although I loved seeing all the glittery dresses that girl skaters were once required to wear at competitions—and even during regular practice ice at some rinks—they made me uncomfortable to perform in myself. I loved having long hair, too, but didn't like that it made people look at me and automatically think *girl*.

When I got older, I met other trans people for the first time in my life. At one point, I thought I identified fully as a man. I asked people to call me a traditionally male name, I cut my hair short, and I started using pronouns like *he*, *him*, and *his*.

I was delighted when people started seeing me as a man, because it felt fresh and new and closer to how I saw myself than when they assumed I was a woman. Like Ana, I gradually began to realize that this didn't quite fit how I felt and internally saw myself. When I finally discovered the term *nonbinary*, a weight felt like it had lifted off me, one I'd been carrying since I was a kid skating in Georgia and Minnesota ice rinks. And when I came out to the people closest to me, it really did feel like stepping into the light after hiding someplace dark.

In this story, Ana realizes that her discomfort comes not from what her body looks like but how other people around her interpret her gender based on a number of identifying factors: her name, the length of her hair, the clothes she wears, the color of her figure skates, and even the bathroom she chooses to enter. There's a term to define this discomfort: *dysphoria.*

Dysphoria is an emotional condition where a person feels distress or a disconnect with the sex they were assigned at birth. In Ana's case, her discomfort is linked to social situations and the assumptions other people make about her gender. This is known as social dysphoria. Body dysphoria is another type, where a person feels uncomfortable with parts or all of their physical body.

Some people experience only one type of dysphoria. Others both. One type of dysphoria may be a cause of more stress than the other. In a similar vein, some people know they are nonbinary at a young age. For others like me, it takes a longer time to figure things out.

If there's only one thing you take away from Ana's story—and mine—I hope it's that there is no one right way to be nonbinary, no expiration date for discovering your identity. Ana's experience is hers alone, just like yours is unique to you. If you have questions or would like more information about gender identity, I encourage you to check out some wonderful, reputable online resources, like Gender Spectrum (genderspectrum.org), GLSEN (glsen.org), PFLAG (pflag.org), the Trevor Project (thetrevorproject.org), Trans Youth Equality Foundation (TYEF, transyouthequality.org), and Trans Youth Family Allies (TYF, imatyfa.org).

Ana now knows she's nonbinary. She's come out to the people she cares about, but she hasn't made any changes to her pronouns. For now, it's enough that her family and friends know she's nonbinary, that they love and support her. This could change for her one day, and it may become important for her to choose different pronouns—or several, if the first set she tries doesn't feel quite right.

The wonderful thing about identity is it's yours. Whether you're twelve like Ana when you figure things out or already an adult, you alone get to decide who you are.

ACKNOWLEDGMENTS

Writing a novel is like preparing for a new skating season: A lot goes on behind the scenes that most people don't see. This book wouldn't have had its moment in the spotlight without the help of some very awesome people.

Thank you, Jordan Hamessley, my wonderful agent and fellow figure skating fan. Like a seasoned coach, you've offered insight and boundless patience in answering my frajillion questions. Thanks for loving Ana's story as much as I do. Thanks also to the team at New Leaf Literary, a truly innovative agency founded by the incomparable Joanna Volpe and supported by enthusiastic, book-loving people. I'm honored to be a leaf on your tree.

Editors are the choreographers of the literary world, and I've had the good fortune of working with not one but three at Little, Brown Books for Young Readers. Thank you, Lisa Yoskowitz, for seeing Ana's potential and encouraging me to help her reach it during an intense summer of revisions. Thanks to Hannah Milton, whose notes gave me the inspiration for so many new scenes. And thank you, Alexandra Hightower, for seeing me through line edits and beyond, plus helping ensure readers are introduced to Ana in a way that is respectful to real-life nonbinary kids.

Thank you, Ellen Shi, for creating a gorgeous cover that gives readers the first glimpse of Ana's world. Thanks to Angelie Yap and Karina Granda for the beautiful cover design; to production mavens Marisa Finkelstein and Olivia Davis; copy editor Sarah Van Bonn; school and library marketing specialist Michelle Campbell; marketing superstars Stefanie Hoffman, Mara Brashem, and Savannah Kennelly; publicist Katharine McAnarney; associate publisher Jackie Engel; publisher Megan Tingley; and the rest of the Little, Brown Books for Young Readers team who had a hand in bringing Ana's story to readers.

Before a skater starts working with a coach and choreographer, they often take lessons in a skate-school program, just like Hayden. I developed my first inkling of an idea for this story in the Children's Book Academy Middle Grade Mastery class. Its founder, Mira Reisberg, made my attendance possible thanks to a diversity scholarship.

Thank you to my CBA classmates who provided

early feedback, especially L. D. Arwood, Chris Ann Derby, Vicki Hammond, Claudette Hoffmann, Eunice Kim Dove, Ismaïla Mokadem, Samantha San Miguel, Sharon J. Wilson, and M. O. Yuksel.

A skating program is only jumps, spins, and fancy steps without lots of practice to get it ready for the big event. Likewise, writing a novel involves considering others' feedback and tweaking accordingly. For that, #WriteMentor came along exactly when I needed it. Founder Stuart White created a stellar mentorship program, and my mentor, Caroline Murphy, provided invaluable guidance. Thank you, both, as well as to the #WM community as a whole.

A skater needs camaraderie during long hours of training, and the same goes for writers. I couldn't have asked for a better friend than Kathleen Nelson. Your feedback is always on point, but what I truly value is our shared love of kidlit.

Same goes for you, Nicole Melleby. I'm so glad to know another author as excited about queer representation in children's literature as I am. Thanks for being a big authorly sibling to me (even though I'm technically older—funny how that works).

Thank you, Liz Edelbrock, Rebecca Gibson, Sabrina Kleckner, and Rebecca Petruck, who all offered feedback during summer 2018.

Thanks, Melony Breeze, Mary Chadd, April Holm, Mallory Lass, Taj McCoy, John Pacheco, Sandra Proudman, and Ethan Weisinger, for the support and friendship.

An extra special thanks to Joy Ding, without whom *Ana*'s "Breathe In" prologue would not be a thing. I'm lucky to call you my friend for so many reasons.

Thanks to the skating community that supported me on my own athletic journey. This includes coaches Lorie Charbonneau, Sarah France, Karin Freund, Suzy Jackson, Chris Kinser, Ari Lieb, and Jayne Throckmorton, as well as practice pals Kaitlyn Landes, Keith Newcombe, and Whitney Westbrook. Much love to all adult skaters, especially those I met at the 7K and SQSA camps. Kudos as well to my synchronized skating team, IceSymmetrics.

My parents, Vicky and David Sass, encouraged me to explore my passions fully. My love of music comes from them, as does my work ethic. I am convinced I wouldn't be a writer now if you hadn't read to me every night as a child, Mom. And to this day, Dad, your musical talent spurs me to achieve more with my writing. A shout-out to my brother, Michael, and his family, as well. Michael, your early support gave me the courage to be myself around others.

Lastly, thank you, Deven Cao. I've been saying I would become an author since the day we met, and you never doubted me, even though it took years to fulfill that promise. Thanks for your endless support and quirky sense of humor. Life with you has been the best adventure.